ASTOUNDING STORIES OF SUPER-SCIENCE

On Sale the First Thursday of Each Month

W. M. CLAYTON,	HARRY BATES,	DOUGLAS M. DOLD,
Publisher	Editor	Consulting Editor

The Clayton Standard on a Magazine Guarantees:

That the stories therein are clean, interesting, vivid; by leading writers of the day and purchased under conditions approved by the Authors' League of America;

That such magazines are manufactured in Union shops by American workmen;

That each newsdealer and agent is insured a fair profit;

That an intelligent censorship guards their advertising pages.

The other Clayton magazines are:

ACE-HIGH MAGAZINE, RANCH ROMANCES, COWBOY STORIES, CLUES, FIVE-NOVELS MONTHLY, WIDE WORLD ADVENTURES, ALL STAR DETECTIVE STORIES, FLYERS, RANGELAND LOVE STORY MAGAZINE, SKY-HIGH LIBRARY MAGAZINE, MISS 1930, *and* FOREST AND STREAM

More Than Two Million Copies Required to Supply the Monthly Demand for Clayton Magazines.

Republished, and reedited from the public domain.

**ISBN-13:
978-1519759405**

**ISBN-10:
1519759401**

	CONTENTS	
VOL. I, No. 2		FEBRUARY, 1930
COVER DESIGN	H. W. WESSOLOWSKI	

Painted in Water-colors from a Scene in "Spawn of the Stars."

OLD CROMPTON'S SECRET   HARL VINCENT   5
> *Tom's Extraordinary Machine Glowed—and the Years Were Banished from Old Crompton's Body. But There Still Remained, Deep-seated in His Century-old Mind, the Memory of His Crime.*

SPAWN OF THE STARS   CHARLES WILLARD DIFFIN   23
> *The Earth Lay Powerless Beneath Those Loathsome, Yellowish Monsters That, Sheathed in Cometlike Globes, Sprang from the Skies to Annihilate Man and Reduce His Cities to Ashes.*

THE CORPSE ON THE GRATING   HUGH B. CAVE   53
> *In the Gloomy Depths of the Old Warehouse Dale Saw a Thing That Drew a Scream of Horror to His Dry Lips. It Was a Corpse—the Mold of Decay on Its Long-dead Features—and Yet It Was Alive!*

CREATURES OF THE LIGHT   SOPHIE WENZEL ELLIS   65
> *He Had Striven to Perfect the Faultless Man of the Future, and Had Succeeded—Too Well. For in the Pitilessly Cold Eyes of Adam, His Super-human Creation, Dr. Mundson Saw Only Contempt—and Annihilation—for the Human Race.*

INTO SPACE   STERNER ST. PAUL   103
> *What Was the Extraordinary Connection Between Dr. Livermore's Sudden Disappearance and the Coming of a New Satellite to the Earth?*

THE BEETLE HORDE   VICTOR ROUSSEAU   115
> *Bullets, Shrapnel, Shell—Nothing Can Stop the Trillions of Famished, Man-sized Beetles Which, Led by a Madman, Sweep Down Over the Human Race.*

MAD MUSIC   ANTHONY PELCHER   143
> *The Sixty Stories of the Perfectly Constructed Colossus Building Had Mysteriously Crashed! What Was the Connection Between This Catastrophe and the Weird Strains of the Mad Musician's Violin?*

THE THIEF OF TIME   CAPTAIN S. P. MEEK   161
> *The Teller Turned to the Stacked Pile of Bills. They Were Gone! And No One Had Been Near!*

Single Copies, 20 Cents (In Canada, 25 Cents)   Yearly Subscription, $2.00

Issued monthly by Publishers' Fiscal Corporation, 80 Lafayette St., New York, N.Y. W. M. Clayton, President; Nathan Goldmann, Secretary. Application for entry as second-class mail pending at the Post Office at New York, under Act of March 3, 1879. Application for registration of title as Trade Mark pending in the U.S. Patent Office. Member Newsstand Group—Men's List. For advertising rates address E. R. Crowe & Co., Inc., 25 Vanderbilt Ave., New York; or 225 North Michigan Ave., Chicago.

Old Crompton's Secret

By Harl Vincent

Tom tripped on a wire and fell, with his ferocious adversary on top.

Tom's extraordinary machine glowed-and the years were banished from Old Crompton's body. But there still remained, deep-seated in his century-old mind, the memory of his crime.

Two miles west of the village of Laketon there lived an aged recluse who was known only as Old Crompton. As far back as the villagers could remember he had visited the town regularly twice a month, each time tottering his lonely way homeward with a load of provisions. He appeared to be well supplied with funds, but purchased sparingly as became a miserly hermit. And so vicious was his tongue that few cared to converse with him, even the young hoodlums of the town hesitating to harass him with the banter usually accorded the other bizarre characters of the streets.

The oldest inhabitants knew nothing of his past history, and they had long since lost their curiosity in the matter. He was a fixture, as was the old town hall with its surrounding park. His lonely cabin was shunned by all who chanced to pass along the old dirt road that led through the woods to nowhere and was rarely used.

His only extravagance was in the matter of books, and the village book store profited considerably by his purchases. But, at the instigation of Cass Harmon, the bookseller, it was whispered about that Old Crompton was a believer in the black art—that he had made a pact with the devil himself and was leagued with him and his imps. For the books he bought were strange ones; ancient volumes that Cass must needs order from New York or Chicago and that cost as much as ten and even fifteen dollars a copy; translations of the writings of the alchemists and astrologers and philosophers of the dark ages.

It was no wonder Old Crompton was looked at askance by the simple-living and deeply religious natives of the small Pennsylvania town.

But there came a day when the hermit was to have a neighbor, and the town buzzed with excited speculation as to what would happen.

The property across the road from Old Crompton's hut belonged to Alton Forsythe, Laketon's wealthiest resident—hundreds of acres of scrubby woodland that he considered well nigh worthless. But Tom Forsythe, the only son, had returned from college and his ambitions were of a nature strange to his townspeople and utterly incomprehensible to his father. Something vague about biology and chemical experiments and the like is what he spoke of, and, when his parents objected on the grounds of possible explosions and other weird accidents, he prevailed upon his father to have a secluded laboratory built for him in the woods.

When the workmen started the small frame structure not a quarter of a mile from his own hut, Old Crompton was furious. He raged and stormed, but to no avail. Tom Forsythe had his heart set on the project and he was somewhat of a successful debater himself. The fire that flashed from his cold gray eyes matched that from the pale blue ones of the elderly anchorite. And the law was on his side.

So the building was completed and Tom Forsythe moved in, bag and baggage.

For more than a year the hermit studiously avoided his neighbor, though, truth to tell, this required very little effort. For Tom Forsythe became almost as much of a recluse as his predecessor, remaining indoors for days at a time and visiting the home of his people scarcely oftener than Old Crompton visited the village. He too became the target of village gossip and his name was ere long linked with that of the old man in similar animadversion. But he cared naught for the opinions of his townspeople nor for the dark looks of suspicion that greeted him on his rare appearances in the public places. His chosen work engrossed him so deeply that all else counted for nothing. His parents remonstrated with him in vain. Tom laughed away their recriminations and fears, continuing with his labors more strenuously than ever. He never troubled his mind over the nearness of Old Crompton's hut, the existence of which he hardly noticed or considered.

It so happened one day that the old man's curiosity got the better of him and Tom caught him prowling about on his property, peering wonderingly at the many rabbit hutches, chicken coops, dove cotes and the like which cluttered the space to the rear of the laboratory.

Seeing that he was discovered, the old man wrinkled his face into a toothless grin of conciliation.

"Just looking over your place, Forsythe," he said. "Sorry about the fuss I made when you built the house. But I'm an old man, you know, and changes are unwelcome. Now I have forgotten my objections and would like to be friends. Can we?"

Tom peered searchingly into the flinty eyes that were set so deeply in the wrinkled, leathery countenance. He suspected an ulterior motive, but could not find it within him to turn the old fellow down.

"Why—I guess so, Crompton," he hesitated: "I have nothing against you, but I came here for seclusion and I'll not have anyone bothering me in my work."

"I'll not bother you, young man. But I'm fond of pets and I see you have many of them here; guinea pigs, chickens, pigeons, and rabbits. Would you mind if I make friends with some of them?"

"They're not pets," answered Tom dryly, "they are material for use in my experiments. But you may amuse yourself with them if you wish."

"You mean that you cut them up—kill them, perhaps?"

"Not that. But I sometimes change them in physical form, sometimes cause them to become of huge size, sometimes produce pigmy offspring of normal animals."

"Don't they suffer?"

"Very seldom, though occasionally a subject dies. But the benefit that will accrue to mankind is well worth the slight inconvenience to the dumb creatures and the infrequent loss of their lives."

Old Crompton regarded him dubiously. "You are trying to find?" he interrogated.

"The secret of life!" Tom Forsythe's eyes took on the stare of fanaticism. "Before I have finished I shall know the nature of the vital force—how to produce it. I shall prolong human life indefinitely; create artificial life. And the solution is more closely approached with each passing day."

The hermit blinked in pretended mystification. But he understood perfectly, and he bitterly envied the younger man's knowledge and ability that enabled him to delve into the mysteries of nature which had always been so attractive to his own mind. And somehow, he acquired a sudden deep hatred of the coolly confident young man who spoke so positively of accomplishing the impossible.

During the winter months that followed, the strange acquaintance progressed but little. Tom did not invite his neighbor to visit him, nor did Old Crompton go out of his way to impose his presence on the younger man, though each spoke pleasantly enough to the other on the few occasions when they happened to meet.

With the coming of spring they encountered one another more frequently, and Tom found considerable of interest in the quaint, borrowed philosophy of the gloomy old man. Old Crompton, of course, was desperately interested in the things that were hidden in Tom's laboratory, but he never requested permission to see them. He hid his real feelings extremely well and was apparently content to spend as much time as possible with the feathered and furred subjects for experiment, being very careful not to incur Tom's displeasure by displaying too great interest in the laboratory itself.

Then there came a day in early summer when an accident served to draw the two men closer together, and Old Crompton's long-sought opportunity followed.

He was starting for the village when, from down the road, there came a series of tremendous squawkings, then a bellow of dismay in the voice of his young neighbor. He turned quickly and was astonished at the sight of a monstrous rooster which had escaped and was headed straight for him with head down and wings fluttering wildly. Tom followed close behind, but was unable to catch the darting monster. And monster it was, for this rooster stood no less than three feet in height and appeared more ferocious than a large turkey. Old Crompton had his shopping bag, a large one of burlap which he always carried to town, and he summoned enough courage to throw it over the head of the screeching, over-sized fowl. So tangled did the panic-stricken bird become that it was a comparatively simple matter to effect his capture, and the old man rose to his feet triumphant with the bag securely closed over the struggling captive.

"Thanks," panted Tom, when he drew alongside. "I should never have caught him, and his appearance at large might have caused me a great deal of trouble—now of all times."

"It's all right, Forsythe," smirked the old man. "Glad I was able to do it."

Secretly he gloated, for he knew this occurrence would be an open sesame to that laboratory of Tom's. And it proved to be just that.

A few nights later he was awakened by a vigorous thumping at his door, something that had never before occurred during his nearly sixty years occupancy of the tumbledown hut. The moon was high and he cautiously peeped from the window and saw that his late visitor was none other than young Forsythe.

"With you in a minute!" he shouted, hastily thrusting his rheumatic old limbs into his shabby trousers. "Now to see the inside of that laboratory," he chuckled to himself.

It required but a moment to attire himself in the scanty raiment he wore during the warm months, but he could hear Tom muttering and impatiently pacing the flagstones before his door.

"What is it?" he asked, as he drew the bolt and emerged into the brilliant light of the moon.

"Success!" breathed Tom excitedly. "I have produced growing, living matter synthetically. More than this, I have learned the secret of the vital force—the spark of life. Immortality is within easy reach. Come and see for yourself."

They quickly traversed the short distance to the two-story building which comprised Tom's workshop and living quarters. The entire ground floor was taken up by the laboratory, and Old Crompton stared aghast at the wealth of equipment it contained. Furnaces there were, and retorts that reminded him of those pictured in the wood cuts in some of his musty books. Then there were complicated machines with many levers and dials mounted on their faces, and with huge glass bulbs of peculiar shape with coils of wire connecting to knoblike protuberances of their transparent walls. In the exact center of the great single room there was what appeared to be a dissecting table, with a brilliant light overhead and with two of the odd glass bulbs at either end. It was to this table that Tom led the excited old man.

"This is my perfected apparatus," said Tom proudly, "and by its use I intend to create a new race of supermen, men and women who will always retain the vigor and strength of their youth and who can not die excepting by actual destruction of their bodies. Under the influence of the rays all bodily ailments vanish as if by magic, and organic defects are quickly corrected. Watch this now."

He stepped to one of the many cages at the side of the room and returned with a wriggling cottontail in his hands. Old Compton watched anxiously as he picked a nickeled instrument from a tray of surgical appliances and requested his visitor to hold the protesting animal while he covered its head with a handkerchief.

"Ethyl chloride," explained Tom, noting with amusement the look of distaste on the old man's face. "We'll just put him to sleep for a minute while I amputate a leg."

The struggles of the rabbit quickly ceased when the spray soaked the handkerchief and the anaesthetic took effect. With a shining scalpel and a surgical saw, Tom speedily removed one of the forelegs of the animal and then he placed the limp body in the center of the table, removing the handkerchief from its head as he did so. At the end of the table there was a panel with its glittering array of switches and electrical instruments, and Old Crompton observed very closely the manipulations of the controls as Tom started the mechanism. With the ensuing hum of a motor-generator from a corner of the room, the four bulbs adjacent to the table sprang into life, each glowing with a different color and each emitting a different vibratory note as it responded to the energy within.

"Keep an eye on Mr. Rabbit now," admonished Tom.

From the body of the small animal there emanated an intangible though hazily visible aura as the combined effects of the rays grew in intensity. Old Crompton bent over the table and peered amazedly at the stump of the foreleg, from which blood no longer dripped. The stump was healing over! Yes—it seemed to elongate as one watched. A new limb was growing on to replace the old! Then the animal struggled once more, this time to regain consciousness. In a moment it was fully awake and, with a frightened hop, was off the table and hobbling about in search of a hiding place.

Tom Forsythe laughed. "Never knew what happened," he exulted, "and excepting for the temporary limp is not inconvenienced at all. Even that will be gone in a couple of hours, for the new limb will be completely grown by that time."

"But—but, Tom," stammered the old man, "this is wonderful. How do you accomplish it?"

"Ha! Don't think I'll reveal my secret. But this much I will tell you: the life force generated by my apparatus stimulates a certain gland that's normally inactive in warm blooded animals. This gland, when active, possesses the function of growing new members to the body to replace lost ones in much the same manner as this is done in case of the lobster and certain other crustaceans. Of course, the process is extremely rapid when the gland is stimulated by the vital rays from my tubes. But this is only one of the many wonders of the process. Here is something far more remarkable."

He took from a large glass jar the body of a guinea pig, a body that was rigid in death.

"This guinea pig," he explained, "was suffocated twenty-four hours ago and is stone dead."

"Suffocated?"

"Yes. But quite painlessly, I assure you. I merely removed the air from the jar with a vacuum pump and the little creature passed out of the picture very quickly. Now we'll revive it."

Old Crompton stretched forth a skinny hand to touch the dead animal, but withdrew it hastily when he felt the clammy rigidity of the body. There was no doubt as to the lifelessness of this specimen.

Tom placed the dead guinea pig on the spot where the rabbit had been subjected to the action of the rays. Again his visitor watched carefully as he manipulated the controls of the apparatus.

With the glow of the tubes and the ensuing haze of eery light that surrounded the little body, a marked change was apparent. The inanimate form relaxed suddenly and it seemed that the muscles pulsated with an accession of energy. Then one leg was stretched forth spasmodically. There was a convulsive heave as the lungs drew in a first long breath, and, with that, an astonished and very much alive rodent scrambled to its feet, blinking wondering eyes in the dazzling light.

"See? See?" shouted Tom, grasping Old Crompton by the arm in a viselike grip. "It is the secret of life and death! Aristocrats, plutocrats and beggars will beat a path to my door. But, never fear, I shall choose my subjects well. The name of Thomas Forsythe will yet be emblazoned in the Hall of Fame. I shall be master of the world!"

Old Crompton began to fear the glitter in the eyes of the gaunt young man who seemed suddenly to have become demented. And his envy and hatred of his talented host blazed anew as Forsythe gloried in the success of his efforts. Then he was struck with an idea and he affected his most ingratiating manner.

"It is a marvelous thing, Tom," he said, "and is entirely beyond my poor comprehension. But I can see that it is all you say and more. Tell me—can you restore the youth of an aged person by these means?"

"Positively!" Tom did not catch the eager note in the old man's voice. Rather he took the question as an inquiry into the further marvels of his process. "Here," he continued, enthusiastically, "I'll prove that to you also. My dog Spot is around the place somewhere. And he is a decrepit old hound, blind, lame and toothless. You've probably seen him with me."

He rushed to the stairs and whistled. There was an answering yelp from above and the pad of uncertain paws on the bare wooden steps. A dejected old beagle blundered into the room, dragging a crippled hind leg as he fawned upon his master, who stretched forth a hand to pat the unsteady head.

"Guess Spot is old enough for the test," laughed Tom, "and I have been meaning to restore him to his youthful vigor, anyway. No time like the present."

He led his trembling pet to the table of the remarkable tubes and lifted him to its surface. The poor old beast lay trustingly where he was placed, quiet, save for his husky asthmatic breathing.

"Hold him, Crompton," directed Tom as he pulled the starting lever of his apparatus.

And Old Crompton watched in fascinated anticipation as the ethereal luminosity bathed the dog's body in response to the action of the four rays. Somewhat vaguely it came to him that the baggy flesh of his own wrinkled hands took on a new firmness and color where they reposed on the animal's back. Young Forsythe grinned triumphantly as Spot's breathing became more regular and the rasp gradually left it. Then the dog whined in pleasure and wagged his tail with increasing vigor. Suddenly he raised his head, perked his ears in astonishment and looked his master straight in the face with eyes that saw once more. The low throat cry rose to a full and joyous bark. He sprang to his feet from under the restraining hands and jumped to the floor in a lithe-muscled leap that carried him half way across the room. He capered about with the abandon of a puppy, making extremely active use of four sound limbs.

"Why—why, Forsythe," stammered the hermit, "it's absolutely incredible. Tell me—tell me—what is this remarkable force?"

His host laughed gleefully. "You probably wouldn't understand it anyway, but I'll tell you. It is as simple as the nose on your face. The spark of life, the vital force, is merely an extremely complicated electrical manifestation which I have been able to duplicate artificially. This spark or force is all that distinguishes living from inanimate matter, and in living beings the force gradually decreases in power as the years pass, causing loss of health and strength. The chemical composition of bones and tissue alters, joints become stiff, muscles atrophied, and bones brittle. By recharging, as it were, with the vital force, the gland action is intensified, youth and strength is renewed. By repeating the process every ten or fifteen years the same degree of vigor can be maintained indefinitely. Mankind will become immortal. That is why I say I am to be master of the world."

For the moment Old Crompton forgot his jealous hatred in the enthusiasm with which he was imbued. "Tom—Tom," he pleaded in his excitement, "Use me as a subject. Renew my youth. My life has been a sad one and a lonely one, but I would that I might live it over. I should make of it a far different one—something worthwhile. See, I am ready."

He sat on the edge of the gleaming table and made as if to lie down on its gleaming surface. But his young host only stared at him in open amusement.

"What? You?" he sneered, unfeelingly. "Why, you old fossil! I told you I would choose my subjects carefully. They are to be people of standing and wealth, who can contribute to the fame and fortune of one Thomas Forsythe."

"But Tom, I have money," Old Crompton begged. But when he saw the hard mirth in the younger man's eyes, his old animosity flamed anew and he sprang from his position and shook a skinny forefinger in Tom's face.

"Don't do that to me, you old fool!" shouted Tom, "and get out of here. Think I'd waste current on an old cadger like you? I guess not! Now get out. Get out, I say!"

Then the old anchorite saw red. Something seemed to snap in his soured old brain. He found himself kicking and biting and punching at his host, who backed away from the furious onslaught in surprise. Then Tom tripped over a wire and fell to the floor with a force that rattled the windows, his ferocious little adversary on top. The younger man lay still where he had fallen, a trickle of blood showing at his temple.

"My God! I've killed him!" gasped the old man.

With trembling fingers he opened Tom's shirt and listened for his heartbeats. Panic-stricken, he rubbed the young man's wrists, slapped his cheeks, and ran for water to dash in his face. But all efforts to revive him proved futile, and then, in awful fear, Old Crompton dashed into the night, the dog Spot snapping at his heels as he ran.

Hours later the stooped figure of a shabby old man might have been seen stealthily re-entering the lonely workshop where the lights still burned brightly. Tom Forsythe lay rigid in the position in which Old Crompton had left him, and the dog growled menacingly.

Averting his gaze and circling wide of the body, Old Crompton made for the table of the marvelous rays. In minute detail he recalled every move made by Tom in starting and adjusting the apparatus to produce the incredible results he had witnessed. Not a moment was to be wasted now. Already he had hesitated too long, for soon would come the dawn and possible discovery of his crime. But the invention of his victim would save him from the long arm of the law, for, with youth restored, Old Crompton would cease to exist and a new life would open its doors to the starved soul of the hermit. Hermit, indeed! He would begin life anew, an active man with youthful vigor and ambition. Under an assumed name he would travel abroad, would enjoy life, and would later become a successful man of affairs. He had enough money, he told himself. And the police would never find Old Crompton, the murderer of Tom Forsythe! He deposited his small traveling bag on the floor and fingered the controls of Tom's apparatus.

He threw the starting switch confidently and grinned in satisfaction as the answering whine of the motor-generator came to his ears. One by one he carefully made the adjustments in exactly the manner followed by the now silenced discoverer of the process. Everything operated precisely as it had during the preceding experiments. Odd that he should have anticipated some such necessity! But something had told him to observe Tom's movements carefully, and now he rejoiced in the fact that his intuition had led him aright. Painfully he climbed to the table top and stretched his aching body in the warm light of the four huge tubes. His exertions during the struggle with Tom were beginning to tell on him. But the soreness and stiffness of feeble muscles and stubborn joints would soon be but a memory. His pulses quickened at the thought and he breathed deep in a sudden feeling of unaccustomed well-being.

The dog growled continuously from his position at the head of his master, but did not move to interfere with the intruder. And Old Crompton, in the excitement of the momentous experience, paid him not the slightest attention.

His body tingled from head to foot with a not unpleasant sensation that conveyed the assurance of radical changes taking place under the influence of the vital rays. The tingling sensation increased in intensity until it seemed that every corpuscle in his veins danced to the tune of the vibration from those glowing tubes that bathed him in an ever-spreading radiance. Aches and pains vanished from his body, but he soon experienced a sharp stab of new pain in his lower jaw. With an experimental forefinger he rubbed the gum. He laughed aloud as the realization came to him that in those gums where there had been no teeth for more than twenty years there was now growing a complete new set. And the rapidity of the process amazed him beyond measure. The aching area spread quickly and was becoming really uncomfortable. But then—and he consoled himself with the thought—nothing is brought into being without a certain amount of pain. Besides, he was confident that his discomfort would soon be over.

He examined his hand, and found that the joints of two fingers long crippled with rheumatism now moved freely and painlessly. The misty brilliance surrounding his body was paling and he saw that the flesh was taking on a faint green fluorescence instead. The rays had completed their work and soon the transformation would be fully effected. He turned on his side and slipped to the floor with the agility of a youngster. The dog snarled anew, but kept steadfastly to his position.

There was a small mirror over the wash stand at the far end of the room and Old Crompton made haste to obtain the first view of his reflected image. His step was firm and springy, his bearing confident, and he found that his long-stooped shoulders straightened naturally and easily. He felt that he had taken on at least two inches in stature, which was indeed the case. When he reached the mirror he peered anxiously into its dingy surface and what he saw there so startled him that he stepped backward in amazement. This was not Larry Crompton, but an entirely new man. The straggly white hair had given way to soft, healthy waves of chestnut hue. Gone were the seams from the leathery countenance and the eyes looked out clearly and steadily from under brows as thick and dark as they had been in his youth. The reflected features were those of an entire stranger. They were not even reminiscent of the Larry Crompton of fifty years ago, but were the features of a far more vigorous and prepossessing individual than he had ever seemed, even in the best years of his life. The jaw was firm, the once sunken cheeks so well filled out that his high cheek bones were no longer in evidence. It was the face of a man of not more than thirty-eight years of age, reflecting exceptional intelligence and strength of character.

"What a disguise!" he exclaimed in delight. And his voice, echoing in the stillness that followed the switching off of the apparatus, was deep-throated and mellow—the voice of a new man.

Now, serenely confident that discovery was impossible, he picked up his small but heavy bag and started for the door. Dawn was breaking and he wished to put as many miles between himself and Tom's laboratory as could be covered in the next few hours. But at the door he hesitated. Then, despite the furious yapping of Spot, he returned to the table of the rays and, with deliberate thoroughness smashed the costly tubes which had brought about his rehabilitation. With a pinch bar from a nearby tool rack, he wrecked the controls and generating mechanisms beyond recognition. Now he was absolutely secure! No meddling experts could possibly discover the secret of Tom's invention. All evidence would show that the young experimenter had met his death at the hands of Old Crompton, the despised hermit of West Laketon. But none would dream that the handsome man of means who was henceforth to be known as George Voight was that same despised hermit.

He recovered his satchel and left the scene. With long, rapid strides he proceeded down the old dirt road toward the main highway where, instead of turning east into the village, he would turn west and walk to Kernsburg, the neighboring town. There, in not more than two hours time, his new life would really begin!

Had you, a visitor, departed from Laketon when Old Crompton did and returned twelve years later, you would have noticed very little difference in the appearance of the village. The old town hall and the little park were the same, the dingy brick building among the trees being just a little dingier and its wooden steps more worn and sagged. The main street showed evidence of recent repaving, and, in consequence of the resulting increase in through automobile traffic; there were two new gasoline filling stations in the heart of the town. Down the road about a half mile there was a new building, which, upon inquiring from one of the natives, would be proudly designated as the new high school building. Otherwise there were no changes to be observed.

In his dilapidated chair in the untidy office he had occupied for nearly thirty years, sat Asa Culkin, popularly known as "Judge" Culkin. Justice of the peace, sheriff, attorney-at-law, and three times Mayor of Laketon, he was still a controlling factor in local politics and government. And many a knotty legal problem was settled in that gloomy little office. Many a dispute in the town council was dependent for arbitration upon the keen mind and understanding wit of the old judge.

The four o'clock train had just puffed its labored way from the station when a stranger entered his office, a stranger of uncommonly prosperous air. The keen blue eyes of the old attorney appraised him instantly and classified him as a successful man of business, not yet forty years of age, and with a weighty problem on his mind.

"What can I do for you, sir?" he asked, removing his feet from the battered desk top.

"You may be able to help me a great deal, Judge," was the unexpected reply. "I came to Laketon to give myself up."

"Give yourself up?" Culkin rose to his feet in surprise and unconsciously straightened his shoulders in the effort to seem less dwarfed before the tall stranger. "Why, what do you mean?" he inquired.

"I wish to give myself up for murder," answered the amazing visitor, slowly and with decision, "for a murder committed twelve years ago. I should like you to listen to my story first, though. It has been kept too long."

"But I still do not understand." There was puzzlement in the honest old face of the attorney. He shook his gray locks in uncertainty. "Why should you come here? Why come to me? What possible interest can I have in the matter?"

"Just this, Judge. You do not recognize me now, and you will probably consider my story incredible when you hear it. But, when I have given you all the evidence, you will know who I am and will be compelled to believe. The murder was committed in Laketon. That is why I came to you."

"A murder in Laketon? Twelve years ago?" Again the aged attorney shook his head. "But—proceed."

"Yes. I killed Thomas Forsythe."

The stranger looked for an expression of horror in the features of his listener, but there was none. Instead the benign countenance took on a look of deepening amazement, but the smile wrinkles had somehow vanished and the old face was grave in its surprised interest.

"You seem astonished," continued the stranger. "Undoubtedly you were convinced that the murderer was Larry Crompton—Old Crompton, the hermit. He disappeared the night of the crime and has never been heard from since. Am I correct?"

"Yes. He disappeared all right. But continue."

Not by a lift of his eyebrow did Culkin betray his disbelief, but the stranger sensed that his story was somehow not as startling as it should have been.

"You will think me crazy, I presume. But I am Old Crompton. It was my hand that felled the unfortunate young man in his laboratory out there in West Laketon twelve years ago to-night. It was his marvelous invention that transformed the old hermit into the apparently young man you see before you. But I swear that I am none other than Larry Crompton and that I killed young Forsythe. I am ready to pay the penalty. I can bear the flagellation of my own conscience no longer."

The visitor's voice had risen to the point of hysteria. But his listener remained calm and unmoved.

"Now just let me get this straight," he said quietly. "Do I understand that you claim to be Old Crompton, rejuvenated in some mysterious manner, and that you killed Tom Forsythe on that night twelve years ago? Do I understand that you wish now to go to trial for that crime and to pay the penalty?"

"Yes! Yes! And the sooner the better. I can stand it no longer. I am the most miserable man in the world!"

"Hm-m—hm-m," muttered the judge, "this is strange." He spoke soothingly to his visitor. "Do not upset yourself, I beg of you. I will take care of this thing for you, never fear. Just take a seat, Mister—er—"

"You may call me Voight for the present," said the stranger, in a more composed tone of voice, "George Voight. That is the name I have been using since the mur—since that fatal night."

"Very well, Mr. Voight," replied the counsellor with an air of the greatest solicitude, "please have a seat now, while I make a telephone call."

And George Voight slipped into a stiff-backed chair with a sigh of relief. For he knew the judge from the old days and he was now certain that his case would be disposed of very quickly.

With the telephone receiver pressed to his ear, Culkin repeated a number. The stranger listened intently during the ensuing silence. Then there came a muffled "hello" sounding in impatient response to the call.

"Hello, Alton," spoke the attorney, "this is Asa speaking. A stranger has just stepped into my office and he claims to be Old Crompton. Remember the hermit across the road from your son's old laboratory? Well, this man, who bears no resemblance whatever to the old man he claims to be and who seems to be less than half the age of Tom's old neighbor, says that he killed Tom on that night we remember so well."

There were some surprised remarks from the other end of the wire, but Voight was unable to catch them. He was in a cold perspiration at the thought of meeting his victim's father.

"Why, yes, Alton," continued Culkin, "I think there is something in this story, although I cannot believe it all. But I wish you would accompany us and visit the laboratory. Will you?"

"Lord, man, not that!" interrupted the judge's visitor. "I can hardly bear to visit the scene of my crime—and in the company of Alton Forsythe. Please, not that!"

"Now you just let me take care of this, young man," replied the judge, testily. Then, once more speaking into the mouthpiece of the telephone, "All right, Alton. We'll pick you up at your office in five minutes."

He replaced the receiver on its hook and turned again to his visitor. "Please be so kind as to do exactly as I request," he said. "I want to help you, but there is more to this thing than you know and I want you to follow unquestioningly where I lead and ask no questions at all for the present. Things may turn out differently than you expect."

"All right, Judge." The visitor resigned himself to whatever might transpire under the guidance of the man he had called upon to turn him over to the officers of the law.

Seated in the judge's ancient motor car, they stopped at the office of Alton Forsythe a few minutes later and were joined by that red-faced and pompous old man. Few words were spoken during the short run to the well-remembered location of Tom's laboratory, and the man who was known as George Voight caught at his own throat with nervous fingers when they passed the tumbledown remains of the hut in which Old Crompton had spent so many years. With a screeching of well-worn brakes the car stopped before the laboratory, which was now almost hidden behind a mass of shrubs and flowers.

"Easy now, young man," cautioned the judge, noting the look of fear which had clouded his new client's features. The three men advanced to the door through which Old Crompton had fled on that night of horror, twelve years before. The elder Forsythe spoke not a word as he turned the knob and stepped within. Voight shrank from entering, but soon mastered his feelings and followed the other two. The sight that met his eyes caused him to cry aloud in awe.

At the dissecting table, which seemed to be exactly as he had seen it last but with replicas of the tubes he had destroyed once more in place, stood Tom Forsythe! Considerably older and with hair prematurely gray, he was still the young man Old Crompton thought he had killed. Tom Forsythe was not dead after all! And all of his years of misery had gone for nothing. He advanced slowly to the side of the wondering young man, Alton Forsythe and Asa Culkin watching silently from just inside the door.

"Tom—Tom," spoke the stranger, "you are alive? You were not dead when I left you on that terrible night when I smashed your precious tubes? Oh—it is too good to be true! I can scarcely believe my eyes!"

He stretched forth trembling fingers to touch the body of the young man to assure himself that it was not all a dream.

"Why," said Tom Forsythe, in astonishment. "I do not know you, sir. Never saw you in my life. What do you mean by your talk of smashing my tubes, of leaving me for dead?"

"Mean?" The stranger's voice rose now; he was growing excited. "Why, Tom, I am Old Crompton. Remember the struggle, here in this very room? You refused to rejuvenate an unhappy old man with your marvelous apparatus, a temporarily insane old man—Crompton. I was that old man and I fought with you. You fell, striking your head. There was blood. You were unconscious. Yes, for many hours I was sure you were dead and that I had murdered you. But I had watched your manipulations of the apparatus and I subjected myself to the action of the rays. My youth was miraculously restored. I became as you see me now. Detection was impossible, for I looked no more like Old Crompton than you do. I smashed your machinery to avoid suspicion. Then I escaped. And, for twelve years, I have thought myself a murderer. I have suffered the tortures of the damned!"

Tom Forsythe advanced on this remarkable visitor with clenched fists. Staring him in the eyes with cold appraisal, his wrath was all too apparent. The dog Spot, young as ever, entered the room and, upon observing the stranger, set up an ominous growling and snarling. At least the dog recognized him!

"What are you trying to do, catechise me? Are you another of these alienists my father has been bringing around?" The young inventor was furious. "If you are," he continued, "you can get out of here—now! I'll have no more of this meddling with my affairs. I'm as sane as any of you and I refuse to submit to this continual persecution."

The elder Forsythe grunted, and Culkin laid a restraining hand on his arm. "Just a minute now, Tom," he said soothingly. "This stranger is no alienist. He has a story to tell. Please permit him to finish."

Somewhat mollified, Tom Forsythe shrugged his assent.

"Tom," continued the stranger, more calmly now, "what I have said is the truth. I shall prove it to you. I'll tell you things no mortals on earth could know but we two. Remember the day I captured the big rooster for you—the monster you had created? Remember the night you awakened me and brought me here in the moonlight? Remember the rabbit whose leg you amputated and re-grew? The poor guinea pig you had suffocated and whose life you restored? Spot here? Don't you remember rejuvenating him? I was here. And you refused to use your process on me, old man that I was. Then is when I went mad and attacked you. Do you believe me, Tom?"

Then a strange thing happened. While Tom Forsythe gazed in growing belief, the stranger's shoulders sagged and he trembled as with the ague. The two older men who had kept in the background gasped their astonishment as his hair faded to a sickly gray, then became as white as the driven snow. Old Crompton was reverting to his previous state! Within five minutes, instead of the handsome young stranger, there stood before them a bent, withered old man—Old Crompton beyond a doubt. The effects of Tom's process were spent.

"Well I'm damned!" ejaculated Alton Forsythe. "You have been right all along, Asa. And I am mighty glad I did not commit Tom as I intended. He has told us the truth all these years and we were not wise enough to see it."

"We!" exclaimed the judge. "You, Alton Forsythe! I have always upheld him. You have done your son a grave injustice and you owe him your apologies if ever a father owed his son anything."

"You are right, Asa." And, his aristocratic pride forgotten, Alton Forsythe rushed to the side of his son and embraced him.

The judge turned to Old Crompton pityingly. "Rather a bad ending for you, Crompton," he said. "Still, it is better by far than being branded as a murderer."

"Better? Better?" croaked Old Crompton. "It is wonderful, Judge. I have never been so happy in my life!"

The face of the old man beamed, though scalding tears coursed down the withered and seamed cheeks. The two Forsythes looked up from their demonstrations of peacemaking to listen to the amazing words of the old hermit.

"Yes, happy for the first time in my life," he continued. "I am one hundred years of age, gentlemen, and I now look it and feel it. That is as it should be. And my experience has taught me a final lasting lesson. None of you know it, but, when I was but a very young man I was bitterly disappointed in love. Ha! ha! Never think it to look at me now, would you? But I was, and it ruined my entire life. I had a little money—inherited—and I traveled about in the world for a few years, then settled in that old hut across the road where I buried myself for sixty years, becoming crabbed and sour and despicable. Young Tom here was the first bright spot and, though I admired him, I hated him for his opportunities, hated him for that which he had that I had not. With the promise of his invention I thought I saw happiness, a new life for myself. I got what I wanted, though not in the way I had expected. And I want to tell you gentlemen that there is nothing in it. With developments of modern science you may be able to restore a man's youthful vigor of body, but you can't cure his mind with electricity. Though I had a youthful body, my brain was the brain of an old man—memories were there which could not be suppressed. Even had I not had the fancied death of young Tom on my conscience I should still have been miserable. I worked. God, how I worked—to forget! But I could not forget. I was successful in business and made a lot of money. I am more independent—probably wealthier than you, Alton Forsythe, but that did not bring happiness. I longed to be myself once more, to have the aches and pains which had been taken from me. It is natural to age and to die. Immortality would make of us a people of restless misery. We would quarrel and bicker and long for death, which would not come to relieve us. Now it is over for me and I am glad—glad—glad!"

He paused for breath, looking beseechingly at Tom Forsythe. "Tom," he said, "I suppose you have nothing for me in your heart but hatred. And I don't blame you. But I wish—I wish you would try and forgive me. Can you?"

The years had brought increased understanding and tolerance to young Tom. He stared at Old Crompton and the long-nursed anger over the destruction of his equipment melted into a strange mixture of pity and admiration for the courageous old fellow.

"Why, I guess I can, Crompton," he replied. "There was many a day when I struggled hopelessly to reconstruct my apparatus, cursing you with every bit of energy in my make-up. I could cheerfully have throttled you, had you been within reach. For twelve years I have labored incessantly to reproduce the results we obtained on the night of which you speak. People called me insane—even my father wished to have me committed to an asylum. And, until now, I have been unsuccessful. Only to-day has it seemed for the first time that the experiments will again succeed. But my ideas have changed with regard to the uses of the process. I was a cocksure young pup in the old days, with foolish dreams of fame and influence. But I have seen the error of my ways. Your experience, too, convinces me that immortality may not be as desirable as I thought. But there are great possibilities in the way of relieving the sufferings of mankind and in making this a better world in which to live. With your advice and help I believe I can do great things. I now forgive you freely and I ask you to remain here with me to assist in the work that is to come. What do you say to the idea?"

At the reverent thankfulness in the pale eyes of the broken old man who had so recently been a perfect specimen of vigorous youth, Alton Forsythe blew his nose noisily. The little judge smiled benevolently and shook his head as if to say, "I told you so." Tom and Old Crompton gripped hands—mightily.

COMING, NEXT MONTH
BRIGANDS OF THE MOON
By RAY CUMMINGS

Spawn of the Stars

By Charles Willard Diffin

The sky was alive with winged shapes, and high in the air shone the glittering menace, trailing five plumes of gas.

> The Earth lay powerless beneath those loathsome, yellowish monsters that, sheathed in cometlike globes, sprang from the skies to annihilate man and reduce his cities to ashes.

When Cyrus R. Thurston bought himself a single-motored Stoughton job he was looking for new thrills. Flying around the east coast had lost its zest: he wanted to join that jaunty group who spoke so easily of hopping off for Los Angeles.

And what Cyrus Thurston wanted he usually obtained. But if that young millionaire-sportsman had been told that on his first flight this blocky, bulletlike ship was to pitch him headlong into the exact center of the wildest, strangest war this earth had ever seen—well, it is still probable that the Stoughton company would not have lost the sale.

They were roaring through the starlit, calm night, three thousand feet above a sage sprinkled desert, when the trip ended. Slim Riley had the stick when the first blast of hot oil ripped slashingly across the pilot's window. "There goes your old trip!" he yelled. "Why don't they try putting engines in these ships?"

He jammed over the throttle and, with motor idling, swept down toward the endless miles of moonlit waste. Wind? They had been boring into it. Through the opened window he spotted a likely stretch of ground. Setting down the ship on a nice piece of Arizona desert was a mere detail for Slim.

"Let off a flare," he ordered, "when I give the word."

The white glare of it faded the stars as he sideslipped, then straightened out on his hand-picked field. The plane rolled down a clear space and stopped. The bright glare persisted while he stared curiously from the quiet cabin. Cutting the motor he opened both windows, then grabbed Thurston by the shoulder.

"'Tis a curious thing, that," he said unsteadily. His hand pointed straight ahead. The flare died, but the bright stars of the desert country still shone on a glistening, shining bulb.

It was some two hundred feet away. The lower part was lost in shadow, but its upper surfaces shone rounded and silvery like a giant bubble. It towered in the air, scores of feet above the chaparral beside it. There was a round spot of black on its side, which looked absurdly like a door....

"I saw something moving," said Thurston slowly. "On the ground I saw.... Oh, good Lord, Slim, it isn't real!"

Slim Riley made no reply. His eyes were riveted to an undulating, ghastly something that oozed and crawled in the pale light not far from the bulb. His hand was reaching, reaching.... It found what he sought; he leaned toward the window. In his hand was the Very pistol for discharging the flares. He aimed forward and up.

The second flare hung close before it settled on the sandy floor. Its blinding whiteness made the more loathsome the sickening yellow of the flabby flowing thing that writhed frantically in the glare. It was formless, shapeless, a heaving mound of nauseous matter. Yet even in its agonized writhing distortions they sensed the beating pulsations that marked it a living thing.

There were unending ripplings crossing and recrossing through the convolutions. To Thurston there was suddenly a sickening likeness: the thing was a brain from a gigantic skull—it was naked—was suffering....

The thing poured itself across the sand. Before the staring gaze of the speechless men an excrescence appeared—a thick bulb on the mass—that protruded itself into a tentacle. At the end there grew instantly a hooked hand. It reached for the black opening in the great shell, found it, and the whole loathsome shapelessness poured itself up and through the hole.

Only at the last was it still. In the dark opening the last slippery mass held quiet for endless seconds. It formed, as they watched, to a head—frightful—menacing. Eyes appeared in the head; eyes flat and round and black save for a cross slit in each; eyes that stared horribly and unchangingly into theirs. Below them a gaping mouth opened and closed.... The head melted—was gone....

And with its going came a rushing roar of sound.

From under the metallic mass shrieked a vaporous cloud. It drove at them, a swirling blast of snow and sand. Some buried memory of gas attacks woke Riley from his stupor. He slammed shut the windows an instant before the cloud struck, but not before they had seen, in the moonlight, a gleaming, gigantic, elongated bulb rise swiftly—screamingly—into the upper air.

The blast tore at their plane. And the cold in their tight compartment was like the cold of outer space. The men stared, speechless, panting. Their breath froze in that frigid room into steam clouds.

"It—it...." Thurston gasped—and slumped helpless upon the floor.

It was an hour before they dared open the door of their cabin. An hour of biting, numbing cold. Zero—on a warm summer night on the desert! Snow in the hurricane that had struck them!

"'Twas the blast from the thing," guessed the pilot; "though never did I see an engine with an exhaust like that." He was pounding himself with his arms to force up the chilled circulation.

"But the beast—the—the *thing*!" exclaimed Thurston. "It's monstrous; indecent! It thought—no question of that—but no body! Horrible! Just a raw, naked, thinking protoplasm!"

It was here that he flung open the door. They sniffed cautiously of the air. It was warm again—clean—save for a hint of some nauseous odor. They walked forward; Riley carried a flash.

The odor grew to a stench as they came where the great mass had lain. On the ground was a fleshy mound. There were bones showing, and horns on a skull. Riley held the light close to show the body of a steer. A body of raw bleeding meat. Half of it had been absorbed....

"The damned thing," said Riley, and paused vainly for adequate words. "The damned thing was eating.... Like a jelly-fish, it was!"

"Exactly," Thurston agreed. He pointed about. There were other heaps scattered among the low sage.

"Smothered," guessed Thurston, "with that frozen exhaust. Then the filthy thing landed and came out to eat."

"Hold the light for me," the pilot commanded. "I'm goin' to fix that busted oil line. And I'm goin' to do it right now. Maybe the creature's still hungry."

They sat in their room. About them was the luxury of a modern hotel. Cyrus Thurston stared vacantly at the breakfast he was forgetting to eat. He wiped his hands mechanically on a snowy napkin. He looked from the window. There were palm trees in the park, and autos in a ceaseless stream. And people! Sane, sober people, living in a sane world. Newsboys were shouting; the life of the city was flowing.

"Riley!" Thurston turned to the man across the table. His voice was curiously toneless, and his face haggard. "Riley, I haven't slept for three nights. Neither have you. We've got to get this thing straight. We didn't both become absolute maniacs at the same instant, but—it was *not* there, it was *never* there—not *that*...." He was lost in unpleasant recollections. "There are other records of hallucinations."

"Hallucinations—hell!" said Slim Riley. He was looking at a Los Angeles newspaper. He passed one hand wearily across his eyes, but his face was happier than it had been in days.

"We didn't imagine it, we aren't crazy—it's real! Would you read that now!" He passed the paper across to Thurston. The headlines were startling.

"Pilot Killed by Mysterious Airship. Silvery Bubble Hangs Over New York. Downs Army Plane in Burst of Flame. Vanishes at Terrific Speed."

"It's our little friend," said Thurston. And on his face, too, the lines were vanishing; to find this horror a reality was positive relief. "Here's the same cloud of vapor—drifted slowly across the city, the accounts says, blowing this stuff like steam from underneath. Airplanes investigated—an army plane drove into the vapor—terrific explosion—plane down in flames—others wrecked. The machine ascended with meteor speed, trailing blue flame. Come on, boy, where's that old bus? Thought I never wanted to fly a plane again. Now I don't want to do anything but."

"Where to?" Slim inquired.

"Headquarters," Thurston told him. "Washington—let's go!"

From Los Angeles to Washington is not far, as the plane flies. There was a stop or two for gasoline, but it was only a day later that they were seated in the War Office. Thurston's card had gained immediate admittance. "Got the low-down," he had written on the back of his card, "on the mystery airship."

"What you have told me is incredible," the Secretary was saying, "or would be if General Lozier here had not reported personally on the occurrence at New York. But the monster, the thing you have described.... Cy, if I didn't know you as I do I would have you locked up."

"It's true," said Thurston, simply. "It's damnable, but it's true. Now what does it mean?"

"Heaven knows," was the response. "That's where it came from—out of the heavens."

"Not what we saw," Slim Riley broke in. "That thing came straight out of Hell." And in his voice was no suggestion of levity.

"You left Los Angeles early yesterday; have you seen the papers?"

Thurston shook his head.

"They are back," said the Secretary. "Reported over London—Paris—the West Coast. Even China has seen them. Shanghai cabled an hour ago."

"Them? How many are there?"

"Nobody knows. There were five seen at one time. There are more—unless the same ones go around the world in a matter of minutes."

Thurston remembered that whirlwind of vapor and a vanishing speck in the Arizona sky. "They could," he asserted. "They're faster than anything on earth. Though what drives them ... that gas—steam—whatever it is...."

"Hydrogen," stated General Lozier. "I saw the New York show when poor Davis got his. He flew into the exhaust; it went off like a million bombs. Characteristic hydrogen flame trailed the damn thing up out of sight—a tail of blue fire."

"And cold," stated Thurston.

"Hot as a Bunsen burner," the General contradicted. "Davis' plane almost melted."

"Before it ignited," said the other. He told of the cold in their plane.

"Ha!" The General spoke explosively. "That's expansion. That's a tip on their motive power. Expansion of gas. That accounts for the cold and the vapor. Suddenly expanded it would be intensely cold. The moisture of the air would condense, freeze. But how could they carry it? Or"—he frowned for a moment, brows drawn over deep-set gray eyes—"or generate it? But that's crazy—that's impossible!"

"So is the whole matter," the Secretary reminded him. "With the information Mr. Thurston and Mr. Riley have given us, the whole affair is beyond any gage our past experience might supply. We start from the impossible, and we go—where? What is to be done?"

"With your permission, sir, a number of things shall be done. It would be interesting to see what a squadron of planes might accomplish, diving on them from above. Or anti-aircraft fire."

"No," said the Secretary of War, "not yet. They have looked us over, but they have not attacked. For the present we do not know what they are. All of us have our suspicions—thoughts of interplanetary travel—thoughts too wild for serious utterance—but we know nothing.

"Say nothing to the papers of what you have told me," he directed Thurston. "Lord knows their surmises are wild enough now. And for you, General, in the event of any hostile move, you will resist."

"Your order was anticipated, sir." The General permitted himself a slight smile. "The air force is ready."

"Of course," the Secretary of War nodded. "Meet me here to-night—nine o'clock." He included Thurston and Riley in the command. "We need to think ... to think ... and perhaps their mission is friendly."

"Friendly!" The two flyers exchanged glances as they went to the door. And each knew what the other was seeing—a viscous ocherous mass that formed into a head where eyes devilish in their hate stared coldly into theirs....

"Think, we need to think," repeated Thurston later. "A creature that is just one big hideous brain, that can think an arm into existence—think a head where it wishes! What does a thing like that think of? What beastly thoughts could that—that *thing* conceive?"

"If I got the sights of a Lewis gun on it," said Riley vindictively, "I'd make it think."

"And my guess is that is all you would accomplish," Thurston told him. "I am forming a few theories about our visitors. One is that it would be quite impossible to find a vital spot in that big homogeneous mass."

The pilot dispensed with theories: his was a more literal mind. "Where on earth did they come from, do you suppose, Mr. Thurston?"

They were walking to their hotel. Thurston raised his eyes to the summer heavens. Faint stars were beginning to twinkle; there was one that glowed steadily.

"Nowhere on earth," Thurston stated softly, "nowhere on earth."

"Maybe so," said the pilot, "maybe so. We've thought about it and talked about it ... and they've gone ahead and done it." He called to a newsboy; they took the latest editions to their room.

The papers were ablaze with speculation. There were dispatches from all corners of the earth, interviews with scientists and near scientists. The machines were a Soviet invention—they were beyond anything human—they were harmless—they would wipe out civilization—poison gas—blasts of fire like that which had enveloped the army flyer....

And through it all Thurston read an ill-concealed fear, a reflection of panic that was gripping the nation—the whole world. These great machines were sinister. Wherever they appeared came the sense of being watched, of a menace being calmly withheld. And at thought of the obscene monsters inside those spheres, Thurston's lips were compressed and his eyes hardened. He threw the papers aside.

"They are here," he said, "and that's all that we know. I hope the Secretary of War gets some good men together. And I hope someone is inspired with an answer."

"An answer is it?" said Riley. "I'm thinkin' that the answer will come, but not from these swivel-chair fighters. 'Tis the boys in the cockpits with one hand on the stick and one on the guns that will have the answer."

But Thurston shook his head. "Their speed," he said, "and the gas! Remember that cold. How much of it can they lay over a city?"

The question was unanswered, unless the quick ringing of the phone was a reply.

"War Department," said a voice. "Hold the wire." The voice of the Secretary of War came on immediately.

"Thurston?" he asked. "Come over at once on the jump, old man. Hell's popping."

The windows of the War Department Building were all alight as they approached. Cars were coming and going; men in uniform, as the Secretary had said, "on the jump." Soldiers with bayonets stopped them, then passed Thurston and his companion on. Bells were ringing from all sides. But in the Secretary's office was perfect quiet.

General Lozier was there, Thurston saw, and an imposing array of gold-braided men with a sprinkling of those in civilian clothes. One he recognized: MacGregor from the Bureau of Standards. The Secretary handed Thurston some papers.

"Radio," he explained. "They are over the Pacific coast. Hit near Vancouver; Associated Press says city destroyed. They are working down the coast. Same story—blast of hydrogen from their funnel shaped base. Colder than Greenland below them; snow fell in Seattle. No real attack since Vancouver and little damage done—" A message was laid before him.

"Portland," he said. "Five mystery ships over city. Dart repeatedly toward earth, deliver blast of gas and then retreat. Doing no damage. Apparently inviting attack. All commercial planes ordered grounded. Awaiting instructions.

"Gentlemen," said the Secretary, "I believe I speak for all present when I say that, in the absence of first hand information, we are utterly unable to arrive at any definite conclusion or make a definite plan. There is a menace in this, undeniably. Mr. Thurston and Mr. Riley have been good enough to report to me. They have seen one machine at close range. It was occupied by a monster so incredible that the report would receive no attention from me did I not know Mr. Thurston personally.

"Where have they come from? What does it mean—what is their mission? Only God knows.

"Gentlemen, I feel that I must see them. I want General Lozier to accompany me, also Doctor MacGregor, to advise me from the scientific angle. I am going to the Pacific Coast. They may not wait—that is true—but they appear to be going slowly south. I will leave to-night for San Diego. I hope to intercept them. We have strong air-forces there; the Navy Department is cooperating."

He waited for no comment. "General," he ordered, "will you kindly arrange for a plane? Take an escort or not as you think best.

"Mr. Thurston and Mr. Riley will also accompany us. We want all the authoritative data we can get. This on my return will be placed before you, gentlemen, for your consideration." He rose from his chair. "I hope they wait for us," he said.

Time was when a commander called loudly for a horse, but in this day a Secretary of War is not kept waiting for transportation. Sirening motorcycles preceded them from the city. Within an hour, motors roaring wide open, propellers ripping into the summer night, lights slipping eastward three thousand feet below, the Secretary of War for the United States was on his way. And on either side from their plane stretched the arms of a V. Like a flight of gigantic wild geese, fast fighting planes of the Army air service bored steadily into the night, guarantors of safe convoy.

"The Air Service is ready," General Lozier had said. And Thurston and his pilot knew that from East coast to West, swift scout planes, whose idling engines could roar into action at a moment's notice, stood waiting; battle planes hidden in hangars would roll forth at the word—the Navy was cooperating—and at San Diego there were strong naval units, Army units, and Marine Corps.

"They don't know what we can do, what we have up our sleeve: they are feeling us out," said the Secretary. They had stopped more than once for gas and for wireless reports. He held a sheaf of typewritten briefs.

"Going slowly south. They have taken their time. Hours over San Francisco and the bay district. Repeating same tactics; fall with terrific speed to cushion against their blast of gas. Trying to draw us out, provoke an attack, make us show our strength. Well, we shall beat them to San Diego at this rate. We'll be there in a few hours."

The afternoon sun was dropping ahead of them when they sighted the water. "Eckener Pass," the pilot told them, "where the Graf Zeppelin came through. Wonder what these birds would think of a Zepp!

"There's the ocean," he added after a time. San Diego glistened against the bare hills. "There's North Island—the Army field." He stared intently ahead, then shouted: "And there they are! Look there!"

Over the city a cluster of meteors was falling. Dark underneath, their tops shone like pure silver in the sun's slanting glare. They fell toward the city, then buried themselves in a dense cloud of steam, rebounding at once to the upper air, vapor trailing behind them.

The cloud billowed slowly. It struck the hills of the city, then lifted and vanished.

"Land at once," requested the Secretary. A flash of silver countermanded the order.

It hung there before them, a great gleaming globe, keeping always its distance ahead. It was elongated at the base, Thurston observed. From that base shot the familiar blast that turned steamy a hundred feet below as it chilled the warm air. There were round orifices, like ports, ranged around the top, where an occasional jet of vapor showed this to be a method of control. Other spots shone dark and glassy. Were they windows? He hardly realized their peril, so interested was he in the strange machine ahead.

Then: "Dodge that vapor," ordered General Lozier. The plane wavered in signal to the others and swung sharply to the left. Each man knew the flaming death that was theirs if the fire of their exhaust touched that explosive mixture of hydrogen and air. The great bubble turned with them and paralleled their course.

"He's watching us," said Riley, "giving us the once over, the slimy devil. Ain't there a gun on this ship?"

The General addressed his superior. Even above the roar of the motors his voice seemed quiet, assured. "We must not land now," he said. "We can't land at North Island. It would focus their attention upon our defenses. That thing—whatever it is—is looking for a vulnerable spot. We must.... Hold on—there he goes!"

The big bulb shot upward. It slanted above them, and hovered there.

"I think he is about to attack," said the General quietly. And, to the commander of their squadron: "It's in your hands now, Captain. It's your fight."

The Captain nodded and squinted above. "He's got to throw heavier stuff than that," he remarked. A small object was falling from the cloud. It passed close to their ship.

"Half-pint size," said Cyrus Thurston, and laughed in derision. There was something ludicrous in the futility of the attack. He stuck his head from a window into the gale they created. He sheltered his eyes to try to follow the missile in its fall.

They were over the city. The criss-cross of streets made a grill-work of lines; tall buildings were dwarfed from this three thousand foot altitude. The sun slanted across a projecting promontory to make golden ripples on a blue sea and the city sparkled back in the clear air. Tiny white faces were massed in the streets, huddled in clusters where the futile black missile had vanished.

And then—then the city was gone....

A white cloud-bank billowed and mushroomed. Slowly, it seemed to the watcher—so slowly.

It was done in the fraction of a second. Yet in that brief time his eyes registered the chaotic sweep in advance of the cloud. There came a crashing of buildings in some monster whirlwind, a white cloud engulfing it all.... It was rising—was on them.

"God," thought Thurston, "why can't I move!" The plane lifted and lurched. A thunder of sound crashed against them, an intolerable force. They were crushed to the floor as the plane was hurled over and upward.

Out of the mad whirling tangle of flying bodies, Thurston glimpsed one clear picture. The face of the pilot hung battered and blood-covered before him, and over the limp body the hand of Slim Riley clutched at the switch.

"Bully boy," he said dazedly, "he's cutting the motors...." The thought ended in blackness.

There was no sound of engines or beating propellers when he came to his senses. Something lay heavy upon him. He pushed it to one side. It was the body of General Lozier.

He drew himself to his knees to look slowly about, rubbed stupidly at his eyes to quiet the whirl, then stared at the blood on his hand. It was so quiet—the motors—what was it that happened? Slim had reached for the switch....

The whirling subsided. Before him he saw Slim Riley at the controls. He got to his feet and went unsteadily forward. It was a battered face that was lifted to his.

"She was spinning," the puffed lips were muttering slowly. "I brought her out ... there's the field...." His voice was thick; he formed the words slowly, painfully. "Got to land ... can you take it? I'm—I'm—" He slumped limply in his seat.

Thurston's arms were uninjured. He dragged the pilot to the floor and got back of the wheel. The field was below them. There were planes taxiing out; he heard the roar of their motors. He tried the controls. The plane answered stiffly, but he managed to level off as the brown field approached.

Thurston never remembered that landing. He was trying to drag Riley from the battered plane when the first man got to him.

"Secretary of War?" he gasped. "In there.... Take Riley; I can walk."

"We'll get them," an officer assured him. "Knew you were coming. They sure gave you hell! But look at the city!"

Arms carried him stumbling from the field. Above the low hangars he saw smoke clouds over the bay. These and red rolling flames marked what had been an American city. Far in the heavens moved five glinting specks.

His head reeled with the thunder of engines. There were planes standing in lines and more erupting from hangars, where khaki-clad men, faces tense under leather helmets, rushed swiftly about.

"General Lozier is dead," said a voice. Thurston turned to the man. They were bringing the others. "The rest are smashed up some," the officer told him, "but I think they'll pull through."

The Secretary of War for the United States lay beside him. Men with red on their sleeves were slitting his coat. Through one good eye he squinted at Thurston. He even managed a smile.

"Well, I wanted to see them up close," he said. "They say you saved us, old man."

Thurston waved that aside. "Thank Riley—" he began, but the words ended in the roar of an exhaust. A plane darted swiftly away to shoot vertically a hundred feet in the air. Another followed and another. In a cloud of brown dust they streamed endlessly out, zooming up like angry hornets, eager to get into the fight.

"Fast little devils!" the ambulance man observed. "Here come the big boys."

A leviathan went deafeningly past. And again others came on in quick succession. Farther up the field, silvery gray planes with rudders flaunting their red, white and blue rose circling to the heights.

"That's the Navy," was the explanation. The surgeon straightened the Secretary's arm. "See them come off the big airplane carriers!"

If his remarks were part of his professional training in removing a patient's thoughts from his pain, they were effective. The Secretary stared out to sea, where two great flat-decked craft were shooting planes with the regularity of a rapid fire gun. They stood out sharply against a bank of gray fog. Cyrus Thurston forgot his bruised body, forgot his own peril—even the inferno that raged back across the bay: he was lost in the sheer thrill of the spectacle.

Above them the sky was alive with winged shapes. And from all the disorder there was order appearing. Squadron after squadron swept to battle formation. Like flights of wild ducks the true sharp-pointed Vs soared off into the sky. Far above and beyond, rows of dots marked the race of swift scouts for the upper levels. And high in the clear air shone the glittering menace trailing their five plumes of gas.

A deeper detonation was merging into the uproar. It came from the ships, Thurston knew, where anti-aircraft guns poured a rain of shells into the sky. About the invaders they bloomed into clusters of smoke balls. The globes shot a thousand feet into the air. Again the shells found them, and again they retreated.

"Look!" said Thurston. "They got one!"

He groaned as a long curving arc of speed showed that the big bulb was under control. Over the ships it paused, to balance and swing, then shot to the zenith as one of the great boats exploded in a cloud of vapor.

The following blast swept the airdrome. Planes yet on the ground went like dry autumn leaves. The hangars were flattened.

Thurston cowered in awe. They were sheltered, he saw, by a slope of the ground. No ridicule now for the bombs!

A second blast marked when the gas-cloud ignited. The billowing flames were blue. They writhed in tortured convulsions through the air. Endless explosions merged into one rumbling roar.

MacGregor had roused from his stupor; he raised to a sitting position.

"Hydrogen," he stated positively, and pointed where great volumes of flame were sent whirling aloft. "It burns as it mixes with air." The scientist was studying intently the mammoth reaction. "But the volume," he marveled, "the volume! From that small container! Impossible!"

"Impossible," the Secretary agreed, "but...." He pointed with his one good arm toward the Pacific. Two great ships of steel, blackened and battered in that fiery breath, tossed helplessly upon the pitching, heaving sea. They furnished to the scientist's exclamation the only adequate reply.

Each man stared aghast into the pallid faces of his companions. "I think we have underestimated the opposition," said the Secretary of War quietly. "Look—the fog is coming in, but it's too late to save them."

The big ships were vanishing in the oncoming fog. Whirls of vapor were eddying toward them in the flame-blaster air. Above them the watchers saw dimly the five gleaming bulbs. There were airplanes attacking: the tapping of machine-gun fire came to them faintly.

Fast planes circled and swooped toward the enemy. An armada of big planes drove in from beyond. Formations were blocking space above.... Every branch of the service was there, Thurston exulted, the army, Marine Corps, the Navy. He gripped hard at the dry ground in a paralysis of taut nerves. The battle was on, and in the balance hung the fate of the world.

The fog drove in fast. Through straining eyes he tried in vain to glimpse the drama spread above. The world grew dark and gray. He buried his face in his hands.

And again came the thunder. The men on the ground forced their gaze to the clouds, though they knew some fresh horror awaited.

The fog-clouds reflected the blue terror above. They were riven and torn. And through them black objects were falling. Some blazed as they fell. They slipped into unthought maneuvers—they darted to earth trailing yellow and black of gasoline fires. The air was filled with the dread rain of death that was spewed from the gray clouds. Gone was the roaring of motors. The air-force of the San Diego area swept in silence to the earth, whose impact alone could give kindly concealment to their flame-stricken burden.

Thurston's last control snapped. He flung himself flat to bury his face in the sheltering earth.

Only the driving necessity of work to be done saved the sanity of the survivors. The commercial broadcasting stations were demolished, a part of the fuel for the terrible furnace across the bay. But the Naval radio station was beyond on an outlying hill. The Secretary of War was in charge. An hour's work and this was again in commission to flash to the world the story of disaster. It told the world also of what lay ahead. The writing was plain. No prophet was needed to forecast the doom and destruction that awaited the earth.

Civilization was helpless. What of armies and cannon, of navies, of aircraft, when from some unreachable height these monsters within their bulbous machines could drop coldly—methodically—their diminutive bombs. And when each bomb meant shattering destruction; each explosion blasting all within a radius of miles; each followed by the blue blast of fire that melted the twisted framework of buildings and powdered the stones to make of a proud city a desolation of wreckage, black and silent beneath the cold stars. There was no crumb of comfort for the world in the terror the radio told.

Slim Riley was lying on an improvised cot when Thurston and the representative of the Bureau of Standards joined him. Four walls of a room still gave shelter in a half-wrecked building. There were candles burning: the dark was unbearable.

"Sit down," said MacGregor quietly; "we must think...."

"Think!" Thurston's voice had an hysterical note. "I can't think! I mustn't think! I'll go raving crazy...."

"Yes, think," said the scientist. "Had it occurred to you that that is our only weapon left?

"We must think, we must analyze. Have these devils a vulnerable spot? Is there any known means of attack? We do not know. We must learn. Here in this room we have all the direct information the world possesses of this menace. I have seen their machines in operation. You have seen more—you have looked at the monsters themselves. At one of them, anyway."

The man's voice was quiet, methodical. Mr. MacGregor was attacking a problem. Problems called for concentration; not hysterics. He could have poured the contents from a beaker without spilling a drop. His poise was needed: they were soon to make a laboratory experiment.

The door burst open to admit a wild-eyed figure that snatched up their candles and dashed them to the floor.

"Lights out!" he screamed at them. "There's one of 'em coming back." He was gone from the room.

The men sprang for the door, then turned to where Riley was clumsily crawling from his couch. An arm under each of his, and the three men stumbled from the room.

They looked about them in the night. The fog-banks were high, drifting in from the ocean. Beneath them the air was clear; from somewhere above a hidden moon forced a pale light through the clouds. And over the ocean, close to the water, drifted a familiar shape. Familiar in its huge sleek roundness, in its funnel-shaped base where a soft roar made vaporous clouds upon the water. Familiar, too, in the wild dread it inspired.

The watchers were spellbound. To Thurston there came a fury of impotent frenzy. It was so near! His hands trembled to tear at that door, to rip at that foul mass he knew was within.... The great bulb drifted past. It was nearing the shore. But its action! Its motion!

Gone was the swift certainty of control. The thing settled and sank, to rise weakly with a fresh blast of gas from its exhaust. It settled again, and passed waveringly on in the night.

Thurston was throbbingly alive with hope that was certainty. "It's been hit," he exulted; "it's been hit. Quick! After it, follow it!" He dashed for a car. There were some that had been salvaged from the less ruined buildings. He swung it quickly around where the others were waiting.

"Get a gun," he commanded. "Hey, you,"—to an officer who appeared—"your pistol, man, quick! We're going after it!" He caught the tossed gun and hurried the others into the car.

"Wait," MacGregor commanded. "Would you hunt elephants with a pop-gun? Or these things?"

"Yes," the other told him, "or my bare hands! Are you coming, or aren't you?"

The physicist was unmoved. "The creature you saw—you said that it writhed in a bright light—you said it seemed almost in agony. There's an idea there! Yes, I'm going with you, but keep your shirt on, and think."

He turned again to the officer. "We need lights," he explained, "bright lights. What is there? Magnesium? Lights of any kind?"

"Wait." The man rushed off into the dark.

He was back in a moment to thrust a pistol into the car. "Flares," he explained. "Here's a flashlight, if you need it." The car tore at the ground as Thurston opened it wide. He drove recklessly toward the highway that followed the shore.

The high fog had thinned to a mist. A full moon was breaking through to touch with silver the white breakers hissing on the sand. It spread its full glory on dunes and sea: one more of the countless soft nights where peace and calm beauty told of an ageless existence that made naught of the red havoc of men or of monsters. It shone on the ceaseless surf that had beaten these shores before there were men, that would thunder there still when men were no more. But to the tense crouching men in the car it shone only ahead on a distant, glittering speck. A wavering reflection marked the uncertain flight of the stricken enemy.

Thurston drove like a maniac; the road carried them straight toward their quarry. What could he do when he overtook it? He neither knew nor cared. There was only the blind fury forcing him on within reach of the thing. He cursed as the lights of the car showed a bend in the road. It was leaving the shore.

He slackened their speed to drive cautiously into the sand. It dragged at the car, but he fought through to the beach, where he hoped for firm footing. The tide was out. They tore madly along the smooth sand, breakers clutching at the flying wheels.

The strange aircraft was nearer; it was plainly over the shore, they saw. Thurston groaned as it shot high in the air in an effort to clear the cliffs ahead. But the heights were no longer a refuge. Again it settled. It struck on the cliff to rebound in a last futile leap. The great pear shape tilted, then shot end over end to crash hard on the firm sand. The lights of the car struck the wreck, and they saw the shell roll over once. A ragged break was opening—the spherical top fell slowly to one side. It was still rocking as they brought the car to a stop. Filling the lower shell, they saw dimly, was a mucouslike mass that seethed and struggled in the brilliance of their lights.

MacGregor was persisting in his theory. "Keep the lights on it!" he shouted. "It can't stand the light."

While they watched, the hideous, bubbling beast oozed over the side of the broken shell to shelter itself in the shadow beneath. And again Thurston sensed the pulse and throb of life in the monstrous mass.

He saw again in his rage the streaming rain of black airplanes; saw, too, the bodies, blackened and charred as they saw them when first they tried rescue from the crashed ships; the smoke clouds and flames from the blasted city, where people—his people, men and women and little children—had met terrible death. He sprang from the car. Yet he faltered with a revulsion that was almost a nausea. His gun was gripped in his hand as he ran toward the monster.

"Come back!" shouted MacGregor. "Come back! Have you gone mad?" He was jerking at the door of the car.

Beyond the white funnel of their lights a yellow thing was moving. It twisted and flowed with incredible speed a hundred feet back to the base of the cliff. It drew itself together in a quivering heap.

An out-thrusting rock threw a sheltering shadow; the moon was low in the west. In the blackness a phosphorescence was apparent. It rippled and rose in the dark with the pulsing beat of the jellylike mass. And through it were showing two discs. Gray at first, they formed to black, staring eyes.

Thurston had followed. His gun was raised as he neared it. Then out of the mass shot a serpentine arm. It whipped about him, soft, sticky, viscid—utterly loathsome. He screamed once when it clung to his face, then tore savagely and in silence at the encircling folds.

The gun! He ripped a blinding mass from his face and emptied the automatic in a stream of shots straight toward the eyes. And he knew as he fired that the effort was useless; to have shot at the milky surf would have been as vain.

The thing was pulling him irresistibly; he sank to his knees; it dragged him over the sand. He clutched at a rock. A vision was before him: the carcass of a steer, half absorbed and still bleeding on the sand of an Arizona desert....

To be drawn to the smothering embrace of that glutinous mass ... for that monstrous appetite.... He tore afresh at the unyielding folds, then knew MacGregor was beside him.

In the man's hand was a flashlight. The scientist risked his life on a guess. He thrust the powerful light into the clinging serpent. It was like the touch of hot iron to human flesh. The arm struggled and flailed in a paroxysm of pain.

Thurston was free. He lay gasping on the sand. But MacGregor! ... He looked up to see him vanish in the clinging ooze. Another thick tentacle had been projected from the main mass to sweep like a whip about the man. It hissed as it whirled about him in the still air.

The flashlight was gone; Thurston's hand touched it in the sand. He sprang to his feet and pressed the switch. No light responded; the flashlight was out—broken.

A thick arm slashed and wrapped about him.... It beat him to the ground. The sand was moving beneath him; he was being dragged swiftly, helplessly, toward what waited in the shadow. He was smothering.... A blinding glare filled his eyes....

The flares were still burning when he dared look about. MacGregor was pulling frantically at his arm. "Quick—quick!" he was shouting. Thurston scrambled to his feet.

One glimpse he caught of a heaving yellow mass in the white light; it twisted in horrible convulsions. They ran stumblingly—drunkenly—toward the car.

Riley was half out of the machine. He had tried to drag himself to their assistance. "I couldn't make it," he said: "then I thought of the flares."

"Thank Heaven," said MacGregor with emphasis, "it was your legs that were paralyzed, Riley, not your brain."

Thurston found his voice. "Let me have that Very pistol. If light hurts that damn thing, I am going to put a blaze of magnesium into the middle of it if I die for it."

"They're all gone," said Riley.

"Then let's get out of here. I've had enough. We can come back later on."

He got back of the wheel and slammed the door of the sedan. The moonlight was gone. The darkness was velvet just tinged with the gray that precedes the dawn. Back in the deeper blackness at the cliff-base a phosphorescent something wavered and glowed. The light rippled and flowed in all directions over the mass. Thurston felt, vaguely, its mystery—the bulk was a vast, naked brain; its quiverings were like visible thought waves....

The phosphorescence grew brighter. The thing was approaching. Thurston let in his clutch, but the scientist checked him.

"Wait," he implored, "wait! I wouldn't miss this for the world." He waved toward the east, where far distant ranges were etched in palest rose.

"We know less than nothing of these creatures, in what part of the universe they are spawned, how they live, where they live—Saturn!—Mars!—the Moon! But—we shall soon know how one dies!"

The thing was coming from the cliff. In the dim grayness it seemed less yellow, less fluid. A membrane enclosed it. It was close to the car. Was it hunger that drove it, or cold rage for these puny opponents? The hollow eyes were glaring; a thick arm formed quickly to dart out toward the car. A cloud, high above, caught the color of approaching day....

Before their eyes the vile mass pulsed visibly; it quivered and beat. Then, sensing its danger, it darted like some headless serpent for its machine.

It massed itself about the shattered top to heave convulsively. The top was lifted, carried toward the rest of the great metal egg. The sun's first rays made golden arrows through the distant peaks.

The struggling mass released its burden to stretch its vile length toward the dark caves under the cliffs. The last sheltering fog-veil parted. The thing was halfway to the high bank when the first bright shaft of direct sunlight shot through.

Incredible in the concealment of night, the vast protoplasmic pod was doubly so in the glare of day. But it was there before them, not a hundred feet distant. And it boiled in vast tortured convulsions. The clean sunshine struck it, and the mass heaved itself into the air in a nauseous eruption, then fell limply to the earth.

The yellow membrane turned paler. Once more the staring black eyes formed to turn hopelessly toward the sheltering globe. Then the bulk flattened out on the sand. It was a jellylike mound, through which trembled endless quivering palpitations.

The sun struck hot, and before the eyes of the watching, speechless men was a sickening, horrible sight—a festering mass of corruption.

The sickening yellow was liquid. It seethed and bubbled with liberated gases; it decomposed to purplish fluid streams. A breath of wind blew in their direction. The stench from the hideous pool was overpowering, unbearable. Their heads swam in the evil breath.... Thurston ripped the gears into reverse, nor stopped until they were far away on the clean sand.

The tide was coming in when they returned. Gone was the vile putrescence. The waves were lapping at the base of the gleaming machine.

"We'll have to work fast," said MacGregor. "I must know, I must learn." He drew himself up and into the shattered shell.

It was of metal, some forty feet across, its framework a maze of latticed struts. The central part was clear. Here in a wide, shallow pan the monster had rested. Below this was tubing, intricate coils, massive, heavy and strong. MacGregor lowered himself upon it, Thurston was beside him. They went down into the dim bowels of the deadly instrument.

"Hydrogen," the physicist was stating. "Hydrogen—there's our starting point. A generator, obviously, forming the gas—from what? They couldn't compress it! They couldn't carry it or make it, not the volume that they evolved. But they did it, they did it!"

Close to the coils a dim light was glowing. It was a pin-point of radiance in the half-darkness about them. The two men bent closer.

"See," directed MacGregor, "it strikes on this mirror—bright metal and parabolic. It disperses the light, doesn't concentrate it! Ah! Here is another, and another. This one is bent—broken. They are adjustable. Hm! Micrometer accuracy for reducing the light. The last one could reflect through this slot. It's light that does it, Thurston, it's light that does it!"

"Does what?" Thurston had followed the other's analysis of the diffusion process. "The light that would finally reach that slot would be hardly perceptible."

"It's the agent," said MacGregor, "the activator—the catalyst! What does it strike upon? I must know—I must!"

The waves were splashing outside the shell. Thurston turned in a feverish search of the unexplored depths. There was a surprising simplicity, an absence of complicated mechanism. The generator, with its tremendous braces to carry its thrust to the framework itself, filled most of the space. Some of the ribs were thicker, he noticed. Solid metal, as if they might carry great weights. Resting upon them were ranged numbers of objects. They were like eggs, slender, and inches in length. On some were propellers. They worked through the shells on long slender rods. Each was threaded finely—an adjustable arm engaged the thread. Thurston called excitedly to the other.

"Here they are," he said. "Look! Here are the shells. Here's what blew us up!"

He pointed to the slim shafts with their little propellerlike fans. "Adjustable, see? Unwind in their fall ... set 'em for any length of travel ... fires the charge in the air. That's how they wiped out our air fleet."

There were others without the propellers; they had fins to hold them nose downward. On each nose was a small rounded cap.

"Detonators of some sort," said MacGregor. "We've got to have one. We must get it out quick; the tide's coming in." He laid his hands upon one of the slim, egg-shaped things. He lifted, then strained mightily. But the object did not rise; it only rolled sluggishly.

The scientist stared at it amazed. "Specific gravity," he exclaimed, "beyond anything known! There's nothing on earth ... there is no such substance ... no form of matter...." His eyes were incredulous.

"Lots to learn," Thurston answered grimly. "We've yet to learn how to fight off the other four."

The other nodded. "Here's the secret," he said. "These shells liberate the same gas that drives the machine. Solve one and we solve both—then we learn how to combat it. But how to remove it—that is the problem. You and I can never lift this out of here."

His glance darted about. There was a small door in the metal beam. The groove in which the shells were placed led to it; it was a port for launching the projectiles. He moved it, opened it. A dash of spray struck him in the face. He glanced inquiringly at his companion.

"Dare we do it?" he asked. "Slide one of them out?"

Each man looked long into the eyes of the other. Was this, then, the end of their terrible night? One shell to be dropped—then a bursting volcano to blast them to eternity....

"The boys in the planes risked it," said Thurston quietly. "They got theirs." He stopped for a broken fragment of steel. "Try one with a fan on; it hasn't a detonator."

The men pried at the slim thing. It slid slowly toward the open port. One heave and it balanced on the edge, then vanished abruptly. The spray was cold on their faces. They breathed heavily with the realization that they still lived.

There were days of horror that followed, horror tempered by a numbing paralysis of all emotions. There were bodies by thousands to be heaped in the pit where San Diego had stood, to be buried beneath countless tons of debris and dirt. Trains brought an army of helpers; airplanes came with doctors and nurses and the beginning of a mountain of supplies. The need was there; it must be met. Yet the whole world was waiting while it helped, waiting for the next blow to fall.

Telegraph service was improvised, and radio receivers rushed in. The news of the world was theirs once more. And it told of a terrified, waiting world. There would be no temporizing now on the part of the invaders. They had seen the airplanes swarming from the ground—they would know an airdrome next time from the air. Thurston had noted the windows in the great shell, windows of dull-colored glass which would protect the darkness of the interior, essential to life for the horrible occupant, but through which it could see. It could watch all directions at once.

The great shell had vanished from the shore. Pounding waves and the shifting sands of high tide had obliterated all trace. More than once had Thurston uttered devout thanks for the chance shell from an anti-aircraft gun that had entered the funnel beneath the machine, had bent and twisted the arrangement of mirrors that he and MacGregor had seen, and, exploding, had cracked and broken the domed roof of the bulb. They had learned little, but MacGregor was up north within reach of Los Angeles laboratories. And he had with him the slim cylinder of death. He was studying, thinking.

Telephone service had been established for official business. The whole nation-wide system, for that matter, was under military control. The Secretary of War had flown back to Washington. The whole world was on a war basis. War! And none knew where they should defend themselves, nor how.

An orderly rushed Thurston to the telephone. "You are wanted at once; Los Angeles calling."

The voice of MacGregor was cool and unhurried as Thurston listened. "Grab a plane, old man," he was saying, "and come up here on the jump."

The phrase brought a grim smile to Thurston's tired lips. "Hell's popping!" the Secretary of War had added on that evening those long ages before. Did MacGregor have something? Was a different kind of hell preparing to pop? The thoughts flashed through the listener's mind.

"I need a good deputy," MacGregor said. "You may be the whole works—may have to carry on—but I'll tell you it all later. Meet me at the Biltmore."

"In less than two hours," Thurston assured him.

A plane was at his disposal. Riley's legs were functioning again, after a fashion. They kept the appointment with minutes to spare.

"Come on," said MacGregor, "I'll talk to you in the car." The automobile whirled them out of the city to race off upon a winding highway that climbed into far hills. There was twenty miles of this; MacGregor had time for his talk.

"They've struck," he told the two men. "They were over Germany yesterday. The news was kept quiet: I got the last report a half-hour ago. They pretty well wiped out Berlin. No airforce there. France and England sent a swarm of planes, from the reports. Poor devils! No need to tell you what they got. We've seen it first hand. They headed west over the Atlantic, the four machines. Gave England a burst or two from high up, paused over New York, then went on. But they're here somewhere, we think. Now listen:

"How long was it from the time when you saw the first monster until we heard from them again?"

Thurston forced his mind back to those days that seemed so far in the past. He tried to remember.

"Four days," broke in Riley. "It was the fourth day after we found the devil feeding."

"Feeding!" interrupted the scientist. "That's the point I am making. Four days. Remember that!

"And we knew they were down in the Argentine five days ago—that's another item kept from an hysterical public. They slaughtered some thousands of cattle; there were scores of them found where the devils—I'll borrow Riley's word—where the devils had fed. Nothing left but hide and bones.

"And—mark this—that was four days before they appeared over Berlin.

"Why? Don't ask me. Do they have to lie quiet for that period miles up there in space? God knows. Perhaps! These things seem outside the knowledge of a deity. But enough of that! Remember: four days! Let us assume that there is this four days waiting period. It will help us to time them. I'll come back to that later.

"Here is what I have been doing. We know that light is a means of attack. I believe that the detonators we saw on those bombs merely opened a seal in the shell and forced in a flash of some sort. I believe that radiant energy is what fires the blast.

"What is it that explodes? Nobody knows. We have opened the shell, working in the absolute blackness of a room a hundred feet underground. We found in it a powder—two powders, to be exact.

"They are mixed. One is finely divided, the other rather granular. Their specific gravity is enormous, beyond anything known to physical science unless it would be the hypothetical neutron masses we think are in certain stars. But this is not matter as we know matter; it is something new.

"Our theory is this: the hydrogen atom has been split, resolved into components, not of electrons and the proton centers, but held at some halfway point of decomposition. Matter composed only of neutrons would be heavy beyond belief. This fits the theory in that respect. But the point is this: When these solids are formed—they are dense—they represent in a cubic centimeter possibly a cubic mile of hydrogen gas under normal pressure. That's a guess, but it will give you the idea.

"Not compressed, you understand, but all the elements present in other than elemental form for the reconstruction of the atom ... for a million billions of atoms.

"Then the light strikes it. These dense solids become instantly a gas—miles of it held in that small space.

"There you have it: the gas, the explosion, the entire absence of heat—which is to say, its terrific cold—when it expands."

Slim Riley was looking bewildered but game. "Sure, I saw it snow," he affirmed, "so I guess the rest must be O.K. But what are we going to do about it? You say light kills 'em, and fires their bombs. But how can we let light into those big steel shells, or the little ones either?"

"Not through those thick walls," said MacGregor. "Not light. One of our anti-aircraft shells made a direct hit. That might not happen again in a million shots. But there are other forms of radiant energy that do penetrate steel...."

The car had stopped beside a grove of eucalyptus. A barren, sun-baked hillside stretched beyond. MacGregor motioned them to alight.

Riley was afire with optimism. "And do you believe it?" he asked eagerly. "Do you believe that we've got 'em licked?"

Thurston, too, looked into MacGregor's face: Riley was not the only one who needed encouragement. But the gray eyes were suddenly tired and hopeless.

"You ask what I believe," said the scientist slowly. "I believe we are witnessing the end of the world, our world of humans, their struggles, their grave hopes and happiness and aspirations...."

He was not looking at them. His gaze was far off in space.

"Men will struggle and fight with their puny weapons, but these monsters will win, and they will have their way with us. Then more of them will come. The world, I believe, is doomed...."

He straightened his shoulders. "But we can die fighting," he added, and pointed over the hill.

"Over there," he said, "in the valley beyond, is a charge of their explosive and a little apparatus of mine. I intend to fire the charge from a distance of three hundred yards. I expect to be safe, perfectly safe. But accidents happen.

"In Washington a plane is being prepared. I have given instructions through hours of phoning. They are working night and day. It will contain a huge generator for producing my ray. Nothing new! Just the product of our knowledge of radiant energy up to date. But the man who flies that plane will die—horribly. No time to experiment with protection. The rays will destroy him, though he may live a month.

"I am asking you," he told Cyrus Thurston, "to handle that plane. You may be of service to the world—you may find you are utterly powerless. You surely will die. But you know the machines and the monsters; your knowledge may be of value in an attack." He waited. The silence lasted for only a moment.

"Why, sure," said Cyrus Thurston.

He looked at the eucalyptus grove with earnest appraisal. The sun made lovely shadows among their stripped trunks: the world was a beautiful place. A lingering death, MacGregor had intimated—and horrible.... "Why, sure," he repeated steadily.

Slim Riley shoved him firmly aside to stand facing MacGregor.

"Sure, hell!" he said. "I'm your man, Mr. MacGregor.

"What do you know about flying?" he asked Cyrus Thurston. "You're good—for a beginner. But men like you two have got brains, and I'm thinkin' the world will be needin' them. Now me, all I'm good for is holdin' a shtick"—his brogue had returned to his speech, and was evidence of his earnestness.

"And, besides"—the smile faded from his lips, and his voice was suddenly soft—"them boys we saw take their last flip was just pilots to you, just a bunch of good fighters. Well, they're buddies of mine. I fought beside some of them in France.... I belong!"

He grinned happily at Thurston. "Besides," he said, "what do you know about dog-fights?"

MacGregor gripped him by the hand. "You win," he said. "Report to Washington. The Secretary of War has all the dope."

He turned to Thurston. "Now for you! Get this! The enemy machines almost attacked New York. One of them came low, then went back, and the four flashed out of sight toward the west. It is my belief that New York is next, but the devils are hungry. The beast that attacked us was ravenous, remember. They need food and lots of it. You will hear of their feeding, and you can count on four days. Keep Riley informed—that's your job.

"Now I'm going over the hill. If this experiment works, there's a chance we can repeat it on a larger scale. No certainty, but a chance! I'll be back. Full instructions at the hotel in case...." He vanished into the scrub growth.

"Not exactly encouraging," Thurston pondered, "but he's a good man, Mac, a good egg! Not as big a brain as the one we saw, but perhaps it's a better one—cleaner—and it's working!"

They were sheltered under the brow of the hill, but the blast from the valley beyond rocked them like an earthquake. They rushed to the top of the knoll. MacGregor was standing in the valley; he waved them a greeting and shouted something unintelligible.

The gas had mushroomed into a cloud of steamy vapor. From above came snowflakes to whirl in the churning mass, then fall to the ground. A wind came howling about them to beat upon the cloud. It swirled slowly back and down the valley. The figure of MacGregor vanished in its smothering embrace.

"Exit, MacGregor!" said Cyrus Thurston softly. He held tight to the struggling figure of Slim Riley.

"He couldn't live a minute in that atmosphere of hydrogen," he explained. "They can—the devils!—but not a good egg like Mac. It's our job now—yours and mine."

Slowly the gas retreated, lifted to permit their passage down the slope.

Mac Gregor was a good prophet. Thurston admitted that when, four days later, he stood on the roof of the Equitable Building in lower New York.

The monsters had fed as predicted. Out in Wyoming a desolate area marked the place of their meal, where a great herd of cattle lay smothered and frozen. There were ranch houses, too, in the circle of destruction, their occupants frozen stiff as the carcasses that dotted the plains. The country had stood tense for the following blow. Only Thurston had lived in certainty of a few days reprieve. And now had come the fourth day.

In Washington was Riley. Thurston had been in touch with him frequently.

"Sure, it's a crazy machine," the pilot had told him, "and 'tis not much I think of it at all. Neither bullets nor guns, just this big glass contraption and speed. She's fast, man, she's fast ... but it's little hope I have." And Thurston, remembering the scientist's words, was heartless and sick with dreadful certainty.

There were aircraft ready near New York; it was generally felt that here was the next objective. The enemy had looked it over carefully. And Washington, too, was guarded. The nation's capital must receive what little help the aircraft could afford.

There were other cities waiting for destruction. If not this time—later! The horror hung over them all.

The fourth day! And Thurston was suddenly certain of the fate of New York. He hurried to a telephone. Of the Secretary of War he implored assistance.

"Send your planes," he begged. "Here's where we will get it next. Send Riley. Let's make a last stand—win or lose."

"I'll give you a squadron," was the concession. "What difference whether they die there or here...?" The voice was that of a weary man, weary and sleepless and hopeless.

"Good-by Cy, old man!" The click of the receiver sounded in Thurston's ear. He returned to the roof for his vigil.

To wait, to stride nervously back and forth in impotent expectancy. He could leave, go out into open country, but what were a few days or months—or a year—with this horror upon them? It was the end. MacGregor was right. "Good old Mac!"

There were airplanes roaring overhead. It meant.... Thurston abruptly was cold; a chill gripped at his heart.

The paroxysm passed. He was doubled with laughter—or was it he who was laughing? He was suddenly buoyantly carefree. Who was he that it mattered? Cyrus Thurston—an ant! And their ant-hill was about to be snuffed out....

He walked over to a waiting group and clapped one man on the shoulder. "Well, how does it feel to be an ant?" he inquired and laughed loudly at the jest. "You and your millions of dollars, your acres of factories, your steamships, railroads!"

The man looked at him strangely and edged cautiously away. His eyes, like those of the others, had a dazed, stricken look. A woman was sobbing softly as she clung to her husband. From the streets far below came a quavering shrillness of sound.

The planes gathered in climbing circles. Far on the horizon were four tiny glinting specks....

Thurston stared until his eyes were stinging. He was walking in a waking sleep as he made his way to the stone coping beyond which was the street far below. He was dead—dead!—right this minute. What were a few minutes more or less? He could climb over the coping; none of the huddled, fear-gripped group would stop him. He could step out into space and fool them, the devils. They could never kill him....

What was it MacGregor had said? Good egg, MacGregor! "But we can die fighting...." Yes, that was it—die fighting. But he couldn't fight; he could only wait. Well, what were the others doing, down there in the streets—in their homes? He could wait with them, die with them....

He straightened slowly and drew one long breath. He looked steadily and unafraid at the advancing specks. They were larger now. He could see their round forms. The planes were less noisy: they were far up in the heights—climbing—climbing.

The bulbs came slantingly down. They were separating. Thurston wondered vaguely.

What had they done in Berlin? Yes, he remembered. Placed themselves at the four corners of a great square and wiped out the whole city in one explosion. Four bombs dropped at the same instant while they shot up to safety in the thin air. How did they communicate? Thought transference, most likely. Telepathy between those great brains, one to another. A plane was falling. It curved and swooped in a trail of flame, then fell straight toward the earth. They were fighting....

Thurston stared above. There were clusters of planes diving down from on high. Machine-guns stuttered faintly. "Machine-guns—toys! Brave, that was it! 'We can die fighting.'" His thoughts were far off; it was like listening to another's mind.

The air was filled with swelling clouds. He saw them before the blast struck where he stood. The great building shuddered at the impact. There were things falling from the clouds, wrecks of planes, blazing and shattered. Still came others; he saw them faintly through the clouds. They came in from the West; they had gone far to gain altitude. They drove down from the heights—the enemy had drifted—they were over the bay.

More clouds, and another blast thundering at the city. There were specks, Thurston saw, falling into the water.

Again the invaders came down from the heights where they had escaped their own shattering attack. There was the faint roar of motors behind, from the south. The squadron from Washington passed overhead.

They surely had seen the fate that awaited. And they drove on to the attack, to strike at an enemy that shot instantly into the sky leaving crashing destruction about the torn dead.

"Now!" said Cyrus Thurston aloud.

The big bulbs were back. They floated easily in the air, a plume of vapor billowing beneath. They were ranging to the four corners of a great square.

One plane only was left, coming in from the south, a lone straggler, late for the fray. One plane! Thurston's shoulders sagged heavily. All they had left! It went swiftly overhead.... It was fast—fast. Thurston suddenly knew. It was Riley in that plane.

"Go back, you fool!"—he was screaming at the top of his voice—"Back—back—you poor, damned, decent Irishman!"

Tears were streaming down his face. "His buddies," Riley had said. And this was Riley, driving swiftly in, alone, to avenge them....

He saw dimly as the swift plane sped over the first bulb, on and over the second. The soft roar of gas from the machines drowned the sound of his engine. The plane passed them in silence to bank sharply toward the third corner of the forming square.

He was looking them over, Thurston thought. And the damn beasts disregarded so contemptible an opponent. He could still leave. "For God's sake, Riley, beat it—escape!"

Thurston's mind was solely on the fate of the lone voyager—until the impossible was borne in upon him.

The square was disrupted. Three great bulbs were now drifting. The wind was carrying them out toward the bay. They were coming down in a long, smooth descent. The plane shot like a winged rocket at the fourth great, shining ball. To the watcher, aghast with sudden hope, it seemed barely to crawl.

"The ray! The ray...." Thurston saw as if straining eyes had pierced through the distance to see the invisible. He saw from below the swift plane, the streaming, intangible ray. That was why Riley had flown closely past and above them—the ray poured from below. His throat was choking him, strangling....

The last enemy took alarm. Had it seen the slow sinking of its companions, failed to hear them in reply to his mental call? The shining pear shape shot violently upward; the attacking plane rolled to a vertical bank as it missed the threatening clouds of exhaust. "What do you know about dog-fights?" And Riley had grinned ... Riley belonged!

The bulb swelled before Thurston's eyes in its swift descent. It canted to one side to head off the struggling plane that could never escape, did not try to escape. The steady wings held true upon their straight course. From above came the silver meteor; it seemed striking at the very plane itself. It was almost upon it before it belched forth the cushioning blast of gas.

Through the forming clouds a plane bored in swiftly. It rolled slowly, was flying upside down. It was under the enemy! Its ray.... Thurston was thrown a score of feet away to crash helpless into the stone coping by the thunderous crash of the explosion.

There were fragments falling from a dense cloud—fragments of curved and silvery metal ... the wing of a plane danced and fluttered in the air....

"He fired its bombs," whispered Thurston in a shaking voice. "He killed the other devils where they lay—he destroyed this with its own explosive. He flew upside down to shoot up with the ray, to set off its shells...."

His mind was fumbling with the miracle of it. "Clever pilot, Riley, in a dog-fight...." And then he realized.

Cyrus Thurston, millionaire sportsman, sank slowly, numbly to the roof of the Equitable Building that still stood. And New York was still there ... and the whole world....

He sobbed weakly, brokenly. Through his dazed brain flashed a sudden, mind-saving thought. He laughed foolishly through his sobs.

"And you said he'd die horribly, Mac, a horrible death." His head dropped upon his arms, unconscious—and safe—with the rest of humanity.

The Corpse on the Grating

By Hugh B. Cave

It was a corpse, standing before me like some propped-up thing from the grave.

In the gloomy depths of the old warehouse Dale saw a thing that drew a scream of horror to his dry lips. It was a corpse-the mold of decay on its long-dead features-and yet it was alive!

It was ten o'clock on the morning of December 5 when M. S. and I left the study of Professor Daimler. You are perhaps acquainted with M. S. His name appears constantly in the pages of the Illustrated News, in conjunction with some very technical article on psycho-analysis or with some extensive study of the human brain and its functions. He is a psycho-fanatic, more or less, and has spent an entire lifetime of some seventy-odd years in pulling apart human skulls for the purpose of investigation. Lovely pursuit!

> In the gloomy depths of the old warehouse Dale saw a thing that drew a scream of horror to his dry lips. It was a corpse—the mold of decay on its long-dead features—and yet it was alive!

For some twenty years I have mocked him, in a friendly, half-hearted fashion. I am a medical man, and my own profession is one that does not sympathize with radicals.

As for Professor Daimler, the third member of our triangle—perhaps, if I take a moment to outline the events of that evening, the Professor's part in what follows will be less obscure. We had called on him, M. S. and I, at his urgent request. His rooms were in a narrow, unlighted street just off the square, and Daimler himself opened the door to us. A tall, loosely built chap he was, standing in the doorway like a motionless ape, arms half extended.

"I've summoned you, gentlemen," he said quietly, "because you two, of all London, are the only persons who know the nature of my recent experiments. I should like to acquaint you with the results!"

He led the way to his study, then kicked the door shut with his foot, seizing my arm as he did so. Quietly he dragged me to the table that stood against the farther wall. In the same even, unemotional tone of a man completely sure of himself, he commanded me to inspect it.

For a moment, in the semi-gloom of the room, I saw nothing. At length, however, the contents of the table revealed themselves, and I distinguished a motley collection of test tubes, each filled with some fluid. The tubes were attached to each other by some ingenious arrangement of thistles, and at the end of the table, where a chance blow could not brush it aside, lay a tiny phial of the resulting serum. From the appearance of the table, Daimler had evidently drawn a certain amount of gas from each of the smaller tubes, distilling them through acid into the minute phial at the end. Yet even now, as I stared down at the fantastic paraphernalia before me, I could sense no conclusive reason for its existence.

I turned to the Professor with a quiet stare of bewilderment. He smiled.

"The experiment is over," he said. "As to its conclusion, you, Dale, as a medical man, will be sceptical. And you"—turning to M. S.—"as a scientist you will be amazed. I, being neither physician nor scientist, am merely filled with wonder!"

He stepped to a long, square table-like structure in the center of the room. Standing over it, he glanced quizzically at M. S., then at me.

"For a period of two weeks," he went on, "I have kept, on the table here, the body of a man who has been dead more than a month. I have tried, gentlemen, with acid combinations of my own origination, to bring that body back to life. And ... I have—failed!"

"But," he added quickly, noting the smile that crept across my face, "that failure was in itself worth more than the average scientist's greatest achievement! You know, Dale, that heat, if a man is not truly dead, will sometimes resurrect him. In a case of epilepsy, for instance, victims have been pronounced dead only to return to life—sometimes in the grave.

"I say 'if a man be not truly dead.' But what if that man *is* truly dead? Does the cure alter itself in any manner? The motor of your car dies—do you bury it? You do not; you locate the faulty part, correct it, and infuse new life. And so, gentlemen, after remedying the ruptured heart of this dead man, by operation, I proceeded to bring him back to life.

"I used heat. Terrific heat will sometimes originate a spark of new life in something long dead. Gentlemen, on the fourth day of my tests, following a continued application of electric and acid heat, the patient—"

Daimler leaned over the table and took up a cigarette. Lightning it, he dropped the match and resumed his monologue.

"The patient turned suddenly over and drew his arm weakly across his eyes. I rushed to his side. When I reached him, the body was once again stiff and lifeless. And—it has remained so."

The Professor stared at us quietly, waiting for comment. I answered him, as carelessly as I could, with a shrug of my shoulders.

"Professor, have you ever played with the dead body of a frog?" I said softly.

He shook his head silently.

"You would find it interesting sport," I told him. "Take a common dry cell battery with enough voltage to render a sharp shock. Then apply your wires to various parts of the frog's anatomy. If you are lucky, and strike the right set of muscles, you will have the pleasure of seeing a dead frog leap suddenly forward. Understand, he will not regain life. You have merely released his dead muscles by shock, and sent him bolting."

The Professor did not reply. I could feel his eyes on me, and had I turned, I should probably had found M. S. glaring at me in honest hate. These men were students of mesmerism, of spiritualism, and my commonplace contradiction was not over welcome.

"You are cynical, Dale," said M. S. coldly, "because you do not understand!"

"Understand? I am a doctor—not a ghost!"

But M. S. had turned eagerly to the Professor.

"Where is this body—this experiment?" he demanded.

Daimler shook his head. Evidently he had acknowledged failure and did not intend to drag his dead man before our eyes, unless he could bring that man forth alive, upright, and ready to join our conversation!

"I've put it away," he said distantly. "There is nothing more to be done, now that our reverend doctor has insisted in making a matter of fact thing out of our experiment. You understand, I had not intended to go in for wholesale resurrection, even if I had met with success. It was my belief that a dead body, like a dead piece of mechanism, can be brought to life again, provided we are intelligent enough to discover the secret. And by God, it is *still* my belief!"

That was the situation, then, when M. S. and I paced slowly back along the narrow street that contained the Professor's dwelling-place. My companion was strangely silent. More than once I felt his eyes upon me in an uncomfortable stare, yet he said nothing. Nothing, that is, until I had opened the conversation with some casual remark about the lunacy of the man we had just left.

"You are wrong in mocking him, Dale," M. S. replied bitterly. "Daimler is a man of science. He is no child, experimenting with a toy; he is a grown man who has the courage to believe in his powers. One of these days...."

He had intended to say that some day I should respect the Professor's efforts. One of these days! The interval of time was far shorter than anything so indefinite. The first event, with its succeeding series of horrors, came within the next three minutes.

We had reached a more deserted section of the square, a black, uninhabited street extending like a shadowed band of darkness between gaunt, high walls. I had noticed for some time that the stone structure beside us seemed to be unbroken by door or window—that it appeared to be a single gigantic building, black and forbidding. I mentioned the fact to M. S.

"The warehouse," he said simply. "A lonely, God-forsaken place. We shall probably see the flicker of the watchman's light in one of the upper chinks."

At his words, I glanced up. True enough, the higher part of the grim structure was punctured by narrow, barred openings. Safety vaults, probably. But the light, unless its tiny gleam was somewhere in the inner recesses of the warehouse, was dead. The great building was like an immense burial vault, a tomb—silent and lifeless.

We had reached the most forbidding section of the narrow street, where a single arch-lamp overhead cast a halo of ghastly yellow light over the pavement. At the very rim of the circle of illumination, where the shadows were deeper and more silent, I could make out the black mouldings of a heavy iron grating. The bars of metal were designed, I believe, to seal the side entrance of the great warehouse from night marauders. It was bolted in place and secured with a set of immense chains, immovable.

This much I saw as my intent gaze swept the wall before me. This huge tomb of silence held for me a peculiar fascination, and as I paced along beside my gloomy companion, I stared directly ahead of me into the darkness of the street. I wish to God my eyes had been closed or blinded!

He was hanging on the grating. Hanging there, with white, twisted hands clutching the rigid bars of iron, straining to force them apart. His whole distorted body was forced against the barrier, like the form of a madman struggling to escape from his cage. His face—the image of it still haunts me whenever I see iron bars in the darkness of a passage—was the face of a man who has died from utter, stark horror. It was frozen in a silent shriek of agony, staring out at me with fiendish maliciousness. Lips twisted apart. White teeth gleaming in the light. Bloody eyes, with a horrible glare of colorless pigment. And—*dead*.

I believe M. S. saw him at the very instant I recoiled. I felt a sudden grip on my arm; and then, as an exclamation came harshly from my companion's lips, I was pulled forward roughly. I found myself staring straight into the dead eyes of that fearful thing before me, found myself standing rigid, motionless, before the corpse that hung within reach of my arm.

And then, through that overwhelming sense of the horrible, came the quiet voice of my comrade—the voice of a man who looks upon death as nothing more than an opportunity for research.

"The fellow has been frightened to death, Dale. Frightened most horribly. Note the expression of his mouth, the evident struggle to force these bars apart and escape. Something has driven fear to his soul, killed him."

I remember the words vaguely. When M. S. had finished speaking, I did not reply. Not until he had stepped forward and bent over the distorted face of the thing before me, did I attempt to speak. When I did, my thoughts were a jargon.

"What, in God's name," I cried, "could have brought such horror to a strong man? What—"

"Loneliness, perhaps," suggested M. S. with a smile. "The fellow is evidently the watchman. He is alone, in a huge, deserted pit of darkness, for hours at a time. His light is merely a ghostly ray of illumination, hardly enough to do more than increase the darkness. I have heard of such cases before."

He shrugged his shoulders. Even as he spoke, I sensed the evasion in his words. When I replied, he hardly heard my answer, for he had suddenly stepped forward, where he could look directly into those fear twisted eyes.

"Dale," he said at length, turning slowly to face me, "you ask for an explanation of this horror? There *is* an explanation. It is written with an almost fearful clearness on this fellow's mind. Yet if I tell you, you will return to your old skepticism—your damnable habit of disbelief!"

I looked at him quietly. I had heard M. S. claim, at other times, that he could read the thoughts of a dead man by the mental image that lay on that man's brain. I had laughed at him. Evidently, in the present moment, he recalled those laughs. Nevertheless, he faced me seriously.

"I can see two things, Dale," he said deliberately. "One of them is a dark, narrow room—a room piled with indistinct boxes and crates, and with an open door bearing the black number 4167. And in that open doorway, coming forward with slow steps—alive, with arms extended and a frightful face of passion—is a decayed human form. A corpse, Dale. A man who has been dead for many days, and is now—*alive*!"

M.S. turned slowly and pointed with upraised hand to the corpse on the grating.

"That is why," he said simply, "this fellow died from horror."

His words died into emptiness. For a moment I stared at him. Then, in spite of our surroundings, in spite of the late hour, the loneliness of the street, the awful thing beside us, I laughed.

He turned upon me with a snarl. For the first time in my life I saw M. S. convulsed with rage. His old, lined face had suddenly become savage with intensity.

"You laugh at me, Dale," he thundered. "By God, you make a mockery out of a science that I have spent more than my life in studying! You call yourself a medical man—and you are not fit to carry the name! I will wager you, man, that your laughter is not backed by courage!"

I fell away from him. Had I stood within reach, I am sure he would have struck me. Struck me! And I have been nearer to M. S. for the past ten years than any man in London. And as I retreated from his temper, he reached forward to seize my arm. I could not help but feel impressed at his grim intentness.

"Look here, Dale," he said bitterly, "I will wager you a hundred pounds that you will not spend the remainder of this night in the warehouse above you! I will wager a hundred pounds against your own courage that you will not back your laughter by going through what this fellow has gone through. That you will not prowl through the corridors of this great structure until you have found room 4167—*and remain in that room until dawn!*"

There was no choice. I glanced at the dead man, at the face of fear and the clutching, twisted hands, and a cold dread filled me. But to refuse my friend's wager would have been to brand myself an empty coward. I had mocked him. Now, whatever the cost, I must stand ready to pay for that mockery.

"Room 4167?" I replied quietly, in a voice which I made every effort to control, lest he should discover the tremor in it. "Very well, I will do it!"

It was nearly midnight when I found myself alone, climbing a musty, winding ramp between the first and second floors of the deserted building. Not a sound, except the sharp intake of my breath and the dismal creak of the wooden stairs, echoed through that tomb of death. There was no light, not even the usual dim glow that is left to illuminate an unused corridor. Moreover, I had brought no means of light with me—nothing but a half empty box of safety matches which, by some unholy premonition, I had forced myself to save for some future moment. The stairs were black and difficult, and I mounted them slowly, groping with both hands along the rough wall.

I had left M. S. some few moments before. In his usual decisive manner he had helped me to climb the iron grating and lower myself to the sealed alley-way on the farther side. Then, leaving him without a word, for I was bitter against the triumphant tone of his parting words, I proceeded into the darkness, fumbling forward until I had discovered the open door in the lower part of the warehouse.

And then the ramp, winding crazily upward—upward—upward, seemingly without end. I was seeking blindly for that particular room which was to be my destination. Room 4167, with its high number, could hardly be on the lower floors, and so I had stumbled upward....

It was at the entrance of the second floor corridor that I struck the first of my desultory supply of matches, and by its light discovered a placard nailed to the wall. The thing was yellow with age and hardly legible. In the drab light of the match I had difficulty in reading it—but, as far as I can remember, the notice went something like this:

WAREHOUSE RULES

1. No light shall be permitted in any room or corridor, as a prevention against fire.

2. No person shall be admitted to rooms or corridors unless accompanied by an employee.

3. A watchman shall be on the premises from 7 P.M. until 6 A.M. He shall make the round of the corridors every hour during that interval, at a quarter past the hour.

4. Rooms are located by their numbers: the first figure in the room number indicating its floor location.

I could read no further. The match in my fingers burned to a black thread and dropped. Then, with the burnt stump still in my hand, I groped through the darkness to the bottom of the second ramp.

Room 4167, then, was on the fourth floor—the topmost floor of the structure. I must confess that the knowledge did not bring any renewed burst of courage! The top floor! Three black stair-pits would lie between me and the safety of escape. There would be no escape! No human being in the throes of fear could hope to discover that tortured outlet, could hope to grope his way through Stygian gloom down a triple ramp of black stairs. And even though he succeeded in reaching the lower corridors, there was still a blind alley-way, sealed at the outer end by a high grating of iron bars....

Escape! The mockery of it caused me to stop suddenly in my ascent and stand rigid, my whole body trembling violently.

But outside, in the gloom of the street, M. S. was waiting, waiting with that fiendish glare of triumph that would brand me a man without courage. I could not return to face him, not though all the horrors of hell inhabited this gruesome place of mystery. And horrors must surely inhabit it, else how could one account for that fearful thing on the grating below? But I had been through horror before. I had seen a man, supposedly dead on the operating table, jerk suddenly to his feet and scream. I had seen a young girl, not long before, awake in the midst of an operation, with the knife already in her frail body. Surely, after those definite horrors, no *unknown* danger would send me cringing back to the man who was waiting so bitterly for me to return.

Those were the thoughts pregnant in my mind as I groped slowly, cautiously along the corridor of the upper floor, searching each closed door for the indistinct number 4167. The place was like the center of a huge labyrinth, a spider-web of black, repelling passages, leading into some central chamber of utter silence and blackness. I went forward with dragging steps, fighting back the dread that gripped me as I went farther and farther from the outlet of escape. And then, after losing myself completely in the gloom, I threw aside all thoughts of return and pushed on with a careless, surface bravado, and laughed aloud.

So, at length, I reached that room of horror, secreted high in the deeper recesses of the deserted warehouse. The number—God grant I never see it again!—was scrawled in black chalk on the door—4167. I pushed the half-open barrier wide, and entered.

It was a small room, even as M. S. had forewarned me—or as the dead mind of that thing on the grate had forewarned M. S. The glow of my out-thrust match revealed a great stack of dusty boxes and crates, piled against the farther wall. Revealed, too, the black corridor beyond the entrance, and a small, upright table before me.

It was the table, and the stool beside it, that drew my attention and brought a muffled exclamation from my lips. The thing had been thrust out of its usual place, pushed aside as if some frenzied shape had lunged against it. I could make out its former position by the marks on the dusty floor at my feet. Now it was nearer to the center of the room, and had been wrenched sidewise from its holdings. A shudder took hold of me as I looked at it. A living person, sitting on the stool before me, staring at the door, would have wrenched the table in just this manner in his frenzy to escape from the room!

The light of the match died, plunging me into a pit of gloom. I struck another and stepped closer to the table. And there, on the floor, I found two more things that brought fear to my soul. One of them was a heavy flash-lamp—a watchman's lamp—where it had evidently been dropped. Been dropped in flight! But what awful terror must have gripped the fellow to make him forsake his only means of escape through those black passages? And the second thing—a worn copy of a leather-bound book, flung open on the boards below the stool!

The flash-lamp, thank God! had not been shattered. I switched it on, directing its white circle of light over the room. This time, in the vivid glare, the room became even more unreal. Black walls, clumsy, distorted shadows on the wall, thrown by those huge piles of wooden boxes. Shadows that were like crouching men, groping toward me. And beyond, where the single door opened into a passage of Stygian darkness, that yawning entrance was thrown into hideous detail. Had any upright figure been standing there, the light would have made an unholy phosphorescent specter out of it.

I summoned enough courage to cross the room and pull the door shut. There was no way of locking it. Had I been able to fasten it, I should surely have done so; but the room was evidently an unused chamber, filled with empty refuse. This was the reason, probably, why the watchman had made use of it as a retreat during the intervals between his rounds.

But I had no desire to ponder over the sordidness of my surroundings. I returned to my stool in silence, and stooping, picked up the fallen book from the floor. Carefully I placed the lamp on the table, where its light would shine on the open page. Then, turning the cover, I began to glance through the thing which the man before me had evidently been studying.

And before I had read two lines, the explanation of the whole horrible thing struck me. I stared dumbly down at the little book and laughed. Laughed harshly, so that the sound of my mad cackle echoed in a thousand ghastly reverberations through the dead corridors of the building.

It was a book of horror, of fantasy. A collection of weird, terrifying, supernatural tales with grotesque illustrations in funereal black and white. And the very line I had turned to, the line which had probably struck terror to that unlucky devil's soul, explained M. S.'s "decayed human form, standing in the doorway with arms extended and a frightful face of passion!" The description—the same description—lay before me, almost in my friend's words. Little wonder that the fellow on the grating below, after reading this orgy of horror, had suddenly gone mad with fright. Little wonder that the picture engraved on his dead mind was a picture of a corpse standing in the doorway of room 4167!

I glanced at that doorway and laughed. No doubt of it, it was that awful description in M. S.'s untempered language that had made me dread my surroundings, not the loneliness and silence of the corridors about me. Now, as I stared at the room, the closed door, the shadows on the wall, I could not repress a grin.

But the grin was not long in duration. A six-hour siege awaited me before I could hear the sound of human voice again—six hours of silence and gloom. I did not relish it. Thank God the fellow before me had had foresight enough to leave his book of fantasy for my amusement!

I turned to the beginning of the story. A lovely beginning it was, outlining in some detail how a certain Jack Fulton, English adventurer, had suddenly found himself imprisoned (by a mysterious black gang of monks, or something of the sort) in a forgotten cell at the monastery of El Toro. The cell, according to the pages before me, was located in the "empty, haunted pits below the stone floors of the structure...." Lovely setting! And the brave Fulton had been secured firmly to a huge metal ring set in the farther wall, opposite the entrance.

I read the description twice. At the end of it I could not help but lift my head to stare at my own surroundings. Except for the location of the cell, I might have been in they same setting. The same darkness, same silence, same loneliness. Peculiar similarity!

And then: "Fulton lay quietly, without attempt to struggle. In the dark, the stillness of the vaults became unbearable, terrifying. Not a suggestion of sound, except the scraping of unseen rats—"

I dropped the book with a start. From the opposite end of the room in which I sat came a half inaudible scuffling noise—the sound of hidden rodents scrambling through the great pile of boxes. Imagination? I am not sure. At the moment, I would have sworn that the sound was a definite one, that I had heard it distinctly. Now, as I recount this tale of horror, I am not sure.

But I am sure of this: There was no smile on my lips as I picked up the book again with trembling fingers and continued.

"The sound died into silence. For an eternity, the prisoner lay rigid, staring at the open door of his cell. The opening was black, deserted, like the mouth of a deep tunnel, leading to hell. And then, suddenly, from the gloom beyond that opening, came an almost noiseless, padded footfall!"

This time there was no doubt of it. The book fell from my fingers, dropped to the floor with a clatter. Yet even through the sound of its falling, I heard that fearful sound—the shuffle of a living foot! I sat motionless, staring with bloodless face at the door of room 4167. And as I stared, the sound came again, and again—*the slow tread of dragging footsteps, approaching along the black corridor without*!

I got to my feet like an automaton, swaying heavily. Every drop of courage ebbed from my soul as I stood there, one hand clutching the table, waiting....

And then, with an effort, I moved forward. My hand was outstretched to grasp the wooden handle of the door. And—I did not have the courage. Like a cowed beast I crept back to my place and slumped down on the stool, my eyes still transfixed in a mute stare of terror.

I waited. For more than half an hour I waited, motionless. Not a sound stirred in the passage beyond that closed barrier. Not a suggestion of any living presence came to me. Then, leaning back against the wall with a harsh laugh, I wiped away the cold moisture that had trickled over my forehead into my eyes.

It was another five minutes before I picked up the book again. You call me a fool for continuing it? A fool? I tell you, even a story of horror is more comfort than a room of grotesque shadows and silence. Even a printed page is better than grim reality!

And so I read on. The story was one of suspense, madness. For the next two pages I read a cunning description of the prisoner's mental reaction. Strangely enough, it conformed precisely with my own.

"Fulton's head had fallen to his chest," the script read. "For an endless while he did not stir, did not dare to lift his eyes. And then, after more than an hour of silent agony and suspense, the boy's head came up mechanically. Came up—and suddenly jerked rigid. A horrible scream burst from his dry lips as he stared—stared like a dead man—at the black entrance to his cell. There, standing without motion in the opening, stood a shrouded figure of death. Empty eyes, glaring with awful hate, bored into his own. Great arms, bony and rotten, extended toward him. Decayed flesh—"

I read no more. Even as I lunged to my feet, with that mad book still gripped in my hand, I heard the door of my room grind open. I screamed, screamed in utter horror at the thing I saw there. Dead? Good God, I do not know. It was a corpse, a dead human body, standing before me like some propped-up thing from the grave. A face half eaten away, terrible in its leering grin. Twisted mouth, with only a suggestion of lips, curled back over broken teeth. Hair—writhing, distorted—like a mass of moving, bloody coils. And its arms, ghastly white, bloodless, were extended toward me, with open, clutching hands.

It was alive! Alive! Even while I stood there, crouching against the wall, it stepped forward toward me. I saw a heavy shudder pass over it, and the sound of its scraping feet burned its way into my soul. And then, with its second step, the fearful thing stumbled to its knees. The white, gleaming arms, thrown into streaks of living fire by the light of my lamp, flung violently upwards, twisting toward the ceiling. I saw the grin change to an expression of agony, of torment. And then the thing crashed upon me—dead.

With a great cry of fear I stumbled to the door. I groped out of that room of horror, stumbled along the corridor. No light. I left it behind, on the table, to throw a circle of white glare over the decayed, living-dead intruder who had driven me mad.

My return down those winding ramps to the lower floor was a nightmare of fear. I remember that I stumbled, that I plunged through the darkness like a man gone mad. I had no thought of caution, no thought of anything except escape.

And then the lower door, and the alley of gloom. I reached the grating, flung myself upon it and pressed my face against the bars in a futile effort to escape. The same—as the fear-tortured man—who had—come before—me.

I felt strong hands lifting me up. A dash of cool air, and then the refreshing patter of falling rain.

It was the afternoon of the following day, December 6, when M. S. sat across the table from me in my own study. I had made a rather hesitant attempt to tell him, without dramatics and without dwelling on my own lack of courage, of the events of the previous night.

"You deserved it, Dale," he said quietly. "You are a medical man, nothing more, and yet you mock the beliefs of a scientist as great as Daimler. I wonder—do you still mock the Professor's beliefs?"

"That he can bring a dead man to life?" I smiled, a bit doubtfully.

"I will tell you something, Dale," said M. S. deliberately. He was leaning across the table, staring at me. "The Professor made only one mistake in his great experiment. He did not wait long enough for the effect of his strange acids to work. He acknowledged failure too soon, and got rid of the body." He paused.

"When the Professor stored his patient away, Dale," he said quietly, "he stored it in room 4170, at the great warehouse. If you are acquainted with the place, you will know that room 4170 is directly across the corridor from 4167."

Creatures of the Light

By Sophie Wenzel Ellis

In a night club of many lights and much high-pitched laughter, where he had come for an hour of forgetfulness and an execrable dinner, John Northwood was suddenly conscious that Fate had begun shuffling the cards of his destiny for a dramatic game.

He had striven to perfect the faultless man of the future, and had succeeded-too well. For in the pitilessly cold eyes of Adam, his super-human creation, Dr. Mundson saw only contempt-and annihilation-for the human race.

First, he was aware that the singularly ugly and deformed man at the next table was gazing at him with an intense, almost excited scrutiny. But, more disturbing than this, was the scowl of hate on the face of another man, as handsome as this other was hideous, who sat in a far corner hidden behind a broad column, with rude elbows on the table, gawking first at Northwood and then at the deformed, almost hideous man.

The projector, belching forth its stinking breath of corruption, swung in a mad arc over the ceiling, over the walls.

Northwood's blood chilled over the expression on the handsome, fair-haired stranger's perfectly carved face. If a figure in marble could display a fierce, unnatural passion, it would seem no more eldritch than the hate in the icy blue eyes.

It was not a new experience for Northwood to be stared at: he was not merely a good-looking young fellow of twenty-five, he was scenery, magnificent and compelling. Furthermore, he had been in the public eye for years, first as a precocious child and, later, as a brilliant young scientist. Yet, for all his experience with hero worshippers to put an adamantine crust on his sensibilities, he grew warm-eared under the gaze of these two strangers—this hunchback with a face like a grotesque mask in a Greek play, this other who, even handsomer than himself, chilled the blood queerly with the cold perfection of his godlike masculine beauty.

Northwood sensed something familiar about the hunchback. Somewhere he had seen that huge, round, intelligent face splattered with startling features. The very breadth of the man's massive brow was not altogether unknown to him, nor could Northwood look into the mournful, near-sighted black eyes without trying to recall when and where he had last seen them.

But this other of the marble-perfect nose and jaw, the blond, thick-waved hair, was totally a stranger, whom Northwood fervently hoped he would never know too well.

Trying to analyze the queer repugnance that he felt for this handsome, boldly staring fellow, Northwood decided: "He's like a newly-made wax figure endowed with life."

Shivering over his own fantastic thought, he again glanced swiftly at the hunchback, who he noticed was playing with his coffee, evidently to prolong the meal.

One year of calm-headed scientific teaching in a famous old eastern university had not made him callous to mysteries. Thus, with a feeling of high adventure, he finished his supper and prepared to go. From the corner of his eye, he saw the hunchback leave his seat, while the handsome man behind the column rose furtively, as though he, too, intended to follow.

Northwood was out in the dusky street about thirty seconds, when the hunchback came from the foyer. Without apparently noticing Northwood, he hailed a taxi. For a moment, he stood still, waiting for the taxi to pull up at the curb. Standing thus, with the street light limning every unnatural angle of his twisted body and every queer abnormality of his huge features, he looked almost repulsive.

On his way to the taxi, his thick shoulder jostled the younger man. Northwood felt something strike his foot, and, stooping in the crowded street, picked up a black leather wallet.

"Wait!" he shouted as the hunchback stepped into the waiting taxi.

But the man did not falter. In a moment, Northwood lost sight of him as the taxi moved away.

He debated with himself whether or not he should attempt to follow. And while he stood thus in indecision, the handsome stranger approached him.

"Good evening to you," he said curtly. His rich, musical voice, for all its deepness, held a faint hint of the tremulous, birdlike notes heard in the voice of a young child who has not used his vocal chords long enough for them to have lost their exquisite newness.

"Good evening," echoed Northwood, somewhat uncertainly. A sudden aura of repulsion swept coldly over him. Seen close, with the brilliant light of the street directly on his too perfect face, the man was more sinister than in the café. Yet Northwood, struggling desperately for a reason to explain his violent dislike, could not discover why he shrank from this splendid creature, whose eyes and flesh had a new, fresh appearance rarely seen except in very young boys.

"I want what you picked up," went on the stranger.

"It isn't yours!" Northwood flashed back. Ah! that effluvium of hatred which seemed to weave a tangible net around him!

"Nor is it yours. Give it to me!"

"You're insolent, aren't you?"

"If you don't give it to me, you will be sorry." The man did not raise his voice in anger, yet the words whipped Northwood with almost physical violence. "If he knew that I saw everything that happened in there—that I am talking to you at this moment—he would tremble with fear."

"But you can't intimidate me."

"No?" For a long moment, the cold blue eyes held his contemptuously. "No? I can't frighten you—you worm of the Black Age?"

Before Northwood's horrified sight, he vanished; vanished as though he had turned suddenly to air and floated away.

The street was not crowded at that time, and there was no pressing group of bodies to hide the splendid creature. Northwood gawked stupidly, mouth half open, eyes searching wildly everywhere. The man was gone. He had simply disappeared, in this sane, electric-lighted street.

Suddenly, close to Northwood's ear, grated a derisive laugh. "I can't frighten you?" From nowhere came that singularly young-old voice.

As Northwood jerked his head around to meet blank space, a blow struck the corner of his mouth. He felt the warm blood run over his chin.

"I could take that wallet from you, worm, but you may keep it, and see me later. But remember this—the thing inside never will be yours."

The words fell from empty air.

For several minutes, Northwood waited at the spot, expecting another demonstration of the abnormal, but nothing else occurred. At last, trembling violently, he wiped the thick moisture from his forehead and dabbed at the blood which he still felt on his chin.

But when he looked at his handkerchief, he muttered:

"Well, I'll be jiggered!"

The handkerchief bore not the slightest trace of blood.

Under the light in his bedroom, Northwood examined the wallet. It was made of alligator skin, clasped with a gold signet that bore the initial M. The first pocket was empty; the second yielded an object that sent a warm flush to his face.

It was the photograph of a gloriously beautiful girl, so seductively lovely that the picture seemed almost to be alive. The short, curved upper lip, the full, delicately voluptuous lower, parted slightly in a smile that seemed to linger in every exquisite line of her face. She looked as though she had just spoken passionately, and the spirit of her words had inspired her sweet flesh and eyes.

Northwood turned his head abruptly and groaned, "Good Heavens!"

He had no right to palpitate over the picture of an unknown beauty. Only a month ago, he had become engaged to a young woman whose mind was as brilliant as her face was plain. Always he had vowed that he would never marry a pretty girl, for he detested his own masculine beauty sincerely.

He tried to grasp a mental picture of Mary Burns, who had never stirred in him the emotion that this smiling picture invoked. But, gazing at the picture, he could not remember how his fiancée looked.

Suddenly the picture fell from his fingers and dropped to the floor on its face, revealing an inscription on the back. In a bold, masculine hand, he read: "Your future wife."

"Some lucky fellow is headed for a life of bliss," was his jealous thought.

He frowned at the beautiful face. What was this girl to that hideous hunchback? Why did the handsome stranger warn him, "*The thing inside never will be yours?*"

Again he turned eagerly to the wallet.

In the last flap he found something that gave him another surprise: a plain white card on which a name and address were written by the same hand that had penned the inscription on the picture.

Emil Mundson, Ph. D.,
44-1/2 Indian Court

Emil Mundson, the electrical wizard and distinguished scientific writer, friend of the professor of science at the university where Northwood was an assistant professor; Emil Mundson, whom, a week ago, Northwood had yearned mightily to meet.

Now Northwood knew why the hunchback's intelligent, ugly face was familiar to him. He had seen it pictured as often as enterprising news photographers could steal a likeness from the over-sensitive scientist, who would never sit for a formal portrait.

Even before Northwood had graduated from the university where he now taught, he had been avidly interested in Emil Mundson's fantastic articles in scientific journals. Only a week ago, Professor Michael had come to him with the current issue of New Science, shouting excitedly:

"Did you read this, John, this article by Emil Mundson?" His shaking, gnarled old fingers tapped the open magazine.

Northwood seized the magazine and looked avidly at the title of the article, "Creatures of the Light."

"No, I haven't read it," he admitted. "My magazine hasn't come yet."

"Run through it now briefly, will you? And note with especial care the passages I have marked. In fact, you needn't bother with anything else just now. Read this—and this—and this." He pointed out penciled paragraphs.

Northwood read:

Man always has been, always will be a creature of the light. He is forever reaching for some future point of perfected evolution which, even when his most remote ancestor was a fish creature composed of a few cells, was the guiding power that brought him up from the first stinking sea and caused him to create gods in his own image.

It is this yearning for perfection which sets man apart from all other life, which made him *man* even in the rudimentary stages of his development. He was man when he wallowed in the slime of the new world and yearned for the air above. He will still be man when he has evolved into that glorious creature of the future whose body is deathless and whose mind rules the universe.

Professor Michael, looking over Northwood's shoulder, interrupted the reading:

"*Man always has been man,*" he droned emphatically. "That's not original with friend Mundson, of course; yet it is a theory that has not received sufficient investigation." He indicated another marked paragraph. "Read this thoughtfully, John. It's the crux of Mundson's thought."

Northwood continued:

Since the human body is chemical and electrical, increased knowledge of its powers and limitations will enable us to work with Nature in her sublime but infinitely slow processes of human evolution. We need not wait another fifty thousand years to be godlike creatures. Perhaps even now we may be standing at the beginning of the splendid bridge that will take us to that state of perfected evolution when we shall be Creatures who have reached the Light.

Northwood looked questioningly at the professor. "Queer, fantastic thing, isn't it?"

Professor Michael smoothed his thin, gray hair with his dried-out hand. "Fantastic?" His intellectual eyes behind the thick glasses sought the ceiling. "Who can say? Haven't you ever wondered why all parents expect their children to be nearer perfection than themselves, and why is it a natural impulse for them to be willing to sacrifice themselves to better their offspring?" He paused and moistened his pale, wrinkled lips. "Instinct, Northwood. We Creatures of the Light know that our race shall reach that point in evolution when, as perfect creatures, we shall rule all matter and live forever." He punctuated the last words with blows on the table.

Northwood laughed dryly. "How many thousands of years are you looking forward, Professor?"

The professor made an obscure noise that sounded like a smothered sniff. "You and I shall never agree on the point that mental advancement may wipe out physical limitations in the human race, perhaps in a few hundred years. It seems as though your profound admiration for Dr. Mundson would win you over to this pet theory."

"But what sane man can believe that even perfectly developed beings, through mental control, could overcome Nature's fixed laws?"

"We don't know! We don't know!" The professor slapped the magazine with an emphatic hand. "Emil Mundson hasn't written this article for nothing. He's paving the way for some announcement that will startle the scientific world. I know him. In the same manner he gave out veiled hints of his various brilliant discoveries and inventions long before he offered them to the world."

"But Dr. Mundson is an electrical wizard. He would not be delving seriously into the mysteries of evolution, would he?"

"Why not?" The professor's wizened face screwed up wisely. "A year ago, when he was back from one of those mysterious long excursions he takes in that weirdly different aircraft of his, about which he is so secretive, he told me that he was conducting experiments to prove his belief that the human brain generates electric current, and that the electrical impulses in the brain set up radioactive waves that some day, among other miracles, will make thought communication possible. Perfect man, he says, will perform mental feats which will give him complete mental domination over the physical."

Northwood finished reading and turned thoughtfully to the window. His profile in repose had the straight-nosed, full-lipped perfection of a Greek coin. Old, wizened Professor Michael, gazing at him covertly, smothered a sigh.

"I wish you knew Dr. Mundson," he said. "He, the ugliest man in the world, delights in physical perfection. He would revel in your splendid body and brilliant mind."

Northwood blushed hotly. "You'll have to arrange a meeting between us."

"I have." The professor's thin, dry lips pursed comically. "He'll drop in to see you within a few days."

And now John Northwood sat holding Dr. Mundson's card and the wallet which the scientist had so mysteriously dropped at his feet.

Here was high adventure, perhaps, for which he had been singled out by the famous electrical wizard. While excitement mounted in his blood, Northwood again examined the photograph. The girl's strange eyes, odd in expression rather than in size or shape, seemed to hold him. The young man's breath came quicker.

"It's a challenge," he said softly. "It won't hurt to see what it's all about."

His watch showed eleven o'clock. He would return the wallet that night. Into his coat pocket he slipped a revolver. One sometimes needed weapons in Indian Court.

He took a taxi, which soon turned from the well-lighted streets into a section where squalid houses crowded against each other, and dirty children swarmed in the streets in their last games of the day.

Indian Court was little more than an alley, dark and evil smelling.

The chauffeur stopped at the entrance and said:

"If I drive in, I'll have to back out, sir. Number forty-four and a half is the end house, facing the entrance."

"You've been here before?" asked Northwood.

"Last week I drove the queerest bird here—a fellow as good-looking as you, who had me follow the taxi occupied by a hunchback with a face like Old Nick." The man hesitated and went on haltingly: "It might sound goofy, mister, but there was something funny about my fare. He jumped out, asked me the charge, and, in the moment I glanced at my taxi-meter, he disappeared. Yes, sir. Vanished, owing me four dollars, six bits. It was almost ghostlike, mister."

Northwood laughed nervously and dismissed him. He found his number and knocked at the dilapidated door. He heard a sudden movement in the lighted room beyond, and the door opened quickly.

Dr. Mundson faced him.

"I knew you'd come!" he said with a slight Teutonic accent. "Often I'm not wrong in sizing up my man. Come in."

Northwood cleared his throat awkwardly. "You dropped your wallet at my feet, Dr. Mundson. I tried to stop you before you got away, but I guess you did not hear me."

He offered the wallet, but the hunchback waved it aside.

"A ruse, of course," he confessed. "It just was my way of testing what your Professor Michael told about you—that you are extraordinarily intelligent, virile, and imaginative. Had you sent the wallet to me, I should have sought elsewhere for my man. Come in."

Northwood followed him into a living room evidently recently furnished in a somewhat hurried manner. The furniture, although rich, was not placed to best advantage. The new rug was a trifle crooked on the floor, and the lamp shades clashed in color with the other furnishings.

Dr. Mundson's intense eyes swept over Northwood's tall, slim body.

"Ah, you're a man!" he said softly. "You are what all men would be if we followed Nature's plan that only the fit shall survive. But modern science is permitting the unfit to live and to mix their defective beings with the developing race!" His huge fist gesticulated madly. "Fools! Fools! They need me and perfect men like you."

"Why?"

"Because you can help me in my plan to populate the earth with a new race of godlike people. But don't question me too closely now. Even if I should explain, you would call me insane. But watch; gradually I shall unfold the mystery before you, so that you will believe."

He reached for the wallet that Northwood still held, opened it with a monstrous hand, and reached for the photograph. "She shall bring you love. She's more beautiful than a poet's dream."

A warm flush crept over the young man's face.

"I can easily understand," he said, "how a man could love her, but for me she comes too late."

"Pooh! Fiddlesticks!" The scientist snapped his fingers. "This girl was created for you. That other—you will forget her the moment you set eyes on the sweet flesh of this Athalia. She is an hour from Paradise—a maiden of musk and incense." He held the girl's photograph toward the young man. "Keep it. She is yours, if you are strong enough to hold her."

Northwood opened his card case and placed the picture inside, facing Mary's photograph. Again the warning words of the mysterious stranger rang in his memory: "*The thing inside never will be yours.*"

"Where to," he said eagerly; "and when do we start?"

"To the new Garden of Eden," said the scientist, with such a beatific smile that his face was less hideous. "We start immediately. I have arranged with Professor Michael for you to go."

Northwood followed Dr. Mundson to the street and walked with him a few blocks to a garage where the scientist's motor car waited.

"The apartment in Indian Court is just a little eccentricity of mine," explained Dr. Mundson. "I need people in my work, people whom I must select through swift, sure tests. The apartment comes in handy, as to-night."

Northwood scarcely noted where they were going, or how long they had been on the way. He was vaguely aware that they had left the city behind, and were now passing through farms bathed in moonlight.

At last they entered a path that led through a bit of woodland. For half a mile the path continued, and then ended at a small, enclosed field. In the middle of this rested a queer aircraft. Northwood knew it was a flying machine only by the propellers mounted on the top of the huge ball-shaped body. There were no wings, no birdlike hull, no tail.

"It looks almost like a little world ready to fly off into space," he commented.

"It is just about that." The scientist's squat, bunched-out body, settled squarely on long, thin, straddled legs, looked gnomelike in the moonlight. "One cannot copy flesh with steel and wood, but one can make metal perform magic of which flesh is not capable. My sun-ship is not a mechanical reproduction of a bird. It is—but, climb in, young friend."

Northwood followed Dr. Mundson into the aircraft. The moment the scientist closed the metal door behind them, Northwood was instantly aware of some concealed horror that vibrated through his nerves. For one dreadful moment, he expected some terrific agent of the shadows that escaped the electric lights to leap upon him. And this was odd, for nothing could be saner than the globular interior of the aircraft, divided into four wedge-shaped apartments.

Dr. Mundson also paused at the door, puzzled, hesitant.

"Someone has been here!" he exclaimed. "Look, Northwood! The bunk has been occupied—the one in this cabin I had set aside for you."

He pointed to the disarranged bunk, where the impression of a head could still be seen on a pillow.

"A tramp, perhaps."

"No! The door was locked, and, as you saw, the fence around this field was protected with barbed wire. There's something wrong. I felt it on my trip here all the way, like someone watching me in the dark. And don't laugh! I have stopped laughing at all things that seem unnatural. You don't know what is natural."

Northwood shivered. "Maybe someone is concealed about the ship."

"Impossible. Me, I thought so, too. But I looked and looked, and there was nothing."

All evening Northwood had burned to tell the scientist about the handsome stranger in the Mad Hatter Club. But even now he shrank from saying that a man had vanished before his eyes.

Dr. Mundson was working with a succession of buttons and levers. There was a slight jerk, and then the strange craft shot up, straight as a bullet from a gun, with scarcely a sound other than a continuous whistle.

"The vertical rising aircraft perfected," explained Dr. Mundson. "But what would you think if I told you that there is not an ounce of gasoline in my heavier-than-air craft?"

"I shouldn't be surprised. An electrical genius would seek for a less obsolete source of power."

In the bright flare of the electric lights, the scientist's ugly face flushed. "The man who harnesses the sun rules the world. He can make the desert places bloom, the frozen poles balmy and verdant. You, John Northwood, are one of the very few to fly in a machine operated solely by electrical energy from the sun's rays."

"Are you telling me that this airship is operated with power from the sun?"

"Yes. And I cannot take the credit for its invention." He sighed. "The dream was mine, but a greater brain developed it—a brain that may be greater than I suspect." His face grew suddenly graver.

A little later Northwood said: "It seems that we must be making fabulous speed."

"Perhaps!" Dr. Mundson worked with the controls. "Here, I've cut her down to the average speed of the ordinary airplane. Now you can see a bit of the night scenery."

Northwood peeped out the thick glass porthole. Far below, he saw two tiny streaks of light, one smooth and stationery, the other wavering as though it were a reflection in water.

"That can't be a lighthouse!" he cried.

The scientist glanced out. "It is. We're approaching the Florida Keys."

"Impossible! We've been traveling less than an hour."

"But, my young friend, do you realize that my sun-ship has a speed of over one thousand miles an hour, how much over I dare not tell you?"

Throughout the night, Northwood sat beside Dr. Mundson, watching his deft fingers control the simple-looking buttons and levers. So fast was their flight now that, through the portholes, sky and earth looked the same: dark gray films of emptiness. The continuous weird whistle from the hidden mechanism of the sun-ship was like the drone of a monster insect, monotonous and soporific during the long intervals when the scientist was too busy with his controls to engage in conversation.

For some reason that he could not explain, Northwood had an aversion to going into the sleeping apartment behind the control room. Then, towards morning, when the suddenly falling temperature struck a biting chill throughout the sun-ship, Northwood, going into the cabin for fur coats, discovered why his mind and body shrank in horror from the cabin.

After he had procured the fur coats from a closet, he paused a moment, in the privacy of the cabin, to look at Athalia's picture. Every nerve in his body leaped to meet the magnetism of her beautiful eyes. Never had Mary Burns stirred emotion like this in him. He hung over Mary's picture, wistfully, hoping almost prayerfully that he could react to her as he did to Athalia; but her pale, over-intellectual face left him cold.

"Cad!" he ground out between his teeth. "Forgetting her so soon!"

The two pictures were lying side by side on a little table. Suddenly an obscure noise in the room caught his attention. It was more vibration than noise, for small sounds could scarcely be heard above the whistle of the sun-ship. A slight compression of the air against his neck gave him the eery feeling that someone was standing close behind him. He wheeled and looked over his shoulder. Half ashamed of his startled gesture, he again turned to his pictures. Then a sharp cry broke from him.

Athalia's picture was gone.

He searched for it everywhere in the room, in his own pockets, under the furniture. It was nowhere to be found.

In sudden, overpowering horror, he seized the fur coats and returned to the control room.

Dr. Mundson was changing the speed.

"Look out the window!" he called to Northwood.

The young man looked and started violently. Day had come, and now that the sun-ship was flying at a moderate speed, the ocean beneath was plainly visible; and its entire surface was covered with broken floes of ice and small, ragged icebergs. He seized a telescope and focussed it below. A typical polar scene met his eyes: penguins strutted about on cakes of ice, a whale blowing in the icy water.

"A part of the Antarctic that has never been explored," said Dr. Mundson; "and there, just showing on the horizon, is the Great Ice Barrier." His characteristic smile lighted the morose black eyes. "I am enough of the dramatist to wish you to be impressed with what I shall show you within less than an hour. Accordingly, I shall make a landing and let you feel polar ice under your feet."

After less than a minute's search, Dr. Mundson found a suitable place on the ice for a landing, and, with a few deft manipulations of the controls, brought the sun-ship swooping down like an eagle on its prey.

For a long moment after the scientist had stepped out on the ice, Northwood paused at the door. His feet were chained by a strange reluctance to enter this white, dead wilderness of ice. But Dr. Mundson's impatient, "Ready?" drew from him one last glance at the cozy interior of the sun-ship before he, too, went out into the frozen stillness.

They left the sun-ship resting on the ice like a fallen silver moon, while they wandered to the edge of the Barrier and looked at the gray, narrow stretch of sea between the ice pack and the high cliffs of the Barrier. The sun of the commencing six-months' Antarctic day was a low, cold ball whose slanted rays struck the ice with blinding whiteness. There were constant falls of ice from the Barrier, which thundered into the ocean amid great clouds of ice smoke that lingered like wraiths around the edge. It was a scene of loneliness and waiting death.

"What's that?" exclaimed the scientist suddenly.

Out of the white silence shrilled a low whistle, a familiar whistle. Both men wheeled toward the sun-ship.

Before their horrified eyes, the great sphere jerked and glided up, and swerved into the heavens.

Up it soared; then, gaining speed, it swung into the blue distance until, in a moment, it was a tiny star that flickered out even as they watched.

Both men screamed and cursed and flung up their arms despairingly. A penguin, attracted by their cries, waddled solemnly over to them and regarded them with manlike curiosity.

"Stranded in the coldest spot on earth!" groaned the scientist.

"Why did it start itself, Dr. Mundson!" Northwood narrowed his eyes as he spoke.

"It didn't!" The scientist's huge face, red from cold, quivered with helpless rage. "Human hands started it."

"What! Whose hands?"

"*Ach!* Do I know?" His Teutonic accent grew more pronounced, as it always did when he was under emotional stress. "Somebody whose brain is better than mine. Somebody who found a way to hide away from our eyes. *Ach, Gott!* Don't let me think!"

His great head sank between his shoulders, giving him, in his fur suit, the grotesque appearance of a friendly brown bear.

"Doctor Mundson," said Northwood suddenly, "did you have an enemy, a man with the face and body of a pagan god—a great, blond creature with eyes as cold and cruel as the ice under our feet?"

"Wait!" The huge round head jerked up. "How do you know about Adam? You have not seen him, won't see him until we arrive at our destination."

"But I have seen him. He was sitting not thirty feet from you in the Mad Hatter's Club last night. Didn't you know? He followed me to the street, spoke to me, and then—" Northwood stopped. How could he let the insane words pass his lips?

"Then, what? Speak up!"

Northwood laughed nervously. "It sounds foolish, but I saw him vanish like that." He snapped his fingers.

"*Ach, Gott!*" All the ruddy color drained from the scientist's face. As though talking to himself, he continued:

"Then it is true, as he said. He has crossed the bridge. He has reached the Light. And now he comes to see the world he will conquer—came unseen when I refused my permission."

He was silent for a long time, pondering. Then he turned passionately to Northwood.

"John Northwood, kill me! I have brought a new horror into the world. From the unborn future, I have snatched a creature who has reached the Light too soon. Kill me!" He bowed his great, shaggy head.

"What do you mean, Dr. Mundson: that this Adam has arrived at a point in evolution beyond this age?"

"Yes. Think of it! I visioned godlike creatures with the souls of gods. But, Heaven help us, man always will be man: always will lust for conquest. You and I, Northwood, and all others are barbarians to Adam. He and his kind will do what men always do to barbarians—conquer and kill."

"Are there more like him?" Northwood struggled with a smile of unbelief.

"I don't know. I did not know that Adam had reached a point so near the ultimate. But you have seen. Already he is able to set aside what we call natural laws."

Northwood looked at the scientist closely. The man was surely mad—mad in this desert of white death.

"Come!" he said cheerfully. "Let's build an Eskimo snow house. We can live on penguins for days. And who knows what may rescue us?"

For three hours the two worked at cutting ice blocks. With snow for mortar, they built a crude shelter which enabled them to rest out of the cold breath of the spiral polar winds that blew from the south.

Dr. Mundson was sitting at the door of their hut, moodily pulling at his strong, black pipe. As though a fit had seized him, he leaped up and let his pipe fall to the ice.

"Look!" he shouted. "The sun-ship!"

It seemed but a moment before the tiny speck on the horizon had swept overhead, a silver comet on the grayish-blue polar sky. In another moment it had swooped down, eaglewise, scarcely fifty feet from the ice hut.

Dr. Mundson and Northwood ran forward. From the metal sphere stepped the stranger of the Mad Hatter Club. His tall, straight form, erect and slim, swung toward them over the ice.

"Adam!" shouted Dr. Mundson. "What does this mean? How dare you!"

Adam's laugh was like the happy demonstration of a boy. "So? You think you still are master? You think I returned because I reverenced you yet?" Hate shot viciously through the freezing blue eyes. "You worm of the Black Age!"

Northwood shuddered. He had heard those strange words addressed to himself scarcely more than twelve hours ago.

Adam was still speaking: "With a thought I could annihilate you where you are standing. But I have use for you. Get in." He swept his hand to the sun-ship.

Both men hesitated. Then Northwood strode forward until he was within three feet of Adam. They stood thus, eyeing each other, two splendid beings, one blond as a Viking, the other dark and vital.

"Just what is your game?" demanded Northwood.

The icy eyes shot forth a gleam like lightning. "I needn't tell you, of course, but I may as well let you suffer over the knowledge." He curled his lips with superb scorn. "I have one human weakness. I want Athalia." The icy eyes warmed for a fleeting second. "She is anticipating her meeting with you—bah! The taste of these women of the Black Age! I could kill you, of course; but that would only inflame her. And so I take you to her, thrust you down her throat. When she sees you, she will fly to me." He spread his magnificent chest.

"Adam!" Dr. Mundson's face was dark with anger. "What of Eve?"

"Who are you to question my actions? What a fool you were to let me, whom you forced into life thousands of years too soon, grow more powerful than you! Before I am through with all of you petty creatures of the Black Age, you will call me more terrible than your Jehovah! For see what you have called forth from unborn time."

He vanished.

Before the startled men could recover from the shock of it, the vibrant, too-new voice went on:

"I am sorry for you, Mundson, because, like you, I need specimens for my experiments. What a splendid specimen you will be!" His laugh was ugly with significance. "Get in, worms!"

Unseen hands cuffed and pushed them into the sun-ship.

Inside, Dr. Mundson stumbled to the control room, white and drawn of face, his great brain seemingly paralyzed by the catastrophe.

"You needn't attempt tricks," went on the voice. "I am watching you both. You cannot even hide your thoughts from me."

And thus began the strange continuation of the journey. Not once, in that wild half-hour's rush over the polar ice clouds, did they see Adam. They saw and heard only the weird signs of his presence: a puffing cigar hanging in midair, a glass of water swinging to unseen lips, a ghostly voice hurling threats and insults at them.

Once the scientist whispered: "Don't cross him; it is useless. John Northwood, you'll have to fight a demigod for your woman!"

Because of the terrific speed of the sun-ship, Northwood could distinguish nothing of the topographical details below. At the end of half-an-hour, the scientist slowed enough to point out a tall range of snow-covered mountains, over which hovered a play of colored lights like the *aurora australis*.

"Behind those mountains," he said, "is our destination."

Almost in a moment, the sun-ship had soared over the peaks. Dr. Mundson kept the speed low enough for Northwood to see the splendid view below.

In the giant cup formed by the encircling mountain range was a green valley of tropical luxurance. Stretches of dense forest swept half up the mountains and filled the valley cup with tangled verdure. In the center, surrounded by a broad field and a narrow ring of woods, towered a group of buildings. From the largest, which was circular, came the auroralike radiance that formed an umbrella of light over the entire valley.

"Do I guess right," said Northwood, "that the light is responsible for this oasis in the ice?"

"Yes," said Dr. Mundson. "In your American slang, it is canned sunshine containing an overabundance of certain rays, especially the Life Ray, which I have isolated." He smiled proudly. "You needn't look startled, my friend. Some of the most common things store sunlight. On very dark nights, if you have sharp eyes, you can see the radiance given off by certain flowers, which many naturalists say is trapped sunshine. The familiar nasturtium and the marigold opened for me the way to hold sunshine against the long polar night, for they taught me how to apply the Einstein theory of bent light. Stated simply, during the polar night, when the sun is hidden over the rim of the world, we steal some of his rays; during the polar day we concentrate the light."

"But could be stored sunshine alone give enough warmth for the luxuriant growth of those jungles?"

"An overabundance of the Life Ray is responsible for the miraculous growth of all life in New Eden. The Life Ray is Nature's most powerful force. Yet Nature is often niggardly and paradoxical in her use of her powers. In New Eden, we have forced the powers of creation to take ascendency over the powers of destruction."

At Northwood's sudden start, the scientist laughed and continued: "Is it not a pity that Nature, left alone, requires twenty years to make a man who begins to die in another ten years? Such waste is not tolerated in New Eden, where supermen are younger than babes and—"

"Come, worms; let's land."

It was Adam's voice. Suddenly he materialized, a blond god, whose eyes and flesh were too new.

They were in a world of golden skylight, warmth and tropical vegetation. The field on which they had landed was covered with a velvety green growth of very soft, fine-bladed grass, sprinkled with tiny, star-shaped blue flowers. A balmy, sweet-scented wind, downy as the breeze of a dream, blew gently along the grass and tingled against Northwood's skin refreshingly. Almost instantly he had the sensation of perfect well being, and this feeling of physical perfection was part of the ecstasy that seemed to pervade the entire valley. Grass and breeze and golden skylight were saturated with a strange ether of joyousness.

At one end of the field was a dense jungle, cut through by a road that led to the towering building from which, while above in the sun-ship, they had seen the golden light issue.

From the jungle road came a man and a woman, large, handsome people, whose flesh and eyes had the sinister newness of Adam's. Even before they came close enough to speak, Northwood was aware that while they seemed of Adam's breed, they were yet unlike him. The difference was psychical rather than physical; they lacked the aura of hate and horror that surrounded Adam. The woman drew Adam's head down and kissed him affectionately on both cheeks.

Adam, from his towering height, patted her shoulder impatiently and said: "Run on back to the laboratory, grandmother. We're following soon. You have some new human embryos, I believe you told me this morning."

"Four fine specimens, two of them being your sister's twins."

"Splendid! I was sure that creation had stopped with my generation. I must see them." He turned to the scientist and Northwood. "You needn't try to leave this spot. Of course I shall know instantly and deal with you in my own way. Wait here."

He strode over the emerald grass on the heels of the woman.

Northwood asked: "Why does he call that girl grandmother?"

"Because she is his ancestress." He stirred uneasily. "She is of the first generation brought forth in the laboratory, and is no different from you or I, except that, at the age of five years, she is the ancestress of twenty generations."

"My God!" muttered Northwood.

"Don't start being horrified, my friend. Forget about so-called natural laws while you are in New Eden. Remember, here we have isolated the Life Ray. But look! Here comes your Athalia!"

Northwood gazed covertly at the beautiful girl approaching them with a rarely graceful walk. She was tall, slender, round-bosomed, narrow-hipped, and she held her lovely body in the erect poise of splendid health. Northwood had a confused realization of uncovered bronzy hair, drawn to the back of a white neck in a bunch of short curls; of immense soft black eyes; lips the color of blood, and delicate, plump flesh on which the golden skylight lingered graciously. He was instantly glad to see that while she possessed the freshness of young girlhood, her skin and eyes did not have the horrible newness of Adam's.

When she was still twenty feet distant, Northwood met her eyes and she smiled shyly. The rich, red blood ran through her face; and he, too, flushed.

She went to Dr. Mundson and, placing her hands on his thick shoulders, kissed him affectionately.

"I've been worried about you, Daddy Mundson." Her rich contralto voice matched her exotic beauty. "Since you and Adam had that quarrel the day you left, I did not see him until this morning, when he landed the sun-ship alone."

"And you pleaded with him to return for us?"

"Yes." Her eyes drooped and a hot flush swept over her face.

Dr. Mundson smiled. "But I'm back now, Athalia, and I've brought some one whom I hope you will be glad to know."

Reaching for her hand, he placed it simply in Northwood's.

"This is John, Athalia. Isn't he handsomer than the pictures of him which I televisioned to you? God bless both of you."

He walked ahead and turned his back.

A magical half hour followed for Northwood and Athalia. The girl told him of her past life, how Dr. Mundson had discovered her one year ago working in a New York sweat shop, half dead from consumption. Without friends, she was eager to follow the scientist to New Eden, where he promised she would recover her health immediately.

"And he was right, John," she said shyly. "The Life Ray, that marvelous energy ray which penetrates to the utmost depths of earth and ocean, giving to the cells of all living bodies the power to grow and remain animate, has been concentrated by Dr. Mundson in his stored sunshine. The Life Ray healed me almost immediately."

Northwood looked down at the glorious girl beside him, whose eyes already fluttered away from his like shy black butterflies. Suddenly he squeezed the soft hand in his and said passionately:

"Athalia! Because Adam wants you and will get you if he can, let us set aside all the artificialities of civilization. I have loved you madly ever since I saw your picture. If you can say the same to me, it will give me courage to face what I know lies before me."

Athalia, her face suddenly tender, came closer to him.

"John Northwood, I love you."

Her red lips came temptingly close; but before he could touch them, Adam suddenly pushed his body between him and Athalia. Adam was pale, and all the iciness was gone from his blue eyes, which were deep and dark and very human. He looked down at Athalia, and she looked up at him, two handsome specimens of perfect manhood and womanhood.

"Fast work, Athalia!" The new vibrant voice was strained. "I was hoping you would be disappointed in him, especially after having been wooed by me this morning. I could take you if I wished, of course; but I prefer to win you in the ancient manner. Dismiss him!" He jerked his thumb over his shoulder in Northwood's direction.

Athalia flushed vividly and looked at him almost compassionately. "I am not great enough for you, Adam. I dare not love you."

Adam laughed, and still oblivious of Northwood and Dr. Mundson, folded his arms over his breast. With the golden skylight on his burnished hair, he was a valiant, magnificent spectacle.

"Since the beginning of time, gods and archangels have looked upon the daughters of men and found them fair. Mate with me, Athalia, and I, fifty thousand years beyond the creature Mundson has selected for you, will make you as I am, the deathless overlord of life and all nature."

He drew her hand to his bosom.

For one dark moment, Northwood felt himself seared by jealousy, for, through the plump, sweet flesh of Athalia's face, he saw the red blood leap again. How could she withhold herself from this splendid superman?

But her answer, given with faltering voice, was the old, simple one: "I have promised him, Adam. I love him." Tears trembled on her thick lashes.

"So! I cannot get you in the ancient manner. Now I'll use my own."

He seized her in his arms crushed her against him, and, laughing over her head at Northwood, bent his glistening head and kissed her on the mouth.

There was a blinding flash of blue electric sparks—and nothing else. Both Adam and Athalia had vanished.

Adam's voice came in a last mocking challenge: "I shall be what no other gods before me have been—a good sport. I'll leave you both to your own devices, until I want you again."

White-lipped and trembling, Northwood groaned: "What has he done now?"

Dr. Mundson's great head drooped. "I don't know. Our bodies are electric and chemical machines; and a super intelligence has discovered new laws of which you and I are ignorant."

"But Athalia...."

"She is safe; he loves her."

"Loves her!" Northwood shivered. "I cannot believe that those freezing eyes could ever look with love on a woman."

"Adam is a man. At heart he is as human as the first man-creature that wallowed in the new earth's slime." His voice dropped as though he were musing aloud. "It might be well to let him have Athalia. She will help to keep vigor in the new race, which would stop reproducing in another few generations without the injection of Black Age blood."

"Do you want to bring more creatures like Adam into the world?" Northwood flung at him. "You have tampered with life enough, Dr. Mundson. But, although Adam has my sympathy, I'm not willing to turn Athalia over to him."

"Well said! Now come to the laboratory for chemical nourishment and rest under the Life Ray."

They went to the great circular building from whose highest tower issued the golden radiance that shamed the light of the sun, hanging low in the northeast.

"John Northwood," said Dr. Mundson, "with that laboratory, which is the center of all life in New Eden, we'll have to whip Adam. He gave us what he called a 'sporting chance' because he knew that he is able to send us and all mankind to a doom more terrible than hell. Even now we might be entering some hideous trap that he has set for us."

They entered by a side entrance and went immediately to what Dr. Mundson called the Rest Ward. Here, in a large room, were ranged rows of cots, on many of which lay men basking in the deep orange flood of light which poured from individual lamps set above each cot.

"It is the Life Ray!" said Dr. Mundson reverently. "The source of all growth and restoration in Nature. It is the power that bursts open the seed and brings forth the shoot, that increases the shoot into a giant tree. It is the same power that enables the fertilized ovum to develop into an animal. It creates and recreates cells almost instantly; accordingly, it is the perfect substitute for sleep. Stretch out, enjoy its power; and while you rest, eat these nourishing tablets."

Northwood lay on a cot, and Dr. Mundson turned the Life Ray on him. For a few minutes a delicious drowsiness fell upon him, producing a spell of perfect peace which the cells of his being seemed to drink in. For another delirious, fleeting space, every inch of him vibrated with a thrilling sensation of freshness. He took a deep, ecstatic breath and opened his eyes.

"Enough," said Dr. Mundson, switching off the Ray. "After three minutes of rejuvenation, you are commencing again with perfect cells. All ravages from disease and wear have been corrected."

Northwood leaped up joyously. His handsome eyes sparkled, his skin glowed. "I feel great! Never felt so good since I was a kid."

A pleased grin spread over the scientist's homely face. "See what my discovery will mean to the world! In the future we shall all go to the laboratory for recuperation and nourishment. We'll have almost twenty-four hours a day for work and play."

He stretched out on the bed contentedly. "Some day, when my work is nearly done, I shall permit the Life Ray to cure my hump."

"Why not now?"

Dr. Mundson sighed. "If I were perfect, I should cease to be so overwhelmingly conscious of the importance of perfection." He settled back to enjoyment of the Life Ray.

A few minutes later, he jumped up, alert as a boy. "*Ach!* That's fine. Now I'll show you how the Life Ray speeds up development and produces four generations of humans a year."

With restored energy, Northwood began thinking of Athalia. As he followed Dr. Mundson down a long corridor, he yearned to see her again, to be certain that she was safe. Once he imagined he felt a gentle, soft-fleshed touch against his hand, and was disappointed not to see her walking by his side. Was she with him, unseen? The thought was sweet.

Before Dr. Mundson opened the massive bronze door at the end of the corridor, he said:

"Don't be surprised or shocked over anything you see here, John Northwood. This is the Baby Laboratory."

They entered a room which seemed no different from a hospital ward. On little white beds lay naked children of various sizes, perfect, solemn-eyed youngsters and older children as beautiful as animated statues. Above each bed was a small Life Ray projector. A white-capped nurse went from bed to bed.

"They are recuperating from the daily educational period," said the scientist. "After a few minutes of this they will go into the growing room, which I shall have to show you through a window. Should you and I enter, we might be changed in a most extraordinary manner." He laughed mischievously. "But, look, Northwood!"

He slid back a panel in the wall, and Northwood peered in through a thick pane of clear glass. The room was really an immense outdoor arena, its only carpet the fine-bladed grass, its roof the blue sky cut in the middle by an enormous disc from which shot the aurora of trapped sunshine which made a golden umbrella over the valley. Through openings in the bottom of the disc poured a fine rain of rays which fell constantly upon groups of children, youths and young girls, all clad in the merest scraps of clothing. Some were dancing, others were playing games, but all seemed as supremely happy as the birds and butterflies which fluttered about the shrubs and flowers edging the arena.

"I don't expect you to believe," said Dr. Mundson, "that the oldest young man in there is three months old. You cannot see visible changes in a body which grows as slowly as the human being, whose normal period of development is twenty years or more. But I can give you visible proof of how fast growth takes place under the full power of the Life Ray. Plant life, which, even when left to nature, often develops from seed to flower within a few weeks or months, can be seen making its miraculous changes under the Life Ray. Watch those gorgeous purple flowers over which the butterflies are hovering."

Northwood followed his pointing finger. Near the glass window through which they looked grew an enormous bank of resplendent violet colored flowers, which literally enshrouded the entire bush with their royal glory. At first glance it seemed as though a violent wind were snatching at flower and bush, but closer inspection proved that the agitation was part of the plant itself. And then he saw that the movements were the result of perpetual composition and growth.

He fastened his eyes on one huge bud. He saw it swell, burst, spread out its passionate purple velvet, lift the broad flower face to the light for a joyous minute. A few seconds later a butterfly lighted airily to sample its nectar and to brush the pollen from its yellow dusted wings. Scarcely had the winged visitor flown away than the purple petals began to wither and fall away, leaving the seed pod on the stem. The visible change went on in this seed pod. It turned rapidly brown, dried out, and then sent the released seeds in a shower to the rich black earth below. Scarcely had the seeds touched the ground than they sent up tiny green shoots that grew larger each moment. Within ten minutes there was a new plant a foot high. Within half an hour, the plant budded, blossomed, and cast forth its own seed.

"You understand?" asked the scientist. "Development is going on as rapidly among the children. Before the first year has passed, the youngest baby will have grandchildren; that is, if the baby tests out fit to pass its seed down to the new generation. I know it sounds absurd. Yet you saw the plant."

"But Doctor," Northwood rubbed his jaw thoughtfully, "Nature's forces of destruction, of tearing down, are as powerful as her creative powers. You have discovered the ultimate in creation and upbuilding. But perhaps—oh, Lord, it is too awful to think!"

"Speak, Northwood!" The scientist's voice was impatient.

"It is nothing!" The pale young man attempted a smile. "I was only imagining some of the horror that could be thrust on the world if a supermind like Adam's should discover Nature's secret of death and destruction and speed it up as you have sped the life force."

"*Ach Gott!*" Dr. Mundson's face was white. "He has his own laboratory, where he works every day. Don't talk so loud. He might be listening. And I believe he can do anything he sets out to accomplish."

Close to Northwood's ear fell a faint, triumphant whisper: "Yes, he can do anything. How did you guess, worm?"

It was Adam's voice.

"Now come and see the Leyden jar mothers," said Dr. Mundson. "We do not wait for the child to be born to start our work."

He took Northwood to a laboratory crowded with strange apparatus, where young men and women worked. Northwood knew instantly that these people, although unusually handsome and strong, were not of Adam's generation. None of them had the look of newness which marked those who had grown up under the Life Ray.

"They are the perfect couples whom I combed the world to find," said the scientist. "From their eugenic marriages sprang the first children that passed through the laboratory. I had hoped," he hesitated and looked sideways at Northwood, "I had dreamed of having the children of you and Athalia to help strengthen the New Race."

A wave of sudden disgust passed over Northwood.

"Thanks," he said tartly. "When I marry Athalia, I intend to have an old-fashioned home and a Black Age family. I don't relish having my children turned into—experiments."

"But wait until you see all the wonders of the laboratory! That is why I am showing you all this."

Northwood drew his handkerchief and mopped his brow. "It sickens me, Doctor! The more I see, the more pity I have for Adam—and the less I blame him for his rebellion and his desire to kill and to rule. Heavens! What a terrible thing you have done, experimenting with human life."

"Nonsense! Can you say that all life—all matter—is not the result of scientific experiment? Can you?" His black gaze made Northwood uncomfortable. "Buck up, young friend, for now I am going to show you a marvelous improvement on Nature's bungling ways—the Leyden jar mother." He raised his voice and called, "Lilith!"

The woman whom they had met on the field came forward.

"May we take a peep at Lona's twins?" asked the scientist. "They are about ready to go to the growing dome, are they not?"

"In five more minutes," said the woman. "Come see."

She lifted one of the black velvet curtains that lined an entire side of the laboratory and thereby disclosed a globular jar of glass and metal, connected by wires to a dynamo. Above the jar was a Life Ray projector. Lilith slid aside a metal portion of the jar, disclosing through the glass underneath the squirming, kicking body of a baby, resting on a bed of soft, spongy substance, to which it was connected by the navel cord.

"The Leyden jar mother," said Dr. Mundson. "It is the dream of us scientists realized. The human mother's body does nothing but nourish and protect her unborn child, a job which science can do better. And so, in New Eden, we take the young embryo and place it in the Leyden jar mother, where the Life Ray, electricity, and chemical food shortens the period of gestation to a few days."

At that moment a bell under the Leyden jar began to ring. Dr. Mundson uncovered the jar and lifted out the child, a beautiful, perfectly formed boy, who began to cry lustily.

"Here is one baby who'll never be kissed," he said. "He'll be nourished chemically, and, at the end of the week, will no longer be a baby. If you are patient, you can actually see the processes of development taking place under the Life Ray, for babies develop very fast."

Northwood buried his face in his hands. "Lord! This is awful. No childhood; no mother to mould his mind! No parents to watch over him, to give him their tender care!"

"Awful, fiddlesticks! Come see how children get their education, how they learn to use their hands and feet so they need not pass through the awkwardness of childhood."

He led Northwood to a magnificent building whose façade of white marble was as simply beautiful as a Greek temple. The side walls, built almost entirely of glass, permitted the synthetic sunshine to sweep from end to end. They first entered a library, where youths and young girls poured over books of all kinds. Their manner of reading mystified Northwood.

With a single sweep of the eye, they seemed to devour a page, and then turned to the next. He stepped closer to peer over the shoulder of a beautiful girl. She was reading "Euclid's Elements of Geometry," in Latin, and she turned the pages as swiftly as the other girl occupying her table, who was devouring "Paradise Lost."

Dr. Mundson whispered to him: "If you do not believe that Ruth here is getting her Euclid, which she probably never saw before to-day, examine her from the book; that is, if you are a good enough Latin scholar."

Ruth stopped her reading to talk to him, and, in a few minutes, had completely dumbfounded him with her pedantic replies, which fell from lips as luscious and unformed as an infant's.

"Now," said Dr. Mundson, "test Rachael on her Milton. As far as she has read, she should not misquote a line, and her comments will probably prove her scholarly appreciation of Milton."

Word for word, Rachael was able to give him "Paradise Lost" from memory, except the last four pages, which she had not read. Then, taking the book from him, she swept her eyes over these pages, returned the book to him, and quoted copiously and correctly.

Dr. Mundson gloated triumphantly over his astonishment. "There, my friend. Could you now be satisfied with old-fashioned children who spend long, expensive years in getting an education? Of course, your children will not have the perfect brains of these, yet, developed under the Life Ray, they should have splendid mentality.

"These children, through selective breeding, have brains that make everlasting records instantly. A page in a book, once seen, is indelibly retained by them, and understood. The same is true of a lecture, of an explanation given by a teacher, of even idle conversation. Any man or woman in this room should be able to repeat the most trivial conversation days old."

"But what of the arts, Dr. Mundson? Surely even your supermen and women cannot instantly learn to paint a masterpiece or to guide their fingers and their brains through the intricacies of a difficult musical composition."

"No?" His dark eyes glowed. "Come see!"

Before they entered another wing of the building, they heard a violin being played masterfully.

Dr. Mundson paused at the door.

"So that you may understand what you shall see, let me remind you that the nerve impulses and the coordinating means in the human body are purely electrical. The world has not yet accepted my theory, but it will. Under superman's system of education, the instantaneous records made on the brain give immediate skill to the acting parts of the body. Accordingly, musicians are made over night."

He threw open the door. Under a Life Ray projector, a beautiful, Juno-esque woman was playing a violin. Facing her, and with eyes fastened to hers, stood a young man, whose arms and slender fingers mimicked every motion she made. Presently she stopped playing and handed the violin to him. In her own masterly manner, he repeated the score she had played.

"That is Eve," whispered Dr. Mundson. "I had selected her as Adam's wife. But he does not want her, the most brilliant woman of the New Race."

Northwood gave the woman an appraising look. "Who wants a perfect woman? I don't blame Adam for preferring Athalia. But how is she teaching her pupil?"

"Through thought vibration, which these perfect people have developed until they can record permanently the radioactive waves of the brains of others."

Eve turned, caught Northwood's eyes in her magnetic blue gaze, and smiled as only a goddess can smile upon a mortal she has marked as her own. She came toward him with outflung hands.

"So you have come!" Her vibrant contralto voice, like Adam's, held the birdlike, broken tremulo of a young child's. "I have been waiting for you, John Northwood."

Her eyes, as blue and icy as Adam's, lingered long on him, until he flinched from their steely magnetism. She slipped her arm through his and drew him gently but firmly from the room, while Dr. Mundson stood gaping after them.

They were on a flagged terrace arched with roses of gigantic size, which sent forth billows of sensuous fragrance. Eve led him to a white marble seat piled with silk cushions, on which she reclined her superb body, while she regarded him from narrowed lids.

"I saw your picture that he televisioned to Athalia," she said. "What a botch Dr. Mundson has made of his mating." Her laugh rippled like falling water. "I want you, John Northwood!"

Northwood started and blushed furiously. Smile dimples broke around her red, humid lips.

"Ah, you're old-fashioned!"

Her large, beautiful hand, fleshed more tenderly than any woman's hand he had ever seen, went out to him appealingly. "I can bring you amorous delight that your Athalia never could offer in her few years of youth. And I'll never grow old, John Northwood."

She came closer until he could feel the fragrant warmth of her tawny, ribbon bound hair pulse against his face. In sudden panic he drew back.

"But I am pledged to Athalia!" tumbled from him. "It is all a dreadful mistake, Eve. You and Adam were created for each other."

"Hush!" The lightning that flashed from her blue eyes changed her from seductress to angry goddess. "Created for each other! Who wants a made-to-measure lover?"

The luscious lips trembled slightly, and into the vivid eyes crept a suspicion of moisture. Eternal Eve's weapons! Northwood's handsome face relaxed with pity.

"I want you, John Northwood," she continued shamelessly. "Our love will be sublime." She leaned heavily against him, and her lips were like a blood red flower pressed against white satin. "Come, beloved, kiss me!"

Northwood gasped and turned his head. "Don't, Eve!"

"But a kiss from me will set you apart from all your generation, John Northwood, and you shall understand what no man of the Black Age could possibly fathom."

Her hair had partly fallen from its ribbon bandage and poured its fragrant gold against his shoulder.

"For God's sake, don't tempt me!" he groaned. "What do you mean?"

"That mental and physical and spiritual contact with me will temporarily give you, a three-dimension creature, the power of the new sense, which your race will not have for fifty thousand years."

White-lipped and trembling, he demanded: "Explain!"

Eve smiled. "Have you not guessed that Adam has developed an additional sense? You've seen him vanish. He and I have the sixth sense of Time Perception—the new sense which enables us to penetrate what you of the Black Age call the Fourth Dimension. Even you whose mentalities are framed by three dimensions have this sixth sense instinct. Your very religion is based on it, for you believe that in another life you shall step into Time, or, as you call it, eternity." She leaned closer so that her hair brushed his cheek. "What is eternity, John Northwood? Is it not keeping forever ahead of the Destroyer? The future is eternal, for it is never reached. Adam and I, through our new sense which comprehends Time and Space, can vanish by stepping a few seconds into the future, the Fourth Dimension of Space. Death can never reach us, not even accidental death, unless that which causes death could also slip into the future, which is not yet possible."

"But if the Fourth Dimension is future Time, why can one in the third dimension feel the touch of an unseen presence in the Fourth Dimension—hear his voice, even?"

"Thought vibration. The touch is not really felt nor the voice heard: they are only imagined. The radioactive waves of the brain of even you Black Age people are swift enough to bridge Space and Time. And it is the mind that carries us beyond the third dimension."

Her red mouth reached closer to him, her blue eyes touched hidden forces that slept in remote cells of his being. "You are going into Eternal Time, John Northwood, Eternity without beginning or end. You understand? You feel it? Comprehend it? Now for the contact—kiss me!"

Northwood had seen Athalia vanish under Adam's kiss. Suddenly, in one mad burst of understanding, he leaned over to his magnificent temptress.

For a split second he felt the sweet pressure of baby-soft lips, and then the atoms of his body seemed to fly asunder. Black chaos held him for a frightful moment before he felt sanity return.

He was back on the terrace again, with Eve by his side. They were standing now. The world about him looked the same, yet there was a subtle change in everything.

Eve laughed softly. "It is puzzling, isn't it? You're seeing everything as in a mirror. What was left before is now right. Only you and I are real. All else is but a vision, a dream. For now you and I are existing one minute in future time, or, more simply, we are in the Fourth Dimension. To everything in the third dimension, we are invisible. Let me show you that Dr. Mundson cannot see you."

They went back to the room beyond the terrace. Dr. Mundson was not present.

"There he goes down the jungle path," said Eve, looking out a window. She laughed. "Poor old fellow. The children of his genius are worrying him."

They were standing in the recess formed by a bay window. Eve picked up his hand and laid it against her face, giving him the full, blasting glory of her smiling blue eyes.

Northwood, looking away miserably, uttered a low cry. Coming over the field beyond were Adam and Athalia. By the trimming on the blue dress she wore, he could see that she was still in the Fourth Dimension, for he did not see her as a mirror image.

A look of fear leaped to Eve's face. She clutched Northwood's arm, trembling.

"I don't want Adam to see that I have passed you beyond," she gasped. "We are existing but one minute in the future. Always Adam and I have feared to pass too far beyond the sweetness of reality. But now, so that Adam may not see us, we shall step five minutes into what-is-yet-to-be. And even he, with all his power, cannot see into a future that is more distant than that in which he exists."

She raised her humid lips to his. "Come, beloved."

Northwood kissed her. Again came the moment of confusion, of the awful vacancy that was like death, and then he found himself and Eve in the laboratory, following Adam and Athalia down a long corridor. Athalia was crying and pleading frantically with Adam. Once she stopped and threw herself at his feet in a gesture of dramatic supplication, arms outflung, streaming eyes wide open with fear.

Adam stooped and lifted her gently and continued on his way, supporting her against his side.

Eve dug her fingers into Northwood's arm. Horror contorted her face, horror mixed with rage.

"My mind hears what he is saying, understands the vile plan he has made, John Northwood. He is on his way to his laboratory to destroy not only you and most of these in New Eden, but me as well. He wants only Athalia."

Striding forward like an avenging goddess, she pulled Northwood after her.

"Hurry!" she whispered. "Remember, you and I are five minutes in the future, and Adam is only one. We are witnessing what will occur four minutes from now. We yet have time to reach the laboratory before him and be ready for him when he enters. And because he will have to go back to Present Time to do his work of destruction, I will be able to destroy him. Ah!"

Fierce joy burned in her flashing blue eyes, and her slender nostrils quivered delicately. Northwood, peeping at her in horror, knew that no mercy could be expected of her. And when she stopped at a certain door and inserted a key, he remembered Athalia. What if she should enter with Adam in Present Time?

They were inside Adam's laboratory, a huge apartment filled with queer apparatus and cages of live animals. The room was a strange paradox. Part of the equipment, the walls, and the floor was glistening with newness, and part was moulding with extreme age. The powers of disintegration that haunt a tropical forest seemed to be devouring certain spots of the room. Here, in the midst of bright marble, was a section of wall that seemed as old as the pyramids. The surface of the stone had an appalling mouldiness, as though it had been lifted from an ancient graveyard where it had lain in the festering ground for unwholesome centuries.

Between cracks in this stained and decayed section of stone grew fetid moss that quivered with the microscopic organisms that infest age-rotten places. Sections of the flooring and woodwork also reeked with mustiness. In one dark, webby corner of the room lay a pile of bleached bones, still tinted with the ghastly grays and pinks of putrefaction. Northwood, overwhelmingly nauseated, withdrew his eyes from the bones, only to see, in another corner, a pile of worm-eaten clothing that lay on the floor in the outline of a man.

Faint with the reek of ancient mustiness, Northwood retreated to the door, dizzy and staggering.

"It sickens you," said Eve, "and it sickens me also, for death and decay are not pleasant. Yet Nature, left to herself, reduces all to this. Every grave that has yawned to receive its prey hides corruption no less shocking. Nature's forces of creation and destruction forever work in partnership. Never satisfied with her composition, she destroys and starts again, building, building towards the ultimate of perfection. Thus, it is natural that if Dr. Mundson isolated the Life Ray, Nature's supreme force of compensation, isolation of the Death Ray should closely follow. Adam, thirsting for power, has succeeded. A few sweeps of his unholy ray of decomposition will undo all Dr. Mundson's work in this valley and reduce it to a stinking holocaust of destruction. And the time for his striking has come!"

She seized his face and drew it toward her. "Quick!" she said. "We'll have to go back to the third dimension. I could leave you safe in the fourth, but if anything should happen to me, you would be stranded forever in future time."

She kissed his lips. In a moment, he was back in the old familiar world, where right is right and left is left. Again the subtle change wrought by Eve's magic lips had taken place.

Eve went to a machine standing in a corner of the room.

"Come here and get behind me, John Northwood. I want to test it before he enters."

Northwood stood behind her shoulder.

"Now watch!" she ordered. "I shall turn it on one of those cages of guinea pigs over there."

She swung the projector around, pointed it at the cage of small, squealing animals, and threw a lever. Instantly a cone of black mephitis shot forth, a loathsome, bituminous stream of putrefaction that reeked of the grave and the cesspool, of the utmost reaches of decay before the dust accepts the disintegrated atoms. The first touch of seething, pitchy destruction brought screams of sudden agony from the guinea pigs, but the screams were cut short as the little animals fell in shocking, instant decay. The very cage which imprisoned them shriveled and retreated from the hellish, devouring breath that struck its noisome rot into the heart of the wood and the metal, reducing both to revolting ruin.

Eve cut off the frightful power, and the black cone disappeared, leaving the room putrid with its defilement.

"And Adam would do that to the world," she said, her blue eyes like electric-shot icicles. "He would do it to you, John Northwood—and to me!" Her full bosom strained under the passion beneath.

"Listen!" She raised her hand warningly. "He comes! The destroyer comes!"

A hand was at the door. Eve reached for the lever, and, the same moment, Northwood leaned over her imploringly.

"If Athalia is with him!" he gasped. "You will not harm her?"

A wild shriek at the door, a slight scuffle, and then the doorknob was wrenched as though two were fighting over it.

"For God's sake, Eve!" implored Northwood. "Wait! Wait!"

"No! She shall die, too. You love her!"

Icy, cruel eyes cut into him, and a new-fleshed hand tried to push him aside. The door was straining open. A beloved voice shrieked. "John!"

Eve and Northwood both leaped for the lever. Under her tender white flesh she was as strong as a man. In the midst of the struggle, her red, humid lips approached his—closer. Closer. Their merest pressure would thrust him into Future Time, where the laboratory and all it contained would be but a shadow, and where he would be helpless to interfere with her terrible will.

He saw the door open and Adam stride into the room. Behind him, lying prone in the hall where she had probably fainted, was Athalia. In a mad burst of strength he touched the lever together with Eve.

The projector, belching forth its stinking breath of corruption swung in a mad arc over the ceiling, over the walls—and then straight at Adam.

Then, quicker than thought, came the accident. Eve, attempting to throw Northwood off, tripped, fell half over the machine, and, with a short scream of despair, dropped into the black path of destruction.

Northwood paused, horrified. The Death Ray was pointed at an inner wall of the room, which, even as he looked, crumbled and disappeared, bringing down upon him dust more foul than any obscenity the bowels of the earth might yield. In an instant the black cone ate through the outer parts of the building, where crashing stone and screams that were more horrible because of their shortness followed the ruin that swept far into the fair reaches of the valley.

The paralyzing odor of decay took his breath, numbed his muscles, until, of all that huge building, the wall behind him and one small section of the room by the doorway alone remained whole. He was trying to nerve himself to reach for the lever close to that quiet formless thing still partly draped over the machine, when a faint sound in the door electrified him. At first, he dared not look, but his own name, spoken almost in a gasp, gave him courage.

Athalia lay on the floor, apparently untouched.

He jerked the lever violently before running to her, exultant with the knowledge that his own efforts to keep the ray from the door had saved her.

"And you're not hurt!" He gathered her close.

"John! I saw it get Adam." She pointed to a new mound of mouldy clothes on the floor. "Oh, it is hideous for me to be so glad, but he was going to destroy everything and everyone except me. He made the ray projector for that one purpose."

Northwood looked over the pile of putrid ruins which a few minutes ago had been a building. There was not a wall left intact.

"His intention is accomplished, Athalia," he said sadly. "Let's get out before more stones fall."

In a moment they were in the open. An ominous stillness seemed to grip the very air—the awful silence of the polar wastes which lay not far beyond the mountains.

"How dark it is, John!" cried Athalia. "Dark and cold!"

"The sunshine projector!" gasped Northwood. "It must have been destroyed. Look, dearest! The golden light has disappeared."

"And the warm air of the valley will lift immediately. That means a polar blizzard." She shuddered and clung closer to him. "I've seen Antarctic storms, John. They're death."

Northwood avoided her eyes. "There's the sun-ship. We'll give the ruins the once over in case there are any survivors; then we'll save ourselves."

Even a cursory examination of the mouldy piles of stone and dust convinced them that there could be no survivors. The ruins looked as though they had lain in those crumbling piles for centuries. Northwood, smothering his repugnance, stepped among them—among the green, slimy stones and the unspeakable revolting débris, staggering back and faint and shocked when he came upon dust that was once human.

"God!" he groaned, hands over eyes. "We're alone, Athalia! Alone in a charnal house. The laboratory housed the entire population, didn't it?"

"Yes. Needing no sleep nor food, we did not need houses. We all worked here, under Dr. Mundson's generalship, and, lately under Adam's, like a little band of soldiers fighting for a great cause."

"Let's go to the sun-ship, dearest."

"But Daddy Mundson was in the library," sobbed Athalia. "Let's look for him a little longer."

Sudden remembrance came to Northwood. "No, Athalia! He left the library. I saw him go down the jungle path several minutes before I and Eve went to Adam's laboratory."

"Then he might be safe!" Her eyes danced. "He might have gone to the sun-ship."

Shivering, she slumped against him. "Oh, John! I'm cold."

Her face was blue. Northwood jerked off his coat and wrapped it around her, taking the intense cold against his unprotected shoulders. The low, gray sky was rapidly darkening, and the feeble light of the sun could scarcely pierce the clouds. It was disturbing to know that even the summer temperature in the Antarctic was far below zero.

"Come, girl," said Northwood gravely. "Hurry! It's snowing."

They started to run down the road through the narrow strip of jungle. The Death Ray had cut huge swathes in the tangle of trees and vines, and now areas of heaped débris, livid with the colors of recent decay, exhaled a mephitic humidity altogether alien to the snow that fell in soft, slow flakes. Each hesitated to voice the new fear: had the sun-ship been destroyed?

By the time they reached the open field, the snow stung their flesh like sharp needles, but it was not yet thick enough to hide from them a hideous fact.

The sun-ship was gone.

It might have occupied one of several black, foul areas on the green grass, where the searching Death Ray had made the very soil putrefy, and the rocks crumble into shocking dust.

Northwood snatched Athalia to him, too full of despair to speak. A sudden terrific flurry of snow whirled around them, and they were almost blown from their feet by the icy wind that tore over the unprotected field.

"It won't be long," said Athalia faintly. "Freezing doesn't hurt, John, dear."

"It isn't fair, Athalia! There never would have been such a marriage as ours. Dr. Mundson searched the world to bring us together."

"For scientific experiment!" she sobbed. "I'd rather die, John. I want an old-fashioned home, a Black Age family. I want to grow old with you and leave the earth to my children. Or else I want to die here now under the kind, white blanket the snow is already spreading over us." She drooped in his arms.

Clinging together, they stood in the howling wind, looking at each other hungrily, as though they would snatch from death this one last picture of the other.

Northwood's freezing lips translated some of the futile words that crowded against them. "I love you because you are not perfect. I hate perfection!"

"Yes. Perfection is the only hopeless state, John. That is why Adam wanted to destroy, so that he might build again."

They were sitting in the snow now, for they were very tired. The storm began whistling louder, as though it were only a few feet above their heads.

"That sounds almost like the sun-ship," said Athalia drowsily.

"It's only the wind. Hold your face down so it won't strike your flesh so cruelly."

"I'm not suffering. I'm getting warm again." She smiled at him sleepily.

Little icicles began to form on their clothing, and the powdery snow frosted their uncovered hair.

Suddenly came a familiar voice: "*Ach Gott!*"

Dr. Mundson stood before them, covered with snow until he looked like a polar bear.

"Get up!" he shouted. "Quick! To the sun-ship!"

He seized Athalia and jerked her to her feet. She looked at him sleepily for a moment, and then threw herself at him and hugged him frantically.

"You're not dead?"

Taking each by the arm, he half dragged them to the sun-ship, which had landed only a few feet away. In a few minutes he had hot brandy for them.

While they sipped greedily, he talked, between working the sun-ship's controls.

"No, I wouldn't say it was a lucky moment that drew me to the sun-ship. When I saw Eve trying to charm John, I had what you American slangists call a hunch, which sent me to the sun-ship to get it off the ground so that Adam couldn't commandeer it. And what is a hunch but a mental penetration into the Fourth Dimension?" For a long moment, he brooded, absent-minded. "I was in the air when the black ray, which I suppose is Adam's deviltry, began to destroy everything it touched. From a safe elevation I saw it wreck all my work." A sudden spasm crossed his face. "I've flown over the entire valley. We're the only survivors—thank God!"

"And so at last you confess that it is not well to tamper with human life?" Northwood, warmed with hot brandy, was his old self again.

"Oh, I have not altogether wasted my efforts. I went to elaborate pains to bring together a perfect man and a perfect woman of what Adam called our Black Age." He smiled at them whimsically.

"And who can say to what extent you have thus furthered natural evolution?" Northwood slipped his arm around Athalia. "Our children might be more than geniuses, Doctor!"

Dr. Mundson nodded his huge, shaggy head gravely.

"The true instinct of a Creature of the Light," he declared.

Remember
ASTOUNDING STORIES
Appears on Newsstands
THE FIRST THURSDAY IN EACH MONTH

Into Space

By Sterner St. Paul

A loud hum filled the air, and suddenly the projectile rose, gaining speed rapidly.

What was the extraordinary connection between Dr. Livermore's sudden disappearance and the coming of a new satellite to earth?

Many of my readers will remember the mysterious radio messages which were heard by both amateur and professional short wave operators during the nights of the twenty-third and twenty-fourth of last September, and even more will remember the astounding discovery made by Professor Montescue of the Lick Observatory on the night of September twenty-fifth. At the time, some inspired writers tried to connect the two events, maintaining that the discovery of the fact that the earth had a new satellite coincident with the receipt of the mysterious messages was evidence that the new planetoid was inhabited and that the messages were attempts on the part of the inhabitants to communicate with us.

The fact that the messages were on a lower wave length than any receiver then in existence could receive with any degree of clarity, and the additional fact that they appeared to come from an immense distance lent a certain air of plausibility to these ebullitions in the Sunday magazine sections. For some weeks the feature writers harped on the subject, but the hurried construction of new receivers which would work on a lower wave length yielded no results, and the solemn pronouncements of astronomers to the effect that the new celestial body could by no possibility have an atmosphere on account of its small size finally put an end to the talk. So the matter lapsed into oblivion.

While quite a few people will remember the two events I have noted, I doubt whether there are five hundred people alive who will remember anything at all about the disappearance of Dr. Livermore of the University of Calvada on September twenty-third. He was a man of some local prominence, but he had no more than a local fame, and few papers outside of California even noted the event in their columns. I do not think that anyone ever tried to connect up his disappearance with the radio messages or the discovery of the new earthly satellite; yet the three events were closely bound up together, and but for the Doctor's disappearance, the other two would never have happened.

Dr. Livermoore taught physics at Calvada, or at least he taught the subject when he remembered that he had a class and felt like teaching. His students never knew whether he would appear at class or not; but he always passed everyone who took his courses and so, of course, they were always crowded. The University authorities used to remonstrate with him, but his ability as a research worker was so well known and recognized that he was allowed to go about as he pleased. He was a bachelor who lived alone and who had no interests in life, so far as anyone knew, other than his work.

I first made contact with him when I was a freshman at Calvada, and for some unknown reason he took a liking to me. My father had insisted that I follow in his footsteps as an electrical engineer; as he was paying my bills, I had to make a show at studying engineering while I clandestinely pursued my hobby, literature. Dr. Livermore's courses were the easiest in the school and they counted as science, so I regularly registered for them, cut them, and attended a class in literature as an auditor. The Doctor used to meet me on the campus and laughingly scold me for my absence, but he was really in sympathy with my ambition and he regularly gave me a passing mark and my units of credit without regard to my attendance, or, rather, lack of it.

When I graduated from Calvada I was theoretically an electrical engineer. Practically I had a pretty good knowledge of contemporary literature and knew almost nothing about my so-called profession. I stalled around Dad's office for a few months until I landed a job as a cub reporter on the San Francisco *Graphic* and then I quit him cold. When the storm blew over, Dad admitted that you couldn't make a silk purse out of a sow's ear and agreed with a grunt to my new line of work. He said that I would probably be a better reporter than an engineer because I couldn't by any possibility be a worse one, and let it go at that. However, all this has nothing to do with the story. It just explains how I came to be acquainted with Dr. Livermore, in the first place, and why he sent for me on September twenty-second, in the second place.

The morning of the twenty-second the City Editor called me in and asked me if I knew "Old Liverpills."

"He says that he has a good story ready to break but he won't talk to anyone but you," went on Barnes. "I offered to send out a good man, for when Old Liverpills starts a story it ought to be good, but all I got was a high powered bawling out. He said that he would talk to you or no one and would just as soon talk to no one as to me any longer. Then he hung up. You'd better take a run out to Calvada and see what he has to say. I can have a good man rewrite your drivel when you get back."

I was more or less used to that sort of talk from Barnes so I paid no attention to it. I drove my flivver down to Calvada and asked for the Doctor.

"Dr. Livermore?" said the bursar. "Why, he hasn't been around here for the last ten months. This is his sabbatical year and he is spending it on a ranch he owns up at Hat Creek, near Mount Lassen. You'll have to go there if you want to see him."

I knew better than to report back to Barnes without the story, so there was nothing to it but to drive up to Hat Creek, and a long, hard drive it was. I made Redding late that night; the next day I drove on to Burney and asked for directions to the Doctor's ranch.

"So you're going up to Doc Livermore's, are you?" asked the Postmaster, my informant. "Have you got an invitation?"

I assured him that I had.

"It's a good thing," he replied, "because he don't allow anyone on his place without one. I'd like to go up there myself and see what's going on, but I don't want to get shot at like old Pete Johnson did when he tried to drop in on the Doc and pay him a little call. There's something mighty funny going on up there."

Naturally I tried to find out what was going on but evidently the Postmaster, who was also the express agent, didn't know. All he could tell me was that a "lot of junk" had come for the Doctor by express and that a lot more had been hauled in by truck from Redding.

"What kind of junk?" I asked him.

"Almost everything, Bub: sheet steel, machinery, batteries, cases of glass, and Lord knows what all. It's been going on ever since he landed there. He has a bunch of Indians working for him and he don't let a white man on the place."

Forced to be satisfied with this meager information, I started old Lizzie and lit out for the ranch. After I had turned off the main trail I met no one until the ranch house was in sight. As I rounded a bend in the road which brought me in sight of the building, I was forced to put on my brakes at top speed to avoid running into a chain which was stretched across the road. An Indian armed with a Winchester rifle stood behind it, and when I stopped he came up and asked my business.

"My business is with Dr. Livermore," I said tartly.

"You got letter?" he inquired.

"No," I answered.

"No ketchum letter, no ketchum Doctor," he replied, and walked stolidly back to his post.

"This is absurd," I shouted, and drove Lizzie up to the chain. I saw that it was merely hooked to a ring at the end, and I climbed out and started to take it down. A thirty-thirty bullet embedded itself in the post an inch or two from my head, and I changed my mind about taking down that chain.

"No ketchum letter, no ketchum Doctor," said the Indian laconically as he pumped another shell into his gun.

I was balked, until I noticed a pair of telephone wires running from the house to the tree to which one end of the chain was fastened.

"Is that a telephone to the house?" I demanded.

The Indian grunted an assent.

"Dr. Livermore telephoned me to come and see him," I said. "Can't I call him up and see if he still wants to see me?"

The Indian debated the question with himself for a minute and then nodded a doubtful assent. I cranked the old coffee mill type of telephone which I found, and presently heard the voice of Dr. Livermore.

"This is Tom Faber, Doctor," I said. "The *Graphic* sent me up to get a story from you, but there's an Indian here who started to murder me when I tried to get past your barricade."

"Good for him," chuckled the Doctor. "I heard the shot, but didn't know that he was shooting at you. Tell him to talk to me."

The Indian took the telephone at my bidding and listened for a minute.

"You go in," he agreed when he hung up the receiver.

He took down the chain and I drove on up to the house, to find the Doctor waiting for me on the veranda.

"Hello, Tom," he greeted me heartily. "So you had trouble with my guard, did you?"

"I nearly got murdered," I said ruefully.

"I expect that Joe would have drilled you if you had tried to force your way in," he remarked cheerfully. "I forgot to tell him that you were coming to-day. I told him you would be here yesterday, but yesterday isn't to-day to that Indian. I wasn't sure you would get here at all, in point of fact, for I didn't know whether that old fool I talked to in your office would send you or some one else. If anyone else had been sent, he would have never got by Joe, I can tell you. Come in. Where's your bag?"

"I haven't one," I replied. "I went to Calvada yesterday to see you, and didn't know until I got there that you were up here."

The Doctor chuckled.

"I guess I forgot to tell where I was," he said. "That man I talked to got me so mad that I hung up on him before I told him. It doesn't matter, though. I can dig you up a new toothbrush, and I guess you can make out with that. Come in."

I followed him into the house, and he showed me a room fitted with a crude bunk, a washstand, a bowl and a pitcher.

"You won't have many luxuries here, Tom," he said, "but you won't need to stay here for more than a few days. My work is done: I am ready to start. In fact, I would have started yesterday instead of to-day, had you arrived. Now don't ask any questions; it's nearly lunch time."

"What's the story, Doctor?" I asked after lunch as I puffed one of his excellent cigars. "And why did you pick me to tell it to?"

"For several reasons," he replied, ignoring my first question. "In the first place, I like you and I think that you can keep your mouth shut until you are told to open it. In the second place, I have always found that you had the gift of vision or imagination and have the ability to believe. In the third place, you are the only man I know who had the literary ability to write up a good story and at the same time has the scientific background to grasp what it is all about. Understand that unless I have your promise not to write this story until I tell you that you can, not a word will I tell you."

I reflected for a moment. The *Graphic* would expect the story when I got back, but on the other hand I knew that unless I gave the desired promise, the Doctor wouldn't talk.

"All right," I assented, "I'll promise."

"Good!" he replied. "In that case, I'll tell you all about it. No doubt you, like the rest of the world, think that I'm crazy?"

"Why, not at all," I stammered. In point of fact, I had often harbored such a suspicion.

"Oh, that's all right," he went on cheerfully. "I *am* crazy, crazy as a loon, which, by the way, is a highly sensible bird with a well balanced mentality. There is no doubt that I am crazy, but my craziness is not of the usual type. Mine is the insanity of genius."

He looked at me sharply as he spoke, but long sessions at poker in the San Francisco Press Club had taught me how to control my facial muscles, and I never batted an eye. He seemed satisfied, and went on.

"From your college work you are familiar with the laws of magnetism," he said. "Perhaps, considering just what your college career really was, I might better say that you are supposed to be familiar with them."

I joined with him in his laughter.

"It won't require a very deep knowledge to follow the thread of my argument," he went on. "You know, of course, that the force of magnetic attraction is inversely proportional to the square of the distances separating the magnet and the attracted particles, and also that each magnetized particle had two poles, a positive and a negative pole, or a north pole and a south pole, as they are usually called?"

I nodded.

"Consider for a moment that the laws of magnetism, insofar as concerns the relation between distance and power of attraction, are exactly matched by the laws of gravitation."

"But there the similarity between the two forces ends," I interrupted.

"But there the similarity does *not* end," he said sharply. "That is the crux of the discovery which I have made: that magnetism and gravity are one and the same, or, rather, that the two are separate, but similar manifestations of one force. The parallel between the two grows closer with each succeeding experiment. You know, for example, that each magnetized particle has two poles. Similarly each gravitized particle, to coin a new word, had two poles, one positive and one negative. Every particle on the earth is so oriented that the negative poles point toward the positive center of the earth. This is what causes the commonly known phenomena of gravity or weight."

"I can prove the fallacy of that in a moment," I retorted.

"There are none so blind as those who will not see," he quoted with an icy smile. "I can probably predict your puerile argument, but go ahead and present it."

"If two magnets are placed so that the north pole of one is in juxtaposition to the South Pole of the other, they attract one another," I said. "If the position of the magnets be reversed so that the two similar poles are opposite, they will repel. If your theory were correct, a man standing on his head would fall off the earth."

"Exactly what I expected," he replied. "Now let me ask you a question. Have you ever seen a small bar magnet placed within the field of attraction of a large electromagnet? Of course you have, and you have noticed that, when the north pole of the bar magnet was pointed toward the electromagnet, the bar was attracted. However, when the bar was reversed and the South Pole pointed toward the electromagnet, the bar was still attracted. You doubtless remember that experiment."

"But in that case the magnetism of the electromagnet was so large that the polarity of the small magnet was reversed!" I cried.

"Exactly, and the field of gravity of the earth is so great compared to the gravity of a man that when he stands on his head, his polarity is instantly reversed."

I nodded. His explanation was too logical for me to pick a flaw in it.

"If that same bar magnet were held in the field of the electromagnet with its north pole pointed toward the magnet and then, by the action of some outside force of sufficient power, its polarity were reversed, the bar would be repelled. If the magnetism were neutralized and held exactly neutral, it would be neither repelled nor attracted, but would act only as the force of gravity impelled it. Is that clear?"

"Perfectly," I assented.

"That, then, paves the way for what I have to tell you. I have developed an electrical method of neutralizing the gravity of a body while it is within the field of the earth, and also, by a slight extension, a method of entirely reversing its polarity."

I nodded calmly.

"Do you realize what this means?" he cried.

"No," I replied, puzzled by his great excitement.

"Man alive," he cried, "it means that the problem of aerial flight is entirely revolutionized, and that the era of interplanetary travel is at hand! Suppose that I construct an airship and then render it neutral to gravity. It would weigh nothing, *absolutely nothing*! The tiniest propeller would drive it at almost incalculable speed with a minimum consumption of power, for the only resistance to its motion would be the resistance of the air. If I were to reverse the polarity, it would be repelled from the earth with the same force with which it is now attracted, and it would rise with the same acceleration as a body falls toward the earth. It would travel to the moon in two hours and forty minutes."

"Air resistance would—"

"There is no air a few miles from the earth. Of course, I do not mean that such a craft would take off from the earth and land on the moon three hours later. There are two things which would interfere with that. One is the fact that the propelling force, the gravity of the earth, would diminish as the square of the distance from the center of the earth, and the other is that when the band of neutral attraction, or rather repulsion, between the earth and the moon had been reached, it would be necessary to decelerate so as to avoid a smash on landing. I have been over the whole thing and I find that it would take twenty-nine hours and fifty-two minutes to make the whole trip. The entire thing is perfectly possible. In fact, I have asked you here to witness and report the first interplanetary trip to be made."

"Have you constructed such a device?" I cried.

"My space ship is finished and ready for your inspection," he replied. "If you will come with me, I will show it to you."

Hardly knowing what to believe, I followed him from the house and to a huge barnlike structure, over a hundred feet high, which stood nearby. He opened the door and switched on a light, and there before me stood what looked at first glance to be a huge artillery shell, but of a size larger than any ever made. It was constructed of sheet steel, and while the lower part was solid, the upper sections had huge glass windows set in them. On the point was a mushroom shaped protuberance. It measured perhaps fifty feet in diameter and was one hundred and forty feet high, the Doctor informed me. A ladder led from the floor to a door about fifty feet from the ground.

I followed the Doctor up the ladder and into the space flier. The door led us into a comfortable living room through a double door arrangement.

"The whole hull beneath us," explained the Doctor, "is filled with batteries and machinery except for a space in the center, where a shaft leads to a glass window in the bottom so that I can see behind me, so to speak. The space above is filled with storerooms and the air purifying apparatus. On this level is my bedroom, kitchen, and other living rooms, together with a laboratory and an observatory. There is a central control room located on an upper level, but it need seldom be entered, for the craft can be controlled by a system of relays from this room or from any other room in the ship. I suppose that you are more or less familiar with imaginative stories of interplanetary travel?"

I nodded an assent.

"In that case there is no use in going over the details of the air purifying and such matters," he said. "The story writers have worked out all that sort of thing in great detail, and there is nothing novel in my arrangements. I carry food and water for six months and air enough for two months by constant renovating. Have you any question you wish to ask?"

"One objection I have seen frequently raised to the idea of interplanetary travel is that the human body could not stand the rapid acceleration which would be necessary to attain speed enough to ever get anywhere. How do you overcome this?"

"My dear boy, who knows what the human body can stand? When the locomotive was first invented learned scientists predicted that the limit of speed was thirty miles an hour, as the human body could not stand a higher speed. To-day the human body stands a speed of three hundred and sixty miles an hour without ill effects. At any rate, on my first trip I intend to take no chances. We know that the body can stand an acceleration of thirty-two feet per second without trouble. That is the rate of acceleration due to gravity and is the rate at which a body increases speed when it falls. This is the acceleration which I will use.

"Remember that the space traveled by a falling body in a vacuum is equal to one half the acceleration multiplied by the square of the elapsed time. The moon, to which I intend to make my first trip, is only 280,000 miles, or 1,478,400,000 feet, from us. With an acceleration of thirty-two feet per second, I would pass the moon two hours and forty minutes after leaving the earth. If I later take another trip, say to Mars, I will have to find a means of increasing my acceleration, possibly by the use of the rocket principle. Then will be time enough to worry about what my body will stand."

A short calculation verified the figures the Doctor had given me, and I stood convinced.

"Are you really going?" I asked.

"Most decidedly. To repeat, I would have started yesterday, had you arrived. As it is, I am ready to start at once. We will go back to the house for a few minutes while I show you the location of an excellent telescope through which you may watch my progress, and instruct you in the use of an ultra-short-wave receiver which I am confident will pierce the Heaviside layer. With this I will keep in communication with you, although I have made no arrangements for you to send messages to me on this trip. I intend to go to the moon and land. I will take atmosphere samples through an airport and, if there is an atmosphere which will support life, I will step out on the surface. If there is not, I will return to the earth."

A few minutes was enough for me to grasp the simple manipulations which I would have to perform, and I followed him again to the space flier.

"How are you going to get it out?" I asked.

"Watch," he said.

He worked some levers and the roof of the barn folded back, leaving the way clear for the departure of the huge projectile. I followed him inside and he climbed the ladder.

"When I shut the door, go back to the house and test the radio," he directed.

The door clanged shut and I hastened into the house. His voice came plainly enough. I went back to the flier and waved him a final farewell, which he acknowledged through a window; then I returned to the receiver. A loud hum filled the air, and suddenly the projectile rose and flew out through the open roof, gaining speed rapidly until it was a mere speck in the sky. It vanished. I had no trouble in picking him up with the telescope. In fact, I could see the Doctor through one of the windows.

"I have passed beyond the range of the atmosphere, Tom," came his voice over the receiver, "and I find that everything is going exactly as it should. I feel no discomfort, and my only regret is that I did not install a transmitter in the house so that you could talk to me; but there is no real necessity for it. I am going to make some observations now, but I will call you again with a report of progress in half-an-hour."

For the rest of the afternoon and all of that night I received his messages regularly, but with the coming of daylight they began to fade. By nine o'clock I could get only a word here and there. By noon I could hear nothing. I went to sleep hoping that the night would bring better reception, nor was I disappointed. About eight o'clock I received a message, rather faintly, but none the less distinctly.

"I regret more than ever that I did not install a transmitter so that I could learn from you whether you are receiving my messages," his voice said faintly. "I have no idea of whether you can hear me or not, but I will keep on repeating this message every hour while my battery holds out. It is now thirty hours since I left the earth and I should be on the moon, according to my calculations. But I am not, and never will be. I am caught at the neutral point where the gravity of the earth and the moon are exactly equal.

"I had relied on my momentum to carry me over this point. Once over it, I expected to reverse my polarity and fall on the moon. My momentum did not do so. If I keep my polarity as it was when left the earth, both the earth and the moon repel me. If I reverse it, they both attract me, and again I cannot move. If I had equipped my space flier with a rocket so that I could move a few miles, or even a few feet, from the dead line, I could proceed, but I did not do so, and I cannot move forward or back. Apparently I am doomed to stay here until my air gives out. Then my body, entombed in my space ship, will endlessly circle the earth as a satellite until the end of time. There is no hope for me, for long before a duplicate of my device equipped with rockets could be constructed and come to my rescue, my air would be exhausted. Good-by, Tom. You may write your story as soon as you wish. I will repeat my message in one hour. Good-by!"

At nine and at ten o'clock the message was repeated. At eleven it started again but after a few sentences the sound suddenly ceased and the receiver went dead. I thought that the fault was with the receiver and I toiled feverishly the rest of the night, but without result. I learned later that the messages heard all over the world ceased at the same hour.

The next morning Professor Montescue announced his discovery of the world's new satellite.

Coming—
MURDER MADNESS
An Extraordinary Four-Part Novel

By MURRAY LEINSTER

The Beetle Horde

By Victor Rousseau

The hideous monsters leaped into the cockpits and began their abominable meal.

CONCLUSION

Bullets, shrapnel, shell–nothing can stop the trillions of famished, man-sized beetles which, led by a madman, sweep down over the human race.

Tommy Travers and James Dodd, of the Travers Antarctic Expedition, crash in their plane somewhere near the South Pole, and are seized by a swarm of man-sized beetles. They are carried down to Submundia, a world under the earth's crust, where the beetles have developed their civilization to an amazing point, using a wretched race of degenerated humans, whom they breed as cattle, for food.

The insect horde is ruled by a human from the outside world—a drug-doped madman. Dodd recognizes this man as Bram, the archaeologist who had been lost years before at the Pole and given up for dead by a world he had hated because it refused to accept his radical scientific theories. His fiendish mind now plans the horrible revenge of leading his unconquerable horde of monster insects forth to ravage the world, destroy the human race and establish a new era—the era of the insect.

The world has to be warned of the impending doom. The two, with Haidia, a girl of Submundia, escape, and pass through menacing dangers to within two miles of the exit. There, suddenly, Tommy sees towering over him a creature that turns his blood cold—a gigantic praying mantis. Before he has time to act, the monster springs at them!

CHAPTER VII

Through the Inferno

Fortunately, the monster miscalculated its leap. The huge legs, whirling through the air, came within a few inches of Tommy's head, but passed over him, and the mantis plunged into the stream. Instantly the water was alive with leaping things with faces of such grotesque horror that Tommy sat paralyzed in his rocking shell, unable to avert his eyes.

Things no more than a foot or two in length, to judge from the slender, eel-like bodies that leaped into the air, but things with catfish heads and tentacles, and eyes waving on stalks; things with clawlike appendages to their ventral fins, and mouths that widened to fearful size, so that the whole head seemed to disappear above them, disclosing fangs like wolves'. Instantly the water was churned into phosphorescent fire as they precipitated themselves upon the struggling mantis, whose enormous form, extending halfway from shore to shore, was covered with the river monsters, gnawing, rending, tearing.

Luckily the struggles of the dying monster carried it downstream instead of up. In a few moments the immediate danger was past. And suddenly Haidia awoke, sat up.

"Where are we?" she cried. "Oh, I can see! I can see! Something has burned away from my eyes! I know this place. A wise man of my people once came here, and returned to tell of it. We must go on. Soon we shall be safe on the wide river. But there is another way that leads to here. We must go on! We must go on!"

Even as she spoke they heard the distant rasping of the beetle-legs. And before the shells were well in mid-current they saw the beetle horde coming round the bend; in the front of them Bram, reclining on his shell couch, and drawn by the eight trained beetles.

Bram saw the fugitives, and a roar of ironic mirth broke from his lips, resounding high above the strident rasping of the beetle-legs, and roaring over the marshes.

"I've got you, Dodd and Travers," he bellowed, as the trained beetles hovered above the shell canoes. "You thought you were clever, but you're at my mercy. Now's your last chance, Dodd. I'll save you still if you'll submit to me, if you'll admit that there were fossil monotremes before the pleistocene epoch. Come, it's so simple! Say it after me: 'The marsupial lion—'"

"You go to hell!" yelled Dodd, nearly upsetting his shell as he shook his fist at his enemy.

High above the rasping sound came Bram's shrill whistle. Just audible to human ears, though probably sounding like the roar of thunder to those of the beetles, there was no need to wonder what it was.

It was the call to slaughter.

Like a black cloud the beetles shot forward. A serried phalanx covered the two men and the girl, hovering a few feet overhead, the long legs dangling to within arm's reach. And a terrible cry of fear broke from Haidia's lips.

Suddenly Tommy remembered Bram's cigarette-lighter. He pulled it from his pocket and ignited it.

Small as the flame was, it was actinically much more powerful than the brighter phosphorescence of the fungi behind them. The beetle-cloud overhead parted. The strident sound was broken into a confused buzzing as the terrified, blinded beetles plopped into the stream.

None of them, fortunately, fell into either of the three shells, but the mass of struggling monsters in the water was hardly less formidable to the safety of the occupants than that menacing cloud overhead.

"Get clear!" Tommy yelled to Dodd, trying to help the shell along with his hands.

He heard Bram's cry of baffled rage, and, looking backward, could not refrain from a laugh of triumph. Bram's trained steeds had taken fright and overset him. Bram had fallen into the red mud beside the stream, from which he was struggling up, plastered from head to feet, and shaking his fists and evidently cursing, though his words could not be heard.

"How about your marsupial lion now, Bram?" yelled Dodd. "No monotremes before the pleistocene! D'you get that? That's my slogan now and for ever more!"

Bram shrieked and raved, and seemed to be inciting the beetles to a renewed assault. The air was still thick with them, but Tommy was waving the cigarette-lighter in a flaming arc, which cleared the way for them.

Then suddenly came disaster. The flame went out! Tommy closed the lighter with a snap and opened it. In vain. In his excitement he must have spilled all the contents, for it would not catch.

Bram saw and yelled derision. The beetle-cloud was thickening. Tommy, now abreast of his companions on the widening stream, saw the imminent end.

And then once more fate intervened. For, leaping through the air out of the places where they had lain concealed, six mantises launched themselves at their beetle prey.

Those awful bounds of the long-legged monsters, the scourges of the insect world, carried them clear from one bank to the other—fortunately for the occupants of the shells. In an instant the beetle-cloud dissolved. And it had all happened in a few seconds. Before Dodd or Tommy had quite taken in the situation, the mantises, each carrying a victim in its grooved legs, had vanished like the beetles. There was no sign of Bram. The three were alone upon the face of the stream, which went swirling upward into renewed darkness.

Tommy saw Dodd bend toward Haidia as she lay on her shell couch. He heard the sound of a noisy kiss. And he lay back in the hollow of his shell, with the feeling that nothing that could happen in the future could be worse than what they had passed through.

Days went by, days when the sense of dawning freedom filled their hearts with hope. Haidia told Dodd and Tommy that, according to the legends of her people, the river ran into the world from which they had been driven by the floods, ages before.

There had been no further signs of Bram or the beetle horde, and Dodd and Tommy surmised that it had been disorganized by the attack of the mantises, and that Bram was engaged in regaining his control over it. But neither of them believed that the respite would be a long one, and for that reason they rested ashore only for the briefest intervals, just long enough to snatch a little sleep, and to eat some of the shrimps that Haidia was adept at finding—or to pull some juicy fruit surreptitiously from a tree.

Incidents there were, nevertheless, during those days. For hours their shells were followed by a school of the luminous river monsters, which, nevertheless, made no attempt to attack them. And once, hearing a cry from Haidia, as she was gathering shrimps, Dodd ran forward to see her battling furiously with a luminous scorpion, eight feet in length, that had sprung at her from its lurking place behind a pear shrub.

Dodd succeeded in stunning and dispatching the monster without suffering any injury from it, but the strain of the period was beginning to tell on all of them. Worst of all, they seemed to have left all the luminous vegetation behind them, and were entering a region of almost total darkness, in which Haidia had to be their eyes.

Something had happened to the girl's sight in the journey over the petrol spring. As a matter of fact, the third, or nictitating membrane, which the humans of Submundia possessed, in common with birds, had been burned away. Haidia could see as well as ever in the dark, but she could bear more light than formerly as well. Unobtrusively she assumed command of the party. She anticipated their wants, dug shrimps in the darkness, and fed Tommy and Dodd with her own hands.

"God, what a girl!" breathed Dodd to his friend. "I've always had the reputation of being a woman-hater, Tommy, but once I get that girl to civilization I'm going to take her to the nearest Little Church Around the Corner in record time."

"I wish you luck, old man, I'm sure," answered Tommy. Dodd's words did not seem strange to him. Civilization was growing very remote to him, and Broadway seemed like a memory of some previous incarnation.

The river was growing narrower again, and swifter, too. On the last day, or night, of their journey—though they did not know that it was to be their last—it swirled so fiercely that it threatened every moment to overset their beetle-shells. Suddenly Tommy began to feel giddy. He gripped the side of his shell with his hand.

"Tommy, we're going round!" shouted Dodd in front of him.

There was no longer any doubt of it. The shells were revolving in a vortex of rushing, foaming water.

"Haidia!" they shouted.

The girl's voice came back thickly across the roaring torrent. The circles grew smaller. Tommy knew that he was being sucked nearer and nearer to the edge of some terrific whirlpool in that inky blackness. Now he could no longer hear Dodd's shouts, and the shell was tipping so that he could feel the water rushing along the edge of it. But for the exercise of centrifugal force he would have been flung from his perilous seat, for he was leaning inward at an angle of forty-five degrees.

Then suddenly his progress was arrested. He felt the shell being drawn to the shore. He leaped out, and Haidia's strong hands dragged the shell out of the torrent, while Tommy sank down, gasping.

"What's the matter?" he heard Dodd demanding.

"There is no more river," said Haidia calmly. "It goes into a hole in the ground. So much I have heard from the wise men of my people. They say that it is near such a place that they fled from the flood in years gone by."

"Then we're near safety," shouted Tommy. "That river must emerge as a stream somewhere in the upper world, Dodd. I wonder where the road lies."

"There is a road here," came Haidia's calm voice. "Let us put on our shells again, since who knows whether there may not be beetles here."

"Did you ever see such a girl as that?" demanded Dodd ecstatically. "First she saves our lives, and then she thinks of everything. Good lord, she'll remember my meals, and to wind my watch for me, and—and—"

But Haidia's voice, some distance ahead, interrupted Dodd's soliloquy, and, hoisting the beetle-shells upon their backs, they started along the rough trail that they could feel with their feet over the stony ground. It was still as dark as pitch, but soon they found themselves traveling up a sunken way that was evidently a dry watercourse. And now and again Haidia's reassuring voice would come from in front of them.

The road grew steeper. There could no longer be any doubt that they were ascending toward the surface of the earth. But even the weight of the beetle-shells and the steepness could not account for the feeling of intense weakness that took possession of them. Time and again they stopped, panting.

"We must be very near the surface, Dodd," said Tommy. "We've surely passed the center of gravity. That's what makes it so difficult."

"Come on," Haidia said in her quiet voice, stretching out her hand through the darkness. And for very shame they had to follow her.

On and on, hour after hour, up the steep ascent, resting only long enough to make them realize their utter fatigue. On because Haidia was leading them, and because in the belief that they were about to leave that awful land behind them their desires lent new strength to their limbs continuously.

Suddenly Haidia uttered a fearful cry. Her ears had caught what became apparent to Dodd and Jimmy several seconds later.

Far down in the hollow of the earth, increased by the echoes that came rumbling up, they heard the distant, strident rasp of the beetle swarm.

Then it was Dodd's turn to support Haidia and whisper consolation in her ears. No thought of resting now. If they were to be overwhelmed at last by the monsters, they meant to be overwhelmed in the upper air.

It was growing insufferably hot. Blasts of air, as if from a furnace, began to rush up and down past them. And the trail was growing steeper still, and slippery as glass.

"What is it, Jim?" Tommy panted, as Dodd, leaving Haidia for a moment, came back to him.

"I'd say lava," Dodd answered. "If only one could see something! I don't know how she finds her way. My impression is that we are coming out through the interior of an extinct volcano."

"But where are there volcanoes in the south polar regions?" inquired Tommy.

"There are Mount Erebus and Mount Terror, in South Victoria Land, active volcanoes discovered by Sir James Ross in 1841, and again by Borchgrevink, in 1899. If that's where we're coming out—well, Tommy, we're doomed, because it's the heart of the polar continent. We might as well turn back."

"But we won't turn back," said Tommy. "I'm damned if we do."

"We're damned if we don't," said Dodd.

"Come along please!" sang Haidia's voice high up the slope.

They struggled on. And now a faint luminosity was beginning to penetrate that infernal darkness. The rasping of the beetle-legs, too, was no longer audible. Perhaps they had thrown Bram off their track! Perhaps in the darkness he had not known which way they had gone after leaving the whirlpool!

That thought encouraged them to a last effort. They pushed their flagging limbs up, upward through an inferno of heated air. Suddenly Dodd uttered a yell and pointed upward.

"God!" ejaculated Tommy. Then he seized Dodd in his arms and nearly crushed him. For high above them, a pin-point in the black void, they saw—a star!

They were almost at the earth's surface!

One more effort, and suddenly the ground seemed to give beneath them. They breathed the outer air, and went sliding down a chute of sand, and stopped, half buried, at the bottom.

CHAPTER VIII

Recaptured

"Where are we?" each demanded of the other, as they staggered out.

It was a moonless night, and the air was chill, but they were certainly nowhere near the polar regions, for there was no trace of snow to be seen anywhere. All about them was sand, with here and there a spiny shrub standing up stiff and erect and solitary.

When they had disengaged themselves from the clinging sand they could see that they were apparently in the hollow of a vast crater, that must have been half a mile in circumference. It was low and worn down to an elevation of not more than two or three hundred feet, and evidently the volcano that had thrown it up had been extinct for millennia.

"Water!" gasped Dodd.

They looked all about them. They could see no signs of a spring anywhere, and both were parched with thirst after their terrific climb.

"We must find water, Haidia," said Tommy. "Why, what's the matter?"

Haidia was pointing upward at the starry heaven, and shivering with fear. "Eyes!" she cried. "Big beetles waiting for us up there!"

"No, no, Haidia," Dodd explained. "Those are stars. They are worlds—places where people live."

"Will you take me up there?" asked Haidia.

"No, this is our world," said Dodd. "And by and by the sun will rise, that's a big ball of fire up there. He watches over the world and gives us light and warmth. Don't be afraid. I'll take care of you."

"Haidia is not afraid with Jimmydodd to take care of her," replied the girl with dignity. "Haidia smells water—over there." She pointed across one side of the crater.

"There we'd better hurry," said Tommy, "because I can't hold out much longer."

The three scrambled over the soft sand, which sucked in their feet to the ankle at every step. It was with the greatest difficulty that they succeeded in reaching the crater's summit, low though it was. Then Dodd uttered a cry, and pointed. In front of them extended a long pool of water, with a scrubby growth around the edges.

The ground was firmer here, and they hurried toward it. Tommy was the first to reach it. He lay down on his face and drank eagerly. He had taken in a quart before he discovered that the water was saline.

At the same time Dodd uttered an exclamation of disgust. Haidia, too, after sipping a little of the fluid, had stood up, chattering excitedly in her own language.

But she was not chattering about the water. She was pointing toward the scrub. "Men there!" she cried. "Men like you and Tommy, Jimmydodd."

Tommy and Dodd looked at each other, the water already forgotten in their excitement at Haidia's information, which neither of them doubted.

Brave as she was, the girl now hung back behind Dodd, letting the two men take precedence of her. The water, saline as it was, had partly quenched their thirst. They felt their strength reviving.

And it was growing light. In the east the sky was already flecked with yellow pink. They felt a thrill of intense excitement at the prospect of meeting others of their kind.

"Where do you think we are?" asked Tommy.

Dodd stopped to look at a shrub that was growing near the edge of the pool. "I don't think, I know, Tommy," he answered. "This is wattle."

"Yes?"

"We're somewhere in the interior regions of the Australian continent—and that's not going to help us much."

"Over there—over there," panted Haidia. "Hold me, Jimmydodd. I can't see. Ah, this terrible light!"

She screwed her eyelids tightly together to shut out the pale light of dawn. The men had already discovered that the third membrane had been burned away.

"We must get her out of here," whispered Dodd to Tommy. "Somewhere where it's dark, before the sun rises. Let's go back to the entrance of the crater."

But Haidia, her arm extended, persisted, "Over there! Over there!"

Suddenly a spear came whirling out of a growth of wattle beside the pool. It whizzed past Tommy's face and dropped into the sand behind. Between the trunks of the wattles they could see the forms of a party of blackfellows, watching them intently.

Tommy held up his arms and moved forward with a show of confidence that he was far from feeling. After what he had escaped in the underworld he was in no mood to be massacred now.

But the blacks were evidently not hostile. It was probable that the spear had not been aimed to kill. At the sight of the two white men, and the white woman, they came forward doubtfully, then more fearlessly, shouting in their language. In another minute Tommy and Dodd were the center of a group of wondering savages.

Especially Haidia. Three or four gins, or black women, had crept out of the scrub, and were already examining her with guttural cries, and fingering the hair garment that she wore.

"Water!" said Tommy, pointing to his throat, and then to the pool, with a frown of disgust.

The blackfellows grinned, and led the three a short distance to a place where a large hollow had been scooped in the sandy floor of the desert. It was full of water, perfectly sweet to the taste. The three drank gratefully.

Suddenly the edge of the sun appeared above the horizon, gilding the sand with gold. The sunlight fell upon the three, and Haidia uttered a terrible cry of distress. She dropped upon the sand, her hands pressed to her eyes convulsively. Tommy and Dodd dragged her into the thickest part of the scrub, where she lay moaning.

They contrived bandages from the remnants of their clothing, and these, damped with cold water, and bound over the girl's eyes, alleviated her suffering somewhat. Meanwhile the blackfellows had prepared a meal of roast opossum. After their long diet of shrimps, it tasted like ambrosia to the two men.

Much to their surprise, Haidia seemed to enjoy it too. The three squatted in the scrub among the friendly blacks, discussing their situation.

"These fellows will save us," said Dodd. "It may be that we're quite near the coast, but, any way, they'll stick to us, even if only out of curiosity. They'll take us somewhere. But as soon as we get Haidia to safety we'll have to go back along our trail. We mustn't lose our direction. Suppose I was laughed at when I get back, called a liar! I tell you, we've got to have something to show, to prove my statements, before I can persuade anybody to fit out an expedition into Submundia. Even those three beetle-shells that we dropped in the crater won't be conclusive evidence for the type of mind that sits in the chairs of science to-day. And, speaking of that, we must get those blacks to carry those shells for us. I tell you, nobody will believe—"

"What's that?" cried Tommy sharply, as a rasping sound rose above the cries of the frightened blacks.

But there was no need to ask. Out of the crater two enormous beetles were winging their way toward them, two beetles larger than any that they had seen.

Fully seven feet in length, they were circling about each other, apparently engaged in a vicious battle.

The fearful beaks stabbed at the flesh beneath the shells, and they alternately stabbed and drew back, all the while approaching the party, which watched them, petrified with terror.

It was evident that the monsters had no conception of the presence of humans. Blinded by the sun, only one thing could have induced them to leave the dark depths of Submundia. That was the mating instinct. The beetles were evidently rival leaders of some swarm, engaged in a duel to the death.

Round and round they went in a dizzy maze, stabbing and thrusting, jaws closing on flesh, until they dropped, close-locked in battle, not more than twenty feet from the little party of blacks and whites, both squirming in the agonies of death.

"I don't think that necessarily means that the swarm is on our trail," said Tommy, a little later, as the three stood beside the shells that they had discarded. "Those two were strays, lost from the swarm and maddened by the mating instinct. Still, it might be as well to wear these things for a while, in case they do follow us."

"You're right," answered Dodd, as he placed one of the shells around Haidia. "We've got to get this little lady to civilization, and we've got to protect our lives in order to give this great new knowledge to the world. If we are attacked, you must sacrifice your life for me, Tommy, so that I can carry back the news."

"Righto!" answered Tommy with alacrity. "You bet I will, Jim."

The glaring sun of mid-afternoon was shining down upon the desert, but Haidia was no longer in pain. It was evident that she was fast becoming accustomed to the sunlight, though she still kept her eyes screwed up tightly, and had to be helped along by Dodd and Jimmy. In high good humor the three reached the encampment, to find that the blacks were feasting on the dead beetles, while the two eldest members of the party had proudly donned the shells.

It was near sunset before they finally started. Dodd and Tommy had managed to make it clear to them that they wished to reach civilization, but how near this was there was, of course, no means of determining. They noted, however, that the party started in a southerly direction.

"I should say," said Dodd, "that we are in South Australia, probably three or four hundred miles from the coast. We've got a long journey before us, but these blackfellows will know how to procure food for us."

They certainly knew how to get water, for, just as it began to grow dark, when the three were already tormented by thirst, they stopped at what seemed a mere hollow among the stones and boulders that strewed the face of the desert, and scooped away the sand, leaving a hole which quickly filled with clear, cold water of excellent taste.

After which they made signs that they were to camp there for the night. The moon was riding high in the sky. As it grew dark, Haidia opened her eyes, saw the luminary, and uttered an exclamation, this time not of fear, but of wonder.

"Moon," said Dodd. "That's all right, girl. She watches over the night, as the sun does over the day."

"Haidia likes the moon better than the sun," said the girl wistfully. "But the moon not strong enough to keep away the beetles."

"If I was you, I'd forget about the beetles, Haidia," said Dodd. "They won't come out of that hole in the ground. You'll never see them again."

And, as he spoke, they heard a familiar rasping sound far in the distance.

"How the wind blows," said Tommy, desperately resolved not to believe his ears. "I think a storm's coming up."

But Haidia, with a scream of fear, was clinging to Dodd, and the blacks were on their feet, spears and boomerangs in their hands, looking northward.

Out of that north a little black cloud was gathering. A cloud that spread gradually, as a thunder-cloud, until it covered a good part of the sky. And still more of the sky, and still more. All the while that faint, distant rasping was audible, but it did not increase in volume. It was as if the beetles had halted until the full number of the swarm had come up out of the crater.

Then the cloud, which by now covered half the sky, began to take geometric form. It grew square, the ragged edges seemed to trim themselves away, streaks of light shot through it at right angles, as if it was marshaling itself into companies.

The doomed men and the girl stood perfectly still, staring at that phenomenon. They knew that only a miracle could save them. They did not even speak, but Haidia clung more tightly to Dodd's arm.

Then suddenly the cloud spread upward and covered the face of the moon.

"Well, this is good-by, Tommy," said Dodd, gripping his friend's hand. "God, I wish I had a revolver, or a knife!" He looked at Haidia.

Suddenly the rasping became a whining shriek. A score of enormous beetles, the advance guards of the army, zoomed out of the darkness into a ray of straggling moonlight. Shrieking, the blacks, who had watched the approaching swarm perfectly immobile, threw away the two shells and bolted.

"Good Lord," Dodd shouted, "did you see the color of their shells, Tommy?" Even in that moment the scientific observer came uppermost in him. "Those red edges? They must be young ones, Tommy. It's the new brood! No wonder Bram stayed behind! He was waiting for them to hatch! The new brood! We're doomed—doomed! All my work wasted!"

The blackfellows did not get very far. A hundred yards from the place where they started to run they dropped, their bodies hidden beneath the clustering monsters, their screams cut short as those frightful beaks sought their throats, and those jaws crunched through flesh and bone.

Circling around Dodd, Tommy, and Haidia, as if puzzled by their appearance, the beetles kept up a continuous, furious droning that sounded like the roar of Niagara mixed with the shrieking of a thousand sirens. The moon was completely hidden, and only a dim, nebulous light showed the repulsive monsters as they flew within a few feet of the heads of the fugitives. The stench was overpowering.

But suddenly a ray of white light shot through the darkness, and, with a changed note, just perceptible to the ears of the two men, but doubtless of the greatest significance to the beetles, the swarm fled apart to right and left, leaving a clear lane, through which appeared—Bram, reclining on his shell-couch above his eight trained beetle steeds!

Hovering overhead, the eight huge monsters dropped lightly to the ground beside the three. Bram sat up, a vicious grin upon his twisted face. In his hand he held a large electric bulb, its sides sheathed in a roughly carved wooden frame; the wire was attached to a battery behind him.

"Well met, my friends!" he shouted exultantly. "I owe you more thanks than I can express for having so providentially left the electrical equipment of your plane undamaged after you crashed at the entrance to Submundia. I had a hunch about it—and the hunch worked!"

He grinned more malevolently as he looked from one man to the other.

"You've run your race," he said. "But I'm going to have a little fun with you before you die. I'm going to use you as an object lesson. You'll find it out in a little while."

"Go ahead, go ahead, Bram," Dodd grinned back at him. "Just a few million years ago, and you were a speck of protoplasm—in that pre-Pleistocene age—swimming among the invertebrate crustaceans that characterized that epoch."

"Invertebrates and monotremes, Dodd," said Bram, almost wistfully. "The mammals were already existent on the earth, as you know—" Suddenly he broke off, as he realized that Dodd was spoofing him. A yell of execration broke from his lips. He uttered a high whistle, and instantly the whiplike lashes of a hundred beetles whizzed through the darkness and remained poised over Dodd's head.

"Not even the marsupial lion, Bram," grinned Dodd, undismayed. "Go ahead, go ahead, but I'll not die with a lie upon my lips!"

CHAPTER IX

The Trail of Death

"There's sure some sort of hoodoo on these Antarctic expeditions, Wilson," said the city editor of *The Daily Record* to the star rewrite man. He glanced through the hastily typed report that had come through on the wireless set erected on the thirty-sixth story of the Record Building. "Tommy Travers gone, eh? And James Dodd, too! There'll be woe and wailing along the Great White Way to-night when this news gets out. They say that half the chorus girls in town considered themselves engaged to Tommy. Nice fellow, too! Always did like him!"

"Queer, that curtain of fog that seems to lie on the actual site of the South Pole," he continued, glancing over the report again. "So Storm thinks that Tommy crashed in it, and that it's a million to one against their ever finding his remains. What's this about beetles? Shells of enormous prehistoric beetles found by Tommy and Dodd! That'll make good copy, Wilson. Let's play that up. Hand it to Jones, and tell him to scare up a catching headline or two."

He beckoned to the boy who was hurrying toward his desk, a flimsy in his hand, glanced through it, and tossed it toward Wilson.

"What do they think this is, April Fool's Day?" he asked. "I'm surprised that the International Press should fall for such stuff as that!"

"Why, to-morrow is the first of April!" exclaimed Wilson, tossing back the cable dispatch with a contemptuous laugh.

"Well, it won't do the I. P. much good to play those tricks on their subscribers," said the city editor testily. "I'm surprised, to say the least. I guess their Adelaide correspondent has gone off his head or something. Using poor Travers's name, too! Of course that fellow didn't know he was dead, but still...."

That was how *The Daily Record* missed being the first to give out certain information that was to stagger the world. The dispatch, which had evidently outrun an earlier one, was as follows:

ADELAIDE, South Australia, March 31.—Further telegraphic communications arriving almost continuously from Settler's Station, signed by Thomas Travers, member of Travers Antarctic Expedition, who claims to have penetrated earth's interior at south pole and to have come out near Victoria Desert. Travers states that swarm of prehistoric beetles, estimated at two trillion, and as large as men, with shells impenetrable by rifle bullets, now besieging Settler's Station, where he and Dodd and Haidia, woman of subterranean race whom they brought away, are shut up in telegraph office. Bram, former member of Greystoke Expedition, said to be in charge of swarm, with intention of obliterating human race. Every living thing at Settler's Station destroyed, and swarm moving south.

It was a small-town paper a hundred miles from New York that took a chance on publishing this report from the International Press, in spite of frantic efforts on the parts of the head office to recall it after it had been transmitted. This paper published the account as an April Fool's Day joke, though later it took to itself the credit for having believed it. But by the time April Fool's Day dawned all the world knew that the account was, if anything, an under-estimate of the fearful things that were happening "down under."

It was known now that the swarm of monsters had originated in the Great Victoria Desert, one of the worst stretches of desolation in the world, situated in the south-east corner of Western Australia. Their numbers were incalculable. Wimbush, the aviator, who was attempting to cross the continent from east to west, reported afterward that he had flown for four days, skirting the edge of the swarm, and that the whole of that time they were moving in the same direction, a thick cloud that left a trail of dense darkness on earth beneath them, like the path of an eclipse. Wimbush escaped them only because he had a ceiling of twenty thousand feet, to which apparently the beetles could not soar.

And this swarm was only about one-fourth of the whole number of the monsters. This was the swarm that was moving westward, and subsequently totally destroyed all living things in Kalgoorlie, Coolgardie, Perth, and all the coastal cities of Western Australia.

Ships were found drifting in the Indian Ocean, totally destitute of crews and passengers; not even their skeletons were found, and it was estimated that the voracious monsters had carried them away bodily, devoured them in the air, and dropped the remains into the water.

All the world knows now how the sea elephant herd on Kerguelen Island was totally destroyed, and of the giant shells that were found lying everywhere on the deserted beaches, in positions that showed the monsters had in the end devoured one another.

Mauritius was the most westerly point reached by a fraction of the swarm. A little over twenty thousand of the beetles reached that lovely island, by count of the shells afterward, and all the world knows now of the desperate and successful fight that the inhabitants waged against them. Men and women, boys and girls, blacks and whites, finding that the devils were invulnerable against rifle fire, sallied forth boldly with knives and choppers, and laid down a life for a life.

On the second day after their appearance, the main swarm, a trillion and a half strong, reached the line of the transcontinental railway, and moved eastward into South Australia, traveling, it was estimated, at the rate of two hundred miles an hour. By the next morning they were in Adelaide, a city of nearly a quarter of a million people. By nightfall every living thing in Adelaide and the suburbs had been eaten, except for a few who succeeded in hiding in walled-up cellars, or in the surrounding marshes.

That night the swarm was on the borders of New South Wales and Victoria, and moving in two divisions toward Melbourne and Sydney.

The northern half, it was quickly seen, was flying "wild," with no particular objective, moving in a solid cohort two hundred miles in length, and devouring game, stock, and humans indiscriminately. It was the southern division, numbering perhaps a trillion, that was under command of Bram, and aimed at destroying Melbourne as Adelaide had been destroyed.

Bram, with his eight beetle steeds, was by this time known and execrated throughout the world. He was pictured as Anti-Christ, and the fulfilment of the prophecies of the Rock of Revelations.

And all this while—or, rather, until the telegraph wires were cut—broken, it was discovered later, by perching beetles—Thomas Travers was sending out messages from his post at Settler's Station.

Soon it was known that prodigious creatures were following in the wake of the devastating horde. Mantises, fifteen feet in height, winged things like pterodactyls, longer than bombing airplanes, followed, preying on the stragglers. But the main bodies never halted, and the inroads that the destroyers made on their numbers were insignificant.

Before the swarm reached Adelaide the Commonwealth Government had taken action. Troops had been called out, and all the available airplanes in the country had been ordered to assemble at Broken Hill, New South Wales, a strategic point commanding the approaches to Sydney and Melbourne. Something like four hundred airplanes were assembled, with several batteries of anti-aircraft guns that had been used in the Great War. Every amateur aviator in Australia was on the spot, with machines ranging from tiny Moths to Handley-Pages—anything that could fly.

Nocturnal though the beetles had been, they no longer feared the light of the sun. In fact, it was ascertained later that they were blind. An opacity had formed over the crystalline lens of the eye. Blind, they were no less formidable than with their sight. They existed only to devour, and their numbers made them irresistible, no matter which way they turned.

As soon as the vanguard of the dark cloud was sighted from Broken Hill, the airplanes went aloft. Four hundred planes, each armed with machine guns, dashed into the serried hosts, drumming out volleys of lead. In a long line, extending nearly to the limits of the beetle formation, thus giving each aviator all the room he needed, the planes gave battle.

The first terror that fell upon the airmen was the discovery that, even at close range, the machine gun bullets failed to penetrate the shells. The force of the impact whirled the beetles around, drove them together in bunches, sent them groping with weaving tentacles through the air—but that was all. On the main body of the invaders no impression was made whatever.

The second terror was the realization that the swarm, driven down here and there from an altitude of several hundred feet, merely resumed their progress on the ground, in a succession of gigantic leaps. Within a few minutes, instead of presenting an inflexible barrier, the line of airplanes was badly broken, each plane surrounded by swarms of the monsters.

Then Bram was seen. And that was the third terror, the sight of the famous beetle steeds, four pairs abreast, with Bram reclining like a Roman emperor upon the surface of the shells. It is true, Bram had no inclination to risk his own life in battle. At the first sight of the aviators he dodged into the thick of the swarm, where no bullet could reach him. Bram managed to transmit an order, and the beetles drew together.

Some thought afterward that it was by thought transference he effected this maneuver, for instantly the beetles, which had hitherto flown in loose order, became a solid wall, a thousand feet in height, closing in on the planes. The propellers struck them and snapped short, and as the planes went weaving down, the hideous monsters leaped into the cockpits and began their abominable meal.

Not a single plane came back. Planes and skeletons, and here and there a shell of a dead beetle, itself completely devoured, were all that was found afterward.

The gunners stayed at their posts till the last moment, firing round after round of shell and shrapnel, with insignificant results. Their skeletons were found not twenty paces from their guns—where the Gunners' Monument now stands.

Half an hour after the flight had first been sighted the news was being radioed to Sydney, Melbourne, and all other Australian cities, advising instant flight to sea as the only chance of safety. That radio message was cut short—and men listened and shuddered. After that came the crowding aboard all craft in the harbors, the tragedies of the *Eustis*, the *All Australia*, the *Sepphoris*, sunk at their moorings. The innumerable sea tragedies. The horde of fugitives that landed in New Zealand. The reign of terror when the mob got out of hand, the burning of Melbourne, the sack of Sydney.

And south and eastward, like a resistless flood, the beetle swarm came pouring. Well had Bram boasted that he would make the earth a desert!

A hundred miles of poisoned carcasses of sheep, extended outside Sydney's suburbs, gave the first promise of success. Long mounds of beetle shells testified to the results; moreover, the beetles that fed on the carcasses of their fellows, were in turn poisoned and died. But this was only a drop in the bucket. What counted was that the swift advance was slowing down. As if exhausted by their efforts, or else satiated with food, the beetles were doing what the soldiers did.

They were digging in!

Twenty-four miles from Sydney, eighteen outside Melbourne, the advance was stayed.

Volunteers who went out from those cities reported that the beetles seemed to be resting in long trenches that they had excavated, so that only their shells appeared above ground. Trees were covered with clinging beetles, every wall, every house was invisible beneath the beetle armor.

Australia had a respite. Perhaps only for a night or day, but still time to draw breath, time to consider, time for the shiploads of fugitives to get farther from the continent that had become a shambles.

And then the cry went up, not only from Australia, but from all the world, "Get Travers!"

CHAPTER X

At Bay

Bram put his fingers to his mouth and whistled, a shrill whistle, yet audible to Dodd, Tommy, and Haidia. Instantly three pairs of beetles appeared out of the throng. Their tentacles went out, and the two men and the girl found themselves hoisted separately upon the backs of the pairs. Next moment they were flying side by side, high in the air above the surrounding swarm.

They could see one another, but it was impossible for them to make their voices heard above the rasping of the beetles' legs. Hours went by, while the moon crossed the sky and dipped toward the horizon. Tommy knew that the moon would set about the hour of dawn. And the stars were already beginning to pale when he saw a line of telegraph poles, then two lines of shining metals, then a small settlement of stone and brick houses.

Tommy was not familiar with the geography of Australia, but he knew this must be the transcontinental line.

Whirling onward, the cloud of beetles suddenly swooped downward. For a moment Tommy could see the frightened occupants of the settlement crowding into the single street, then he shuddered with sick horror as he saw them obliterated by the swarm.

There was no struggle, no attempt at flight or resistance. One moment those forty-odd men were there—the next minute they existed no longer. There was nothing but a swarm of beetles, walking about like men with shells upon their backs.

And now Tommy saw evidences of Bram's devilish control of the swarm. For out of the cloud dropped what seemed to be a phalanx of beetle guards, the military police of beetledom, and, lashing fiercely with their tentacles, they drove back all the swarm that sought to join their companions in their ghoulish feast. There was just so much food and no more; the rest must seek theirs further.

But even beetles, it may be presumed, are not entirely under discipline at all times. The pair of beetles that bore Tommy, suddenly swooped apart, ten or a dozen feet from the ground, and dashed into the thick of the struggling, frenzied mass, flinging their rider to earth.

Tommy struck the soft sand, sat up, half dazed, saw his shell lying a few feet away from him, and retrieved it just as a couple of the monsters came swooping down at him.

He looked about him. Not far away stood Dodd and Haidia, with their shells on their backs. They recognized Tommy and ran toward him.

Not more than twenty yards away stood the railroad station, with several crates of goods on the platform. Next to it was a substantial house of stone, with the front door open.

Tommy pointed to it, and Dodd understood and shouted something that was lost in the furious buzz of the beetles' wings as they devoured their prey. The three raced for the entrance, gained it unmolested, and closed the door.

There was a key in the door, and it was light enough for them to see a chain, which Dodd pulled into position. There was only one story, and there were three rooms, apparently, with the kitchen. Tommy rushed to the kitchen door, locked it, too, and, with almost super-human efforts, dragged the large iron stove against it. He rushed to the window, but it was a mere loophole, not large enough to admit a child. Nevertheless, he stood the heavy table on end so that it covered it. Then he ran back.

Dodd had already barricaded the window of the larger room, which was a bed-sitting room, with a heavy wardrobe, and the wooden bedstead, jamming the two pieces sidewise against the wall, so that they could not be forced apart without being demolished. He was now busy in the smaller room, which seemed to be the station-master's office, dragging an iron safe across the floor. But the window was criss-crossed with iron bars, and it was evident that the safe, which was locked, contained at times considerable money, for the window could hardly have been forced save by a charge of nitro-glycerine or dynamite. However, it was against the door that Dodd placed the safe, and he stood back, panting.

"Good," said Haidia. "That will hold them."

The two men looked at her doubtfully. Did Haidia know what she was talking about?

The sun had risen. A long shaft shot into the room. Outside the beetles were still buzzing as they turned over the vestiges of their prey. There were as yet no signs of attack. Suddenly Tommy grasped Dodd's arm.

"Look!" he shouted, pointing to a corner which had been in gloom a moment before.

There was a table there, and on it a telegraphic instrument. Telegraphy had been one of Tommy's hobbies in boyhood. In a moment he was busy at the table.

Dot-dash-dot-dash! Then suddenly outside a furious hum, and the impact of beetle bodies against the front door.

Tommy got up, grinning. That was the first, interrupted message from Tommy that was received.

Through the barred window the three could see the furious efforts of the beetles to force an entrance. But the very tensile strength of the beetle-shells, which rendered them impervious to bullets, required a laminate construction which rendered them powerless against brick or stone.

Desperately the swarm dashed itself against the walls, until the ground outside was piled high with stunned beetles. Not the faintest impression was made on the defenses.

"Watch them, Jim," said Tom. "I'll go see if the rear's secure."

That thought of his seemed to have been anticipated by the beetles, for as Tommy reached the kitchen the swarm came dashing against door and window, always recoiling. Tommy came back, grinning all over his face.

"You were right, Haidia," he said. "We've held them all right, and the tables are turned on Bram. Also I got a message through, I think," he added to Dodd.

Dash—dot—dash—dot from the instrument. Tommy ran to the table again. Dash—dot went back. For five minutes Tommy labored, while the beetles hammered now on one door, now on another, now on the windows. Then Tommy got up.

"It was some station down the line," he said. "I've told them, and they're sending a man up here to replace the telegraphist, also a couple of cops. They think I'm crazy. I told them again. That's the best I could do."

"DODD! Travers! For the last time—let's talk!"

The cloud of beetles seemed to have thinned, for the sun was shining into the room. Bram's voice was perfectly audible, though he himself was invisible; probably he thought it likely that the defenders had obtained firearms.

"Nothing to say to you, Bram," called Dodd. "We've finished our discussion on the monotremes."

"I want you fellows to stand in with me," came Bram's plaintive tones. "It's so lonesome all by one's self, Dodd."

"Ah, you're beginning to find that out, are you?" Dodd could not resist answering. "You'll be lonelier yet before you're through."

"Dodd, I didn't bring that swarm up here. I swear it. I've been trying to control them from the beginning. I saw what was coming. I believe I can avert this horror, drive them into the sea or something like that. Don't make me desperate, Dodd.

"And listen, old man. About those monotremes—sensible men don't quarrel over things like that. Why can't we agree to differ?"

"Ah, now you're talking, Bram," Dodd answered. "Only you're too late. After what's happened here to-day, we'll have no truck with you. That's final."

"Damn you," shrieked Bram. "I'll batter down this house. I'll—"

"You'll do nothing, Bram, because you can't," Dodd answered. "Travers has wired full information about your devil-horde, and likewise about you, and all Australia will be prepared to give you a warm reception when you arrive."

"I tell you I'm invincible," Bram screamed. "In three days Australia will be a ruin, a depopulated desert. In a week, all southern Asia, in three weeks Europe, in two months America."

"You've been taking too many of those pellets, Bram," Dodd answered. "Stand back now! Stand back, wherever you are, or I'll open the door and throw the slops over you."

Bram's screech rose high above the droning of the wings. In another moment the interior of the room had grown as black as night. The rattle of the beetle shells against the four walls of the house was like the clattering of stage thunder.

All through the darkness Dodd could hear the unhurried clicking of the key.

At last the rattling ceased. The sun shone in again. The ground all around the house was packed with fallen beetles, six feet high, a writhing mass that creaked and clattered as it strove to disengage itself.

Bram's voice once more: "I'm leaving a guard, Dodd. They'll get you if you try to leave. But they won't eat you. I'm going to have you three sliced into little pieces, the Thousand Deaths of the Chinese. The beetles will eat the parts that are sliced away—and you'll live to watch them. I'll be back with a stick or two of dynamite to-morrow."

"Yeah, but listen, Bram," Dodd sang out. "Listen, you old marsupial tiger. When those pipe dreams clear away, I'm going to build a gallows of beetle-shells reaching to the moon, to hang you on!"

Bram's screech of madness died away. The strident rasping of the beetles' legs began again. For hours the three heard it; it was not until nightfall that it died away.

Bram had made good his threat, for all around the house, extending as far as they could see, was the host of beetle-guards. To venture out, even with their shells about them, was clearly a hazardous undertaking. There was neither food nor water in the place.

"We'll just have to hold out," said Dodd, breaking one of the long periods of silence.

Tommy did not answer; he did not hear him, for he was busy at the key. Suddenly he leaped to his feet.

"God, Jimmy," he cried, "that devil's making good his threat! The swarm's in South Australia, destroying every living thing, wiping out whole towns and villages! And they—they believe me now!"

He sank into a chair. For the first time the strain of the awful past seemed to grip him. Haidia came to his side.

"The beetles are finish," she said in her soft voice.

"How d'you know, Haidia?" demanded Dodd.

"The beetles are finish," Haidia repeated quietly, and that was all that Dodd could get out of her. But again the key began to click, and Tommy staggered to the table. Dot—dash—dash—dot. Presently he looked up once more.

"The swarm's halfway to Adelaide," he said. "They want to know if I can help them. Help them!" He burst into hysterical laughter.

Toward evening he came back after an hour at the key. "Line must be broken," he said. "I'm getting nothing."

In the moonlight they could see the huge compound eyes of the beetle guards glittering like enormous diamonds outside. They had not been conscious of thirst during the day, but now, with the coming of the cool night their desire for water became paramount.

"Tommy, there must be water in the station," said Dodd. "I'm going to get a pitcher from the kitchen and risk it, Tommy. Take care of Haidia if—" he added.

But Haidia laid her hand upon his arm. "Do not go, Jimmydodd," she said. "We can be thirsty to-night, and to-morrow the beetles will be finish."

"How d'you know?" asked Dodd again. But now he realized that Haidia had never learned the significance of an interrogation. She only repeated her statement, and again the two men had to remain content.

The long night passed. Outside the many facets of the beetle eyes. Inside the two men, desperate with anxiety, not for themselves, but for the fate of the world, snatching a few moments' sleep from time to time, then looking up to see those glaring eyes from the silent watchers.

Then dawn came stealing over the desert, and the two shook themselves free from sleep. And now the eyes were gone.

But there was immense activity among the beetles. They were scurrying to and fro, and, as they watched, Dodd and Tommy began to see some significance in their movements.

"Why, they're digging trenches!" Tommy shouted. "That's horrible, Jimmy! Are they intending to conduct sapping operations against us like engineers, or what?"

Dodd did not reply, and Tommy hardly expected any answer. As the two men, now joined by Haidia, watched, they saw that the beetles were actually digging themselves into the sand.

Within the space of an hour, by the time the first shafts of sunlight began to stream into the room, there was to be seen only the massive, rounded shells of the monsters as they squatted in the sand.

"Now you may fetch water," said Haidia, smiling at her lover. "No, you do not need the shells," she added. "The beetles are finish. It is as the wise men of my people told me."

Wondering, hesitating, Tommy and Dodd unlocked the front door. They stood upon the threshold ready to bolt back again. But there was no stirring among the beetle hosts.

Growing bolder, they advanced a few steps; then, shamed by Haidia's courage, they followed her, still cautiously to the station.

Dodd shouted as he saw a water-tank, and a receptacle above it with a water-cock. They let Haidia drink, then followed suit, and for a few moments, as they appeased their thirst, the beetles were forgotten.

Then they turned back. There had been no movement in that line of shells that glinted in the morning sunlight.

"Come, I shall show you," said Haidia confidently, advancing toward the trench.

Dodd would have stopped her, but the girl moved forward quickly, eluded him with a graceful, mirthful gesture, and stooped down over the trench.

She rose up, raising in her arms an empty beetle-shell!

Dodd, who had reached the trench before Tommy, turned round and yelled to him excitedly. Tommy ran forward—and then he understood.

The shells were empty. The swarm, whose life cycle Bram had admitted he did not understand, had just moulted!

It had moulted because the bodies, gorged with food, had grown too large for the shells. In time, if left alone, the monsters would grow larger shells, become invincible again. But just now they were defenseless as new-born babes—and knew it.

Deep underneath the empty shells they had burrowed into the ground. Everywhere at the bottom of the deep trenches were the naked, bestial creatures, waving helpless tentacles and squirming over one another as they strove to find shelter and security.

A sudden madness came over Tommy and Dodd. "Dynamite—there must be dynamite!" Dodd shouted, as he ran back to the station.

"Something better than dynamite," shouted Tommy, holding up one of a score of drums of petrol!

CHAPTER XI

The World Set Free

They waited two days at Settler's Station. To push along the line into the desert would have been useless, and both men were convinced that an airplane would arrive for them. But it was not until the second afternoon that the aviator arrived, half-dead with thirst and fatigue, and almost incoherent.

His was the last plane on the Australian continent. He brought the news of the destruction of Adelaide, and of the siege of Melbourne and Sydney, as he termed it. He told Dodd and Tommy that the two cities had been surrounded with trenches and barbed wire. Machine guns and artillery were bombarding the trenches in which the beetles had taken shelter.

"Has any one been out on reconnaissance?" asked Tommy.

Nobody had been permitted to pass through the barbed wire, though there had been volunteers. It meant certain death. But, unless the beetles were sapping deep in the ground, what their purpose was, nobody knew.

Tommy and Dodd led him to the piles of smoking, stinking débris and told him.

That was where the aviator fainted from sheer relief.

"The Commonwealth wants you to take supreme command against the beetles," he told Tommy, when he had recovered. "I'm to bring you back. Not that they expect me back. But—God, what a piece of news! Forgive my swearing—I used to be a parson. Still am, for the matter of that."

"How are you going to bring us three back in your plane?" asked Tommy.

"I shall stay here with Jimmydodd," said Haidia suavely. "There is not the least danger any more. You must destroy the beetles before their shells have grown again, that's all."

"Used to be a parson, you say? Still are?" shouted Dodd excitedly. "Thank God! I mean, I'm glad to hear it. Come inside, and come quick. I want you too, Tommy!"

Then Tommy understood. And it seemed as if Haidia understood, by some instinct that belongs exclusively to women, for her cheeks were flushed as she turned and smiled into Dodd's eyes.

Ten minutes later Tommy hopped into the biplane, leaving the happy married couple at Settler's Station. His eyes grew misty as the plane took the air, and he saw them waving to him from the ground. Dodd and Haidia and he had been through so many adventures, and had reached safety. He must not fail.

He did not fail. He found himself at Sydney in command of thirty thousand men, all enthusiastic for the fight for the human race, soldiers and volunteers ready to fight until they dropped. When the news of the situation was made public, an immense wave of hope ran through the world.

National differences were forgotten, color and creed and race grew more tolerant of one another. A new day had dawned—the day of humanity's true liberation.

Tommy's first act was to call out the fire companies and have the beetles' trenches saturated with petrol from the fire hoses. Then incendiary bullets, shot from guns from a safe distance, quickly converted them into blazing infernos.

But even so only a tithe of the beetle army had been destroyed. Two hundred planes had already been rushed from New Zealand, and their aviators went up and scoured the country far and wide. Everywhere they found trenches, and, where the soil was stony, millions of the beetles clustered helplessly beneath great mounds of discarded shells.

An army of black trackers had been brought in planes from all parts of the country, and they searched out the beetle masses everywhere along the course that the invaders had taken. Then incendiary bombs were dropped from above.

Day after day the beetle massacre went on. By the end of a week the survivors of the invasion began to take heart again. It was certain that the greater portion of the horde had been destroyed.

There was only one thing lacking. No trace of Bram had been seen since his appearance at the head of his beetle army in front of Broken Hill. And louder and more insistent grew the world clamor that he should be found, and put to death in some way more horrible than any yet devised.

The ingenuity of a million minds worked upon this problem. Newspapers all over the world offered prizes for the most suitable form of death. Ingenious Oriental tortures were rediscovered.

The only thing lacking was Bram.

A spy craze ran through Australia. Five hundred Brams were found, and all of them were in imminent danger of death before they were able to prove an alias.

And, oddly enough, it was Tommy and Dodd who found Bram. For Dodd had been brought back east, together with his bride, and given an important command in the Army of Extermination.

Dodd had joined Tommy not far from Broken Hill, where a swarm of a hundred thousand beetles had been found in a little known valley. The monsters had begun to grow new shells, and the news had excited a fresh wave of apprehension. The airplanes had concentrated for an attack upon them, and Tommy and Dodd were riding together, Tommy at the controls, and Dodd observing.

Dodd called through the tube to Tommy, and indicated a mass that was moving through the scrub—some fifty thousand beetles, executing short hops and evidently regaining some vitality. Tommy nodded.

He signaled, and the fleet of planes circled around and began to drop their incendiary bombs. Within a few minutes the beetles were ringed with a wall of fire. Presently the whole terrain was a blazing furnace.

Hours later, when the fires had died away, Tommy and Dodd went down to look at the destruction that had been wrought. The scene was horrible. Great masses of charred flesh and shell were piled up everywhere.

"I guess that's been a pretty thorough job," said Tommy. "Let's get back, Jim."

"What's that?" cried Dodd, pointing. Then, "My God, Tommy, it's one of our men!"

It was a man, but it was not one of their men, that creeping, maimed, half-cinder and half-human thing that was trying to crawl into the hollow of a rock. It was Bram, and recognition was mutual.

Bram dropping, moaning; he was only the shell of a man, and it was incredible how he had managed to survive that ordeal of fire. The remainder of his life, which only his indomitable will had held in that shattered body, was evidently a matter of minutes, but he looked up at Dodd and laughed.

"So—you're—here, damn you!" he snarled. "And—you think—you've won. I've—another card—another invasion of the world—beside which this is child's play. It's an invasion—"

Bram was going, but he pulled himself together with a supreme effort.

"Invasion by—new species of—monotremes," he croaked. "Deep down in—earth. Was saving to—prove you the liar you are. Monotremes—egg-laying platypus big as an elephant—existent long before pleistocene epoch—make you recant, you lying fool!"

Bram died, an outburst of bitter laughter on his lips. Dodd stood silent for a while; then reverently he removed his hat.

"He was a madman and a devil, but he had the potentialities of a god, Tommy," he said.

SUCH WELL-KNOW WRITERS AS

Murray Leinster, Ray Cummings,
Victor Rousseau, R. F. Starzl, A. T. Locke,
Capt. S. P. Meek and Arthur J. Burks

Write for

ASTOUNDING STORIES

Mad Music

By Anthony Pelcher

In an inner room they found a diabolical machine.

The sixty stories of the perfectly constructed Colossus building had mysteriously crashed! What was the connection between this catastrophe and the weird strains of the Mad Musician's violin?

To the accompaniment of a crashing roar, not unlike rumbling thunder, the proud Colossus Building, which a few minutes before had reared its sixty stories of artistic architecture towards the blue dome of the sky, crashed in a rugged, dusty heap of stone, brick, cement and mortar. The steel framework, like the skeleton of some prehistoric monster, still reared to dizzy heights but in a bent and twisted shape of grotesque outline.

No one knew how many lives were snuffed out in the avalanche.

As the collapse occurred in the early dawn it was not believed the death list would be large. It was admitted, however, that autos, cabs and surface cars may have been caught under the falling rock. One train was known to have been wrecked in the subway due to a cave-in from the surface under the ragged mountain of debris.

The litter fairly filled a part of Times Square, the most congested cross-roads on God's footstool. Straggling brick and rock had rolled across the street to the west and had crashed into windows and doors of innocent small tradesmen's shops.

A few minutes after the crash a mad crowd of people had piled from subway exits as far away as Penn Station and Columbus Circle and from cross streets. These milled about, gesticulating and shouting hysterically. All neighboring police stations were hard put to handle the growing mob.

Hundreds of dead and maimed were being carried to the surface from the wrecked train in the subway. Trucks and cabs joined the ambulance crews in the work of transporting these to morgues and hospitals. As the morning grew older and the news of the disaster spread, more milling thousands tried to crowd into the square. Many were craning necks hopelessly on the outskirts of the throng, blocks away, trying vainly to get a view of what lay beyond.

The fire department and finally several companies of militia joined the police in handling the crowd. Newsies, never asleep, yowled their "Wuxtras" and made much small money.

The newspapers devoted solid pages in attempting to describe what had happened. Nervously, efficient reporters had written and written, using all their best adjectives and inventing new ones in attempts to picture the crash and the hysterics which followed.

When the excitement was at its height a middle-aged man, bleeding at the head, clothes torn and dusty, staggered into the West 47th street police station. He found a lone sergeant at the desk.

The police sergeant jumped to his feet as the bedraggled man entered and stumbled to a bench.

"I'm Pat Brennan, street floor watchman of the Colossus," he said. "I ran for it. I got caught in the edge of the wreck and a brick clipped me. I musta been out for some time. When I came around I looked back just once at the wreck and then I beat it over here. Phone my boss."

"I'll let you phone your boss," said the sergeant, "but first tell me just what happened."

"Earthquake, I guess. I saw the floor heaving in waves. Glass was crashing and falling into the street. All windows in the arcade buckled, either in or out. I ran into the street and looked up. God, what a sight! The building from sidewalk to towers was rocking and waving and twisting and buckling and I saw it was bound to crumple, so I lit out and ran. I heard a roar like all Hell broke loose and then something nicked me and my light went out."

"How many got caught in the building?"

"Nobody got out but me, I guess. There weren't many tenants. The building is all rented, but not everybody had moved in yet and those as had didn't spend their nights there. There was a watchman for every five stories. An engineer and his crew. Three elevator operators had come in. There was no names of tenants in or out on my book after 4 A.M. The crash musta come about 6. That's all."

Throughout the country the news of the crash was received with great interest and wonderment, but in one small circle it caused absolute consternation. That was in the offices of the Muller Construction Company, the builders of the Colossus. Jason V. Linane, chief engineer of the company, was in conference with its president, James J. Muller.

Muller sat with his head in his hands, and his face wore an expression of a man in absolute anguish. Linane was pacing the floor, a wild expression in his eyes, and at times he muttered and mumbled under his breath.

In the other offices the entire force from manager to office boys was hushed and awed, for they had seen the expressions on the faces of the heads of the concern when they stalked into the inner office that morning.

Muller finally looked up, rather hopelessly, at Linane.

"Unless we can prove that the crash was due to some circumstance over which we had no control, we are ruined," he said, and there actually were tears in his eyes.

"No doubt about that," agreed Linane, "but I can swear that the Colossus went up according to specifications and that every ounce and splinter of material was of the best. The workmanship was faultless. We have built scores of the biggest blocks in the world and of them all this Colossus was the most perfect. I had prided myself on it. Muller, it was perfection. I simply cannot account for it. I cannot. It should have stood up for thousands of years. The foundation was solid rock. It positively was not an earthquake. No other building in the section was even jarred. No other earthquake was ever localized to one half block of the earth's crust, and we can positively eliminate an earthquake or an explosion as the possible cause. I am sure we are not to blame, but we will have to find the exact cause."

"If there was some flaw?" questioned Muller, although he knew the answer.

"If there was some flaw, then we're sunk. The newspapers are already clamoring for probes, of us, of the building, of the owners and everybody and everything. We have got to have something damned plausible when we go to bat on this proposition or every dollar we have in the world will have to be paid out."

"That is not all," said Muller: "not only will we be penniless, but we may have to go to jail and we will never be able to show our faces in reputable business circles again. Who was the last to go over that building?"

"I sent Teddy Jenks. He is a cub and is swell headed and too big for his pants, but I would bank my life on his judgment. He has the judgment of a much older man and I would also bank my life and reputation on his engineering skill and knowledge. He pronounced the building positively O.K.—100 per cent."

"Where is Jenks?"

"He will be here as soon as his car can drive down from Tarrytown. He should be here now."

As they talked Jenks, the youngest member of the engineering force, entered. He entered like a whirlwind. He threw his hat on the floor and drew out a drawer of a cabinet. He pulled out the plans for the Colossus, big blue prints, some of them yards in extent, and threw them on the floor. Then he dropped to his knees and began poring over them.

"This is a hell of a time for you to begin getting around," exploded Muller. "What were you doing, cabareting all night?"

"It sure is terrible—awful," said Jenks, half to himself.

"Answer me," thundered Muller.

"Oh yes," said Jenks, looking up. He saw the look of anguish on his boss's face and forgot his own excitement in sympathy. He jumped to his feet, placed his arm about the shoulders of the older man and led him to a chair. Linane only scowled at the young man.

"I was delayed because I stopped by to see the wreck. My God, Mr. Muller, it is awful." Jenks drew his hand across his eye as if to erase the scene of the wrecked building. Then patting the older man affectionately on the back he said:

"Buck up. I'm on the job, as usual. I'll find out about it. It could not have been our fault. Why man, that building was as strong as Gibraltar itself!"

"You were the last to inspect it," accused Muller, with a break in his voice.

"Nobody knows that better than I, and I can swear by all that's square and honest that it was no fault of the material or the construction. It must have been—"

"Must have been what?"

"I'll be damned if I know."

"That's like him," said Linane, who, while really kindly intentioned, had always rather enjoyed prodding the young engineer.

"Like me, like the devil," shouted Jenks, glaring at Linane. "I suppose you know all about it, you're so blamed wise."

"No, I don't know," admitted Linane. "But I do know that you don't like me to tell you anything. Nevertheless, I am going to tell you that you had better get busy and find out what caused it, or—"

"That's just what I'm doing," said Jenks, and he dived for his plans on the floor.

Newspaper reporters, many of them, were fighting outside to get in. Muller looked at Linane when a stenographer had announced the reporters for the tenth time.

"We had better let them in," he said, "it looks bad to crawl for cover."

"What are you going to tell them?" asked Linane.

"God only knows," said Muller.

"Let me handle them," said Jenks, looking up confidently.

The newspapermen had rushed the office. They came in like a wild wave. Questions flew like feathers at a cock-fight.

Muller held up his hand and there was something in his grief-stricken eyes that held the gentlemen of the press in silence. They had time to look around. They saw the handsome, dark-haired, brown-eyed Jenks poring over the plans. Dust from the carpet smudged his knees, and he had rubbed some of it over a sweating forehead, but he still looked the picture of self-confident efficiency.

"Gentlemen," said Muller slowly, "I can answer all your questions at once. Our firm is one of the oldest and staunchest in the trade. Our buildings stand as monuments to our integrity—"

"All but one," said a young Irishman.

"You are right. All but one," confessed Muller. "But that one, believe me, has been visited by an act of God. Some form of earthquake or some unlooked for, uncontrolled, almost unbelievable catastrophe has happened. The Muller company stands back of its work to its last dollar. Gentlemen, you know as much as we do. Mr. Jenks there, whose reputation as an engineer is quite sturdy, I assure you, was the last to inspect the building. He passed upon it when it was finished. He is at your service."

Jenks arose, brushed some dust from his knees.

"You look like you'd been praying," bandied the Irishman.

"Maybe I have. Now let me talk. Don't broadside me with questions. I know what you want to know. Let me talk."

The newspapermen were silent.

"There has been talk of probing this disaster, naturally," began Jenks. "You all know, gentlemen, that we will aid any inquiry to our utmost. You want to know what we have to say about it—who is responsible. In a reasonable time I will have a statement to make that will be startling in the extreme. I am not sure of my ground now."

"How about the ground under the Colossus?" said the Irishman.

"Don't let's kid each other," pleaded Jenks. "Look at Mr. Muller: it is as if he had lost his whole family. We are good people. I am doing all I can. Mr. Linane, who had charge of the construction, is doing all he can. We believe we are blameless. If it is proven otherwise we will acknowledge our fault, assume financial responsibility, and take our medicine. Believe me, that building was perfection plus, like all our buildings. That covers the entire situation."

Hundreds of questions were parried and answered by the three engineers, and the reporters left convinced that if the Muller Construction Company was responsible, it was not through any fault of its own.

The fact that Jenks and Linane were not strong for each other, except to recognize each other's ability as engineers, was due to an incident of the past. This incident had caused a ripple of mirth in engineering circles when it happened, and the laugh was on the older man, Linane.

It was when radio was new. Linane, a structural engineer, had paid little attention to radio. Jenks was the kind of an engineer who dabbled in all sciences. He knew his radio.

When Jenks first came to work with a technical sheepskin and a few tons of brass, Linane accorded him only passing notice. Jenks craved the plaudits of the older man and his palship. Linane treated him as a son, but did not warm to his social advances.

"I'm as good an engineer as he is," mused Jenks, "and if he is going to high-hat me, I'll just put a swift one over on him and compel his notice."

The next day Jenks approached Linane in conference and said:

"I've got a curious bet on, Mr. Linane. I am betting sound can travel a mile quicker than it travels a quarter of a mile."

"What?" said Linane.

"I'm betting fifty that sound can travel a mile quicker than it can travel a quarter of a mile."

"Oh no—it can't," insisted Linane.

"Oh yes—it can!" decided Jenks.

"I'll take some of that fool money myself," said Linane.

"How much?" asked Jenks.

"As much as you want."

"All right—five hundred dollars."

"How you going to prove your contention?"

"By stop watches, and your men can hold the watches. We'll bet that a pistol shot can be heard two miles away quicker than it can be heard a quarter of a mile away."

"Sound travels about a fifth of a mile a second. The rate varies slightly according to temperature," explained Linane. "At the freezing point the rate is 1,090 feet per second and increases a little over one foot for every degree Fahrenheit."

"Hot or cold," breezed Jenks, "I am betting you five hundred dollars that sound can travel two miles quicker than a quarter-mile."

"You're on, you damned idiot!" shouted the completely exasperated Linane.

Jenks let Linane's friends hold the watches and his friend held the money. Jenks was to fire the shot.

Jenks fired the shot in front of a microphone on a football field. One of Linane's friends picked the sound up instantaneously on a three-tube radio set two miles away. The other watch holder was standing in the open a quarter of a mile away and his watch showed a second and a fraction.

All hands agreed that Jenks had won the bet fairly. Linane never exactly liked Jenks after that.

Then Jenks rather aggravated matters by a habit. Whenever Linane would make a very positive statement Jenks would look owl-eyed and say: "Mr. Linane, I'll have to sound you out about that." The heavy accent on the word "sound" nettled Linane somewhat.

Linane never completely forgave Jenks for putting over this "fast one." Socially they were always more or less at loggerheads, but neither let this feeling interfere with their work. They worked together faithfully enough and each recognized the ability of the other.

And so it was that Linane and Jenks, their heads together, worked all night in an attempt to find some cause that would tie responsibility for the disaster on mother nature.

They failed to find it and, sleepy-eyed, they were forced to admit failure, so far.

The newspapers, to whom Muller had said that he would not shirk any responsibility, began a hue and cry for the arrest of all parties in any way concerned with the direction of the building of the Colossus.

When the death list from the crash and subway wreck reached 97, the press waxed nasty and demanded the arrest of Muller, Linane and Jenks in no uncertain tones.

Half dead from lack of sleep, the three men were taken by the police to the district attorney's offices and, after a strenuous grilling, were formally placed under arrest on charges of criminal negligence. They put up a $50,000 bond in each case and were permitted to go and seek further to find the cause of what the newspapers now began calling the "Colossal Failure."

Several days were spent by Linane and Jenks in examining the wreckage which was being removed from Times Square, truckload after truckload, to a point outside the city. Here it was again sorted and examined and piled for future disposal.

So far as could be found every brick, stone and ounce of material used in the building was perfect. Attorneys, however, assured Linane, Jenks and Muller that they would have to find the real cause of the disaster if they were to escape possible long prison sentences.

Night after night Jenks courted sleep, but it would not come. He began to grow wan and haggard.

Jenks took to walking the streets at night, mile after mile, thinking, always thinking, and searching his mind for a solution of the mystery.

It was evening. He had walked past the scene of the Colossus crash several times. He found himself on a side street. He looked up and saw in electric lights:

TOWN HALL

Munsterbergen, the Mad Musician
Concert Here To-night.

He took five dollars from his pocket and bought a ticket. He entered with the crowd and was ushered to a seat. He looked neither to the right or left. His eyes were sunken, his face lined with worry.

Something within Jenks caused him to turn slightly. He was curiously aware of a beautiful girl who sat beside him. She had a mass of golden hair which seemed to defy control. It was wild, positively tempestuous. Her eyes were deep blue and her skin as white as fleecy clouds in spring. He was dimly conscious that those glorious eyes were troubled.

She glanced at him. She was aware that he was suffering. A great surge of sympathy welled in her heart. She could not explain the feeling.

A great red plush curtain parted in the center and drew in graceful folds to the edges of the proscenium. A small stage was revealed.

A tousle-headed man with glaring, beady black eyes, dressed in black evening clothes stepped forward and bowed. Under his arm was a violin. He brought the violin forward. His nose, like the beak of some great bird, bobbed up and down in acknowledgment of the plaudits which greeted him. His long nervous fingers began to caress the instrument and his lips began to move.

Jenks was aware that he was saying something, but was not at all interested. What he said was this:

"Maybe, yes, I couldn't talk so good English, but you could understood it, yes? Und now I tell you dot I never play the compositions of any man. I axtemporize exgloosively. I chust blay und blay, und maybe you should listen, yes? If I bleeze you I am chust happy."

Jenks' attention was drawn to him. He noted his wild appearance.

"He sure looks mad enough," mused Jenks.

The violinist flipped the fiddle up under his chin. He drew the bow over the strings and began a gentle melody that reminded one of rain drops falling on calm waters.

Jenks forgot his troubles. He forgot everything. He slumped in his seat and his eyes closed. The rain continued falling from the strings of the violin.

Suddenly the melody changed to a glad little lilting measure, as sweet as love itself. The sun was coming out again and the birds began to sing. There was the trill of a canary with the sun on its cage. There was the song of the thrush, the mocking-bird and the meadow lark. These blended finally into a melodious burst of chirping melody which seemed a chorus of the wild birds of the forest and glen. Then the lilting love measure again. It tore at the heart strings, and brought tears to one's eyes.

Unconsciously the girl next to Jenks leaned towards him. Involuntarily he leaned to meet her. Their shoulders touched. The cloud of her golden hair came to rest against his dark locks. Their hands found each other with gentle pressure. Both were lost to the world.

Abruptly the music changed. There was a succession of broken treble notes that sounded like the crackling of flames. Moans deep and melancholy followed. These grew more strident and prolonged, giving place to abject howls, suggesting the lamentations of the damned.

The hands of the boy and girl gripped tensely. They could not help shuddering.

The violin began to produce notes of a leering, jeering character, growing more horrible with each measure until they burst in a loud guffaw of maniacal laughter.

The whole performance was as if someone had taken a heaven and plunged it into a hell.

The musician bowed jerkily, and was gone.

There was no applause, only wild exclamations. Half the house was on its feet. The other half sat as if glued to chairs.

The boy and the girl were standing, their hands still gripping tensely.

"Come, let's get out of here," said Jenks. The girl took her wrap and Jenks helped her into it. Hand in hand they fled the place.

In the lobby their eyes met, and for the first time they realized they were strangers. Yet deep in their hearts was a feeling that their fates had been sealed.

"My goodness!" burst from the girl.

"It can't be helped now," said Jenks decisively.

"What can't be helped?" asked the girl, although she knew in her heart.

"Nothing can be helped," said Jenks. Then he added: "We should know each other by this time. We have been holding hands for an hour."

The girl's eyes flared. "You have no right to presume on that situation," she said.

Jenks could have kicked himself. "Forgive me," he said. "It was only that I just wanted so to know you. Won't you let me see you home?"

"You may," said the girl simply, and she led the way to her own car.

They drove north.

Their bodies seemed like magnets. They were again shoulder to shoulder, holding hands.

"Will you tell me your name?" pleaded Jenks.

"Surely," replied the girl. "I am Elaine Linane."

"What?" exploded Jenks. "Why, I work with a Linane, an engineer with the Muller Construction Company."

"He is my father," she said.

"Why, we are great friends," said the boy. "I am Jenks, his assistant—at least we work together."

"Yes, I have heard of you," said the girl. "It is strange, the way we met. My father admires your work, but I am afraid you are not great friends." The girl had forgotten her troubles. She chuckled. She had heard the way Jenks had "sounded" her father out.

Jenks was speechless. The girl continued:

"I don't know whether to like you or to hate you. My father is an old dear. You were cruel to him."

Jenks was abject. "I did not mean to be," he said. "He rather belittled me without realizing it. I had to make my stand. The difference in our years made him take me rather too lightly. I had to compel his notice, if I was to advance."

"Oh!" said the girl.

"I am sorry—so sorry."

"You might not have been altogether at fault," said the girl. "Father forgets at times that I have grown up. I resent being treated like a child, but he is the soul of goodness and fatherly care."

"I know that," said Jenks.

Every engineer knows his mathematics. It was this fact, coupled with what the world calls a "lucky break," that solved the Colossus mystery. Nobody can get around the fact that two and two make four.

Jenks had happened on accomplishment to advance in the engineering profession, and it was well for him that he had reached a crisis. He had never believed in luck or in hunches, so it was good for him to be brought face to face with the fact that sometimes the footsteps of man are guided. It made him begin to look into the engineering of the universe, to think more deeply, and to acknowledge a Higher Power.

With Linane he had butted into a stone wall. They were coming to know what real trouble meant. The fact that they were innocent did not make the steel bars of a cage any more attractive. Their troubles began to wrap about them with the clammy intimacy of a shroud. Then came the lucky break.

Next to his troubles, Jenks' favorite topic was the Mad Musician. He tried to learn all he could about this uncanny character at whose concert he had met the girl of his life. He learned two facts that made him perk up and think.

One was that the Mad Musician had had offices and a studio in the Colossus and was one of the first to move in. The other was that the Mad Musician took great delight in shattering glassware with notes of or vibrations from a violin. Nearly everyone knows that a glass tumbler can be shattered by the proper note sounded on a violin. The Mad Musician took delight in this trick. Jenks courted his acquaintance, and saw him shatter a row of glasses of different sizes by sounding different notes on his fiddle. The glasses crashed one after another like gelatine balls hit by the bullets of an expert rifleman.

Then Jenks, the engineer who knew his mathematics, put two and two together. It made four, of course.

"Listen, Linane," he said to his co-worker: "this fiddler is crazier than a flock of cuckoos. If he can crack crockery with violin sound vibrations, is it not possible, by carrying the vibrations to a much higher power, that he could crack a pile of stone, steel, brick and cement, like the Colossus?"

"Possible, but hardly probable. Still," Linane mused, "when you think about it, and put two and two together.... Let's go after him and see what he is doing now."

Both jumped for their coats and hats. As they fared forth, Jenks cinched his argument:

"If a madman takes delight in breaking glassware with a vibratory wave or vibration, how much more of a thrill would he get by crashing a mountain?"

"Wild, but unanswerable," said Linane.

Jenks had been calling on the Mad Musician at his country place. "He had a studio in the Colossus," he reminded Linane. "He must have re-opened somewhere else in town. I wonder where."

"Musicians are great union men," said Linane. "Phone the union."

Teddy Jenks did, but the union gave the last known town address as the Colossus.

"He would remain in the same district around Times Square," reasoned Jenks. "Let's page out the big buildings and see if he is not preparing to crash another one."

"Fair enough," said Linane, who was too busy with the problem at hand to choose his words.

Together the engineers started a canvass of the big buildings in the theatrical district. After four or five had been searched without result they entered the 30-story Acme Theater building.

Here they learned that the Mad Musician had leased a four-room suite just a few days before. This suite was on the fifteenth floor, just half way up in the big structure.

They went to the manager of the building and frankly stated their suspicions. "We want to enter that suite when the tenant is not there," they explained, "and we want him forestalled from entering while we are examining the premises."

"Hadn't we better notify the police?" asked the building manager, who had broken out in a sweat when he heard the dire disaster which might be in store for the stately Acme building.

"Not yet," said Linane. "You see, we are not sure: we have just been putting two and two together."

"We'll get the building detective, anyway," insisted the manager.

"Let him come along, but do not let him know until we are sure. If we are right we will find a most unusual infernal machine," said Linane.

The three men entered the suite with a pass-key. The detective was left outside in the hall to halt anyone who might disturb the searchers. It was as Jenks had thought. In an inner room they found a diabolical machine—a single string stretched across two bridges, one of brass and one of wood. A big horsehair bow attached to a shaft operated by a motor was automatically sawing across the string. The note resulting was evidently higher than the range of the human ear, because no audible sound resulted. It was later estimated that the destructive note was several octaves higher than the highest note on a piano.

The entire machine was enclosed in a heavy wire-net cage, securely bolted to the floor. Neither the string nor bow could be reached. It was evidently the Mad Musician's idea that the devilish contrivance should not be reached by hands other than his own.

How long the infernal machine had been operating no one knew, but the visitors were startled when the building suddenly began to sway perceptibly. Jenks jumped forward to stop the machine but could not find a switch.

"See if the machine plugs in anywhere in a wall socket!" he shouted to Linane, who promptly began examining the walls. Jenks shouted to the building manager to phone the police to clear the streets around the big building.

"Tell the police that the Acme Theater building may crash at any moment," he instructed.

The engineers were perfectly cool in face of the great peril, but the building manager lost his head completely and began to run around in circles muttering: "Oh, my God, save me!" and other words of supplication that blended into an incoherent babel.

Jenks rushed to the man, trying to still his wild hysteria.

The building continued to sway dangerously.

Jenks looked from a window. An enormous crowd was collecting, watching the big building swinging a foot out of plumb like a giant pendulum. The crowd was growing. Should the building fall the loss of life would be appalling. It was mid-morning. The interior of the building teemed with thousands of workers, for all floors above the third were offices.

Teddy Jenks turned suddenly. He heard the watchman in the hall scream in terror. Then he heard a body fall. He rushed to the door to see the Mad Musician standing over the prostrate form of the detective, a devilish grin on his distorted countenance.

The madman turned, saw Jenks, and started to run. Jenks took after him. Up the staircase the madman rushed toward the roof. Teddy followed him two floors and then rushed out to take the elevators. The building in its mad swaying had made it impossible for the lifts to be operated. Teddy realized this with a distraught gulp in his throat. He returned to the stairway and took up the pursuit of the madman.

The corridors were beginning to fill with screaming men and wailing girls. It was a sight never to be forgotten.

Laboriously Jenks climbed story after story without getting sight of the madman. Finally he reached the roof. It was waving like swells on a lake before a breeze. He caught sight of the Mad Musician standing on the street wall, thirty stories from the street, a leer on his devilish visage. He jumped for him.

The madman grasped him and lifted him up to the top of the wall as a cat might have lifted a mouse. Both men were breathing heavily as a result of their 15-story climb.

The madman tried to throw Teddy Jenks to the street below. Teddy clung to him. The two battled desperately as the building swayed.

The dense crowd in the street had caught sight of the two men fighting on the narrow coping, and the shout which rent the air reached the ears of Jenks.

The mind of the engineer was still working clearly, but a wild fear gripped his heart. His strength seemed to be leaving him. The madman pushed him back, bending his spine with brute strength. Teddy was forced to the narrow ledge that had given the two men footing. The fingers of the madman gripped his throat.

He was dimly conscious that the swaying of the building was slowing down. His reason told him that Linane had found the wall socket and had stopped the sawing of the devil's bow on the engine of hell.

He saw the madman draw a big knife. With his last remaining strength he reached out and grasped the wrist above the hand which held the weapon. In spite of all he could do he saw the madman inching the knife nearer and nearer his throat.

Grim death was peering into the bulging eyes of Teddy Jenks, when his engineering knowledge came to his rescue. He remembered the top stories of the Acme building were constructed with a step of ten feet in from the street line, for every story of construction above the 24th floor.

"If we fall," he reasoned, "we can only fall one story." Then he deliberately rolled his own body and the weight of the madman, who held him, over the edge of the coping. At the same time he twisted the madman's wrist so the point of the knife pointed to the madman's body.

There was a dim consciousness of a painful impact. Teddy had fallen underneath, but the force of the two bodies coming together had thrust the knife deep into the entrails of the Mad Musician.

Clouds which had been collecting in the sky began a splattering downpour. The storm grew in fury and lightning tore the heavens, while thunder boomed and crackled. The rain began falling in sheets.

This served to revive the unconscious Teddy. He painfully withdrew his body from under that of the madman. The falling rain, stained with the blood of the Mad Musician, trickled over the edge of the building.

Teddy dragged himself through a window and passed his hand over his forehead, which was aching miserably. He tried to get to his feet and fell back, only to try again. Several times he tried and then, his strength returning, he was able to walk.

He made his way to the studio where he had left Linane and found him there surrounded by police, reporters and others. The infernal machine had been rendered harmless, but was kept intact as evidence.

Catching sight of Teddy, Linane shouted with joy. "I stopped the damned thing," he chuckled, like a pleased schoolboy. Then, observing Teddy's exhausted condition he added:

"Why, you look like you have been to a funeral!"

"I have," said Teddy. "You'll find that crazy fiddler dead on the twenty-ninth story. Look out the window of the thirtieth story," he instructed the police, who had started to recover the body. "He stabbed himself. He is either dead or dying."

It proved that he was dead.

No engineering firm is responsible for the actions of a madman. So the Muller Construction Company was given a clean bill of health.

Jenks and Elaine Linane were with the girl's father in his study. They were asking for the paternal blessing.

Linane was pretending to be hard to convince.

"Now, my daughter," he said, "this young man takes $500 of my good money by sounding me out, as he calls it. Then he comes along and tries to take my daughter away from me. It is positively high-handed. It dates back to the football game—"

"Daddy, dear, don't be like that!" said Elaine, who was on the arm of his chair with her own arms around him.

"I tell you, Elaine, this dates back to the fall of 1927."

"It dates back to the fall of Eve," said Elaine. "When a girl finds her man, no power can keep him from her. If you won't give me to Teddy Jenks, I'll elope with him."

"Well, all right then. Kiss me," said Linane as he turned towards his radio set.

"One and one makes one," said Teddy Jenks.

Every engineer knows his mathematics.

Have you written in to

ASTOUNDING STORIES

*Yet, to Tell the Editors
Just What Kind of
Stories You Would Like
Them to Secure for You?*

The Thief of Time

By Captain S. P. Meek

"That man never entered and stole that money as the picture shows, unless he managed to make himself invisible."

Harvey Winston, paying teller of the First National Bank of Chicago, stripped the band from a bundle of twenty dollar bills, counted out seventeen of them and added them to the pile on the counter before him.

The teller turned to the stacked pile of bills. They were gone! And no one had been near!.

"Twelve hundred and thirty-one tens," he read from the payroll change slip before him. The paymaster of the Cramer Packing Company nodded an assent and Winston turned to the stacked bills in his rear currency rack. He picked up a handful of bundles and turned back to the grill. His gaze swept the counter where, a moment before, he had stacked the twenties, and his jaw dropped.

"You got those twenties, Mr. Trier?" he asked.

"Got them? Of course not, how could I?" replied the paymaster. "There they are...."

His voice trailed off into nothingness as he looked at the empty counter.

"I must have dropped them," said Winston as he turned. He glanced back at the rear rack where his main stock of currency was piled. He stood paralyzed for a moment and then reached under the counter and pushed a button.

The bank resounded instantly to the clangor of gongs and huge steel grills shot into place with a clang, sealing all doors and preventing anyone from entering or leaving the bank. The guards sprang to their stations with drawn weapons and from the inner offices the bank officials came swarming out. The cashier, followed by two men, hurried to the paying teller's cage.

"What is it, Mr. Winston?" he cried.

"I've been robbed!" gasped the teller.

"Who by? How?" demanded the cashier.

"I—I don't know, sir," stammered the teller. "I was counting out Mr. Trier's payroll, and after I had stacked the twenties I turned to get the tens. When I turned back the twenties were gone."

"Where had they gone?" asked the cashier.

"I don't know, sir. Mr. Trier was as surprised as I was, and then I turned back, thinking that I had knocked them off the counter, and I saw at a glance that there was a big hole in my back racks. You can see yourself, sir."

The cashier turned to the paymaster.

"Is this a practical joke, Mr. Trier?" he demanded sharply.

"Of course not," replied the paymaster. "Winston's grill was closed. It still is. Granted that I might have reached the twenties he had piled up, how could I have gone through a grill and taken the rest of the missing money without his seeing me? The money disappeared almost instantly. It was there a moment before, for I noticed when Winston took the twenties from his rack that it was full."

"But someone must have taken it," said the bewildered cashier. "Money doesn't walk off of its own accord or vanish into thin air—"

A bell interrupted his speech.

"There are the police," he said with an air of relief. "I'll let them in."

The smaller of the two men who had followed the cashier from his office when the alarm had sounded stepped forward and spoke quietly. His voice was low and well pitched yet it carried a note of authority and power that held his auditors' attention while he spoke. The voice harmonized with the man. The most noticeable point about him was the inconspicuousness of his voice and manner, yet there was a glint of steel in his gray eyes that told of enormous force in him.

"I don't believe that I would let them in for a few moments, Mr. Rogers," he said. "I think that we are up against something a little different from the usual bank robbery."

"But, Mr. Carnes," protested the cashier, "we must call in the police in a case like this, and the sooner they take charge the better chance there will be of apprehending the thief."

"Suit yourself," replied the little man with a shrug of his shoulders. "I merely offered my advice."

"Will you take charge, Mr. Carnes?" asked the cashier.

"I can't supersede the local authorities in a case like this," replied Carnes. "The secret service is primarily interested in the suppression of counterfeiting and the enforcement of certain federal statutes, but I will be glad to assist the local authorities to the best of my ability, provided they desire my help. My advice to you would be to keep out the patrolmen who are demanding admittance and get in touch with the chief of police. I would ask that his best detective together with an expert finger-print photographer be sent here before anyone else is admitted. If the patrolmen are allowed to wipe their hands over Mr. Winston's counter they may destroy valuable evidence."

"You are right, Mr. Carnes," exclaimed the cashier. "Mr. Jervis, will you tell the police that there is no violence threatening and ask them to wait for a few minutes? I'll telephone the chief of police at once."

As the cashier hurried away to his telephone Carnes turned to his companion who had stood an interested, although silent spectator of the scene. His companion was a marked contrast to the secret service operator. He stood well over six feet in height, and his protruding jaw and shock of unruly black hair combined with his massive shoulders and chest to give him the appearance of a man who labored with his hands—until one looked at them. His hands were in strange contrast to the rest of him. Long, slim, mobile hands they were, with tapering nervous fingers—the hands of a thinker or of a musician. Telltale splotches of acid told of hours spent in a laboratory, a tale that was confirmed by the almost imperceptible stoop of his shoulders.

"Do you agree with my advice, Dr. Bird?" asked Carnes deferentially.

The noted scientist, who from his laboratory in the Bureau of Standards had sent forth many new things in the realms of chemistry and physics, and who, incidentally, had been instrumental in solving some of the most baffling mysteries which the secret service had been called upon to face, grunted.

"It didn't do any harm," he said, "but it is rather a waste of time. The thief wore gloves."

"How in thunder do you know that?" demanded Carnes.

"It's merely common sense. A man who can do what he did had at least some rudiments of intelligence, and even the feeblest-minded crooks know enough to wear gloves nowadays."

Carnes stepped a little closer to the doctor.

"Another reason why I didn't want patrolmen tramping around," he said in an undertone, "is this. If Winston gave the alarm quickly enough, the thief is probably still in the building."

"He's a good many miles away by now," replied Dr. Bird with a shrug of his shoulders.

Carnes' eyes opened widely. "Why?—how?—who?" he stammered. "Have you any idea of who did it, or how it was done?"

"Possibly I have an idea," replied Dr. Bird with a cryptic smile. "My advice to you, Carnes, is to keep away from the local authorities as much as possible. I want to be present when Winston and Trier are questioned and I may possibly wish to ask a few questions myself. Use your authority that far, but no farther. Don't volunteer any information and especially don't let my name get out. We'll drop the counterfeiting case we were summoned here on for the present and look into this a little on our own hook. I will want your aid, so don't get tied up with the police."

"At that, we don't want the police crossing our trail at every turn," protested Carnes.

"They won't," promised the doctor. "They will never get any evidence on this case, if I am right, and neither will we—for the present. Our stunt is to lie low and wait for the next attempt of this nature and thus accumulate some evidence and some idea of where to look."

"Will there be another attempt?" asked Carnes.

"Surely. You don't expect a man who got away with a crime like this to quit operations just because a few flatfeet run around and make a hullabaloo about it, do you? I may be wrong in my assumption, but if I am right, the most important thing is to keep all reference to my name or position out of the press reports."

The cashier hastened up to them.

"Detective-Captain Sturtevant will be here in a few minutes with a photographer and some other men," he said. "Is there anything that we can do in the meantime, Mr. Carnes?"

"I would suggest that Mr. Trier and his guard and Mr. Winston go into your office," replied Carnes. "My assistant and I would like to be present during the questioning, if there are no objections."

"I didn't know that you had an assistant with you," answered the cashier.

Carnes indicated Dr. Bird.

"This gentleman is Mr. Berger, my assistant," he said. "Do you understand?"

"Certainly. I am sure there will be no objection to your presence, Mr. Carnes," replied the cashier as he led the way to his office.

A few minutes later Detective-Captain Sturtevant of the Chicago police was announced. He acknowledged the introductions gruffly and got down to business at once.

"What were the circumstances of the robbery?" he asked.

Winston told his story, Trier and the guard confirming it.

"Pretty thin!" snorted the detective when they had finished. He whirled suddenly on Winston.

"Where did you hide the loot?" he thundered.

"Why—uh—er—what do you mean?" gulped the teller.

"Just what I said," replied the detective. "Where did you hide the loot?"

"I didn't hide it anywhere," said the teller. "It was stolen."

"You had better think up a better one," sneered Sturtevant. "If you think that you can make me believe that that money was stolen from you in broad daylight with two men in plain sight of you who didn't see it, you might just as well get over it. I know that you have some hiding place where you have slipped the stuff and the quicker you come clean and spill it, the better it will be for you. Where did you hide it?"

"I didn't hide it!" cried the teller, his voice trembling. "Mr. Trier can tell you that I didn't touch it from the time I laid it down until I turned back."

"That's right," replied the paymaster. "He turned his back on me for a moment, and when he turned back, it was gone."

"So you're in on it too, are you?" said Sturtevant.

"What do you mean?" demanded the paymaster hotly.

"Oh nothing, nothing at all," replied the detective. "Of course Winston didn't touch it and it disappeared and you never saw it go, although you were within three feet of it all the time. Did *you* see anything?" he demanded of the guard.

"Nothing that I am sure of," answered the guard. "I thought that a shadow passed in front of me for an instant, but when I looked again, it was gone."

Dr. Bird sat forward suddenly. "What did this shadow look like?" he asked.

"It wasn't exactly a shadow," said the guard. "It was as if a person had passed suddenly before me so quickly that I couldn't see him. I seemed to feel that there was someone there, but I didn't rightly *see* anything."

"Did you notice anything of the sort?" demanded the doctor of Trier.

"I don't know," replied Trier thoughtfully. "Now that Williams has mentioned it, I did seem to feel a breath of air or a motion as though something had passed in front of me. I didn't think of it at the time."

"Was this shadow opaque enough to even momentarily obscure your vision?" went on the doctor.

"Not that I am conscious of. It was just a breath of air such as a person might cause by passing very rapidly."

"What made you ask Trier if he had the money when you turned around?" asked the doctor of Winston.

"Say-y-y," broke in the detective. "Who the devil are you, and what do you mean by breaking into my examination and stopping it?"

Carnes tossed a leather wallet on the table.

"There are my credentials," he said in his quiet voice. "I am chief of one section of the United States Secret Service as you will see, and this is Mr. Berger, my assistant. We were in the bank, engaged on a counterfeiting case, when the robbery took place. We have had a good deal of experience along these lines and we are merely anxious to aid you."

Sturtevant examined Carnes' credentials carefully and returned them.

"This is a Chicago robbery," he said, "and we have had a little experience in robberies and in apprehending robbers ourselves. I think that we can get along without your help."

"You have had more experience with robberies than with apprehending robbers if the papers tell the truth," said Dr. Bird with a chuckle.

The detective's face flushed.

"That will be enough from you, Mr. Sherlock Holmes," he said. "If you open your mouth again, I'll arrest you as a material witness and as a possible accomplice."

"That sounds like Chicago methods," said Carnes quietly. "Now listen to me, Captain. My assistant and I are merely trying to assist you in this case. If you don't desire our assistance we'll proceed along our own lines without interfering, but in the meantime remember that this is a National Bank, and that our questions will be answered. The United States is higher than even the Chicago police force, and I am here under orders to investigate a counterfeiting case. If I desire, I can seal the doors of this bank and allow no one in or out until I have the evidence I desire. Do you understand?"

Sturtevant sprang to his feet with an oath, but the sight of the gold badge which Carnes displayed stopped him.

"Oh well," he said ungraciously. "I suppose that no harm will come of letting Winston answer your fool questions, but I'll warn you that I'll report to Washington that you are interfering with the course of justice and using your authority to aid the getaway of a criminal."

"That is your privilege," replied Carnes quietly. "Mr. Winston, will you answer Mr. Berger's question?"

"Why, I asked him because he was right close to the money and I thought that he might have reached through the wicket and picked it up. Then, too—"

He hesitated for a moment and Dr. Bird smiled encouragingly.

"What else?" he asked.

"Why, I can't exactly tell. It just seemed to me that I had heard the rustle that bills make when they are pulled across a counter. When I saw them gone, I thought that he might have taken them. Then when I turned toward him, I seemed to hear the rustle of bills behind me, although I knew that I was alone in the cage. When I looked back the money was gone."

"Did you see or hear anything like a shadow or a person moving?"

"No—yes—I don't know. Just as I turned around it seemed to me that the rear door to my cage had moved and there may have been a shadow for an instant. I don't know. I hadn't thought of it before."

"How long after that did you ring the alarm gongs?"

"Not over a second or two."

"That's all," said Dr. Bird.

"If your high and mightiness has no further questions to ask, perhaps you will let me ask a few," said Sturtevant.

"Go ahead, ask all you wish," replied Dr. Bird with a laugh. "I have all the information I desire here for the present. I may want to ask other questions later, but just now I think we'll be going."

"If you find any strange finger-prints on Winston's counter, I'll be glad to have them compared with our files," said Carnes.

"I am not bothering with finger-prints," snorted the detective. "This is an open and shut case. There would be lots of Winston's finger-prints there and no others. There isn't the slightest doubt that this is an inside case and I have the men I want right here. Mr. Rogers, your bank is closed for to-day. Everyone in it will be searched and then all those not needed to close up will be sent away. I will get a squad of men here to go over your building and locate the hiding place. Your money is still on the premises unless these men slipped it to a confederate who got out before the alarm was given. I'll question the guards about that. If that happened, a little sweating will get it out of them."

"Are you going to arrest me?" demanded Trier in surprise.

"Yes, dearie," answered the detective. "I am going to arrest you and your two little playmates if these Washington experts will allow me to. You will save a lot of time and quite a few painful experiences if you will come clean now instead of later."

"I demand to see my lawyer and to communicate with my firm," said the paymaster.

"Time enough for that when I am through with you," replied the detective.

He turned to Carnes.

"Have I your gracious permission to arrest these three criminals?" he asked.

"Yes indeed, Captain," replied Carnes sweetly. "You have my gracious permission to make just as big an ass of yourself as you wish. We're going now."

"By the way, Captain," said Dr. Bird as he followed Carnes out. "When you get through playing with your prisoners and start to look for the thief, here is a tip. Look for a left-handed man who has a thorough knowledge of chemistry and especially toxicology."

"It's easy enough to see that he was left-handed if he pulled that money out through the grill from the positions occupied by Trier and his guard, but what the dickens led you to suspect that he is a chemist and a toxicologist?" asked Carnes as he and the doctor left the bank.

"Merely a shrewd guess, my dear Watson," replied the doctor with a chuckle. "I am likely to be wrong, but there is a good chance that I am right. I am judging solely from the method used."

"Have you solved the method?" demanded Carnes in amazement. "What on earth was it? The more I have thought about it, the more inclined I am to believe that Sturtevant is right and that it is an inside job. It seems to me impossible that a man could have entered in broad daylight and lifted that money in front of three men and within sight of a hundred more without some one getting a glimpse of him. He must have taken the money out in a grip or a sack or something like that, yet the bank record shows that no one but Trier entered with a grip and no one left with a package for ten minutes before Trier entered."

"There may be something in what you say, Carnes, but I am inclined to have a different idea. I don't think it is the usual run of bank robbery, and I would rather not hazard a guess just now. I am going back to Washington to-night. Before I go any further into the matter, I need some rather specialized knowledge that I don't possess and I want to consult with Dr. Knolles. I'll be back in a week or so and then we can look into that counterfeiting case after we get this disposed of."

"What am I to do?" asked Carnes.

"Sit around the lobby of your hotel, eat three meals a day, and read the papers. If you get bored, I would recommend that you pay a visit to the Art Institute and admire the graceful lions which adorn the steps. Artistic contemplations may well improve your culture."

"All right," replied Carnes. "I'll assume a pensive air and moon at the lions, but I might do better if you told me what I was looking for."

"You are looking for knowledge, my dear Carnes," said the doctor with a laugh. "Remember the saying of the sages: To the wise man, no knowledge is useless."

A huge Martin bomber roared down to a landing at the Maywood airdrome, and a burly figure descended from the rear cockpit and waved his hand jovially to the waiting Carnes. The secret service man hastened over to greet his colleague.

"Have you got that truck I wired you to have ready?" demanded the doctor.

"Waiting at the entrance; but say, I've got some news for you."

"It can wait. Get a detail of men and help us to unload this ship. Some of the cases are pretty heavy."

Carnes hurried off and returned with a gang of laborers, who took from the bomber a dozen heavy packing cases of various sizes, several of them labelled either "Fragile" or "Inflammable" in large type.

"Where do they go, Doctor?" he asked when the last of them had been loaded onto the waiting truck.

"To the First National Bank," replied Dr. Bird, "and Casey here goes with them. You know Casey, don't you, Carnes? He is the best photographer in the Bureau."

"Shall I go along too?" asked Carnes as he acknowledged the introduction.

"No need for it. I wired Rogers and he knows the stuff is coming and what to do with it. Unpack as soon as you get there, Casey, and start setting up as soon as the bank closes."

"All right, Doctor," replied Casey as he mounted the truck beside the driver.

"Where do we go, Doctor?" asked Carnes as the truck rolled off.

"To the Blackstone Hotel for a bath and some clean clothes," replied the doctor. "And now, what is the news you have for me?"

"The news is this, Doctor. I carried out your instructions diligently and, during the daylight hours, the lions have not moved."

Dr. Bird looked contrite.

"I beg your pardon, Carnes," he said. "I really didn't think when I left you so mystified how you must have felt. Believe me, I had my own reasons, excellent ones, for secrecy."

"I have usually been able to maintain silence when asked to," replied Carnes stiffly.

"My dear fellow, I didn't mean to question your discretion. I know that whatever I tell you is safe, but there are angles to this affair that are so weird and improbable that I don't dare to trust my own conclusions, let alone share them. I'll tell you all about it soon. Did you get those tickets I wired for?"

"Of course I got them, but what have two tickets to the A. A. U. track meet this afternoon got to do with a bank robbery?"

"One trouble with you, Carnes," replied the doctor with a judicial air, "is that you have no idea of the importance of proper relaxation. Is it possible that you have no desire to see Ladd, this new marvel who is smashing records right and left, run? He performs for the Illinois Athletic Club this afternoon, and it would not surprise me to see him lower the world's record again. He has already lowered the record for the hundred yard dash from nine and three-fifths to eight and four-fifths. There is no telling what he will do."

"Are we going to waste the whole afternoon just to watch a man run?" demanded Carnes in disgust.

"We will see many men run, my dear fellow, but there is only one in whom I have a deep abiding interest, and that is Mr. Ladd. Have you your binoculars with you?"

"No."

"Then by all means beg, borrow or steal two pairs before this afternoon. We might easily miss half the fun without them. Are our seats near the starting line for the sprints?"

"Yes. The big demand was for seats near the finish line."

"The start will be much more interesting, Carnes. I was somewhat of a minor star in track myself in my college days and it will be of the greatest interest to me to observe the starting form of this new speed artist. Now Carnes, don't ask any more questions. I may be barking up the wrong tree and I don't want to give you a chance to laugh at me. I'll tell you what to watch for at the track."

The sprinters lined up on the hundred yard mark and Dr. Bird and Carnes sat with their glasses glued to their eyes watching the slim figure in the colors of the Illinois Athletic Club, whose large "62" on his back identified him as the new star.

"On your mark!" cried the starter. "Get set!"

"Ah!" cried Dr. Bird. "Did you see that Carnes?"

The starting gun cracked and the runners were off on their short grind. Ladd leaped into the lead and rapidly distanced the field, his legs twinkling under him almost faster than the eye could follow. He was fully twenty yards in the lead when his speed suddenly lessened and the balance of the runners closed up the gap he had opened. His lead was too great for them, and he was still a good ten yards in the lead when he crossed the tape. The official time was posted as eight and nine-tenths seconds.

"Another thirty yards and he would have been beaten," said Carnes as he lowered his glasses.

"That is the way he has won all of his races," replied the doctor. "He piles up a huge lead at first and then loses a good deal at the finish. His speed doesn't hold up. Never mind that, though, it is only an additional point in my favor. Did you notice his jaws just before the gun went?"

"They seemed to clench and then he swallowed, but most of them did some thing like that."

"Watch him carefully for the next heat and see if he puts anything into his mouth. That is the important thing."

Dr. Bird sank into a brown study and paid no attention to the next few events, but he came to attention promptly when the final heat of the hundred yard dash was called. With his glasses he watched Ladd closely as the runner trotted up to the starting line.

"There, Carnes!" he cried suddenly. "Did you see?"

"I saw him wipe his mouth," said Carnes doubtfully.

"All right, now watch his jaws just before the gun goes."

The final heat was a duplicate of the first preliminary. Ladd took an early lead which he held for three-fourths of the distance to the tape, then his pace slackened and he finished only a bare ten yards ahead of the next runner. The time tied his previous world's record of eight and four-fifths seconds.

"He crunched and swallowed all right, Doctor," said Carnes.

"That is all I wanted to be sure of. Now Carnes, here is something for you to do. Get hold of the United States Commissioner and get a John Doe warrant and go back to the hotel with it and wait for me. I may phone you at any minute and I may not. If I don't, wait in your room until you hear from me. Don't leave it for a minute."

"Where are you going, Doctor?"

"I'm going down and congratulate Mr. Ladd. An old track man like me can't let such an opportunity pass."

"I don't know what this is all about, Doctor," replied Carnes, "but I know you well enough to obey orders and to keep my mouth shut until it is my turn to speak."

Few men could resist Dr. Bird when he set out to make a favorable impression, and even a world's champion is apt to be flattered by the attention of one of the greatest scientists of his day, especially when that scientist has made an enviable reputation as an athlete in his college days and can talk the jargon of the champion's particular sport. Henry Ladd promptly capitulated to the charm of the doctor and allowed himself to be led away to supper at Bird's club. The supper passed off pleasantly, and when the doctor requested an interview with the young athlete in a private room, he gladly consented. They entered the room together, remained for an hour and a half, and then came out. The smile had left Ladd's face and he appeared nervous and distracted. The doctor talked cheerfully with him but kept a firm grip on his arm as they descended the stairs together. They entered a telephone booth where the doctor made several calls, and then descended to the street, where they entered a taxi.

"Maywood airdrome," the doctor told the driver.

Two hours later the big Martin bomber which had carried the doctor to Chicago roared away into the night, and Bird turned back, reentered the taxi, and headed for the city alone.

When Carnes received the telephone call, which was one of those the doctor made from the booth in his club, he hurried over to the First National Bank. His badge secured him an entrance and he found Casey busily engaged in rigging up an elaborate piece of apparatus on one of the balconies where guards were normally stationed during banking hours.

"Dr. Bird said to tell you to keep on the job all night if necessary," he told Casey. "He thinks he will need your machine to-morrow."

"I'll have it ready to turn on the power at four A.M.," replied Casey.

Carnes watched him curiously for a while as he soldered together the electrical connections and assembled an apparatus which looked like a motion picture projector.

"What are you setting up?" he asked at length.

"It is a high speed motion picture camera," replied Casey, "with a telescopic lens. It is a piece of apparatus which Dr. Bird designed while he was in Washington last week and which I made from his sketches, using some apparatus we had on hand. It's a dandy, all right."

"What is special about it?"

"The speed. You know how fast an ordinary movie is taken, don't you? No? Well, it's sixteen exposures per second. The slow pictures are taken sometimes at a hundred and twenty-eight or two hundred and fifty-six exposures per second, and then shown at sixteen. This affair will take half a million pictures per second."

"I didn't know that a film would register with that short an exposure."

"That's slow," replied Casey with a laugh. "It all depends on the light. The best flash-light powder gives a flash about one ten-thousandth of a second in duration, but that is by no means the speed limit of the film. The only trouble is enough light and sufficient shutter speed. Pictures have been taken by means of spark photography with an exposure of less than one three-millionth of a second. The whole secret of this machine lies in the shutter. This big disc with the slots in the edge is set up before the lens and run at such a speed that half a million slots per second pass before the lens. The film, which is sixteen millimeter X-ray film, travels behind the lens at a speed of nearly five miles per second. It has to be gradually worked up to this speed, and after the whole thing is set up, it takes it nearly four hours to get to full speed."

"At that speed, it must take a million miles of film before you get up steam."

"It would, if the film were being exposed. There is only about a hundred yards of film all told, which will run over these huge drums in an endless belt. There is a regular camera shutter working on an electric principle which remains closed. When the switch is tripped, the shutter opens in about two thirty-thousandths of a second, stays open just one one-hundredth of a second, and then closes. This time is enough to expose nearly all of our film. When we have our picture, I shut the current down, start applying a magnetic brake, and let it slow down. It takes over an hour to stop it without breaking the film. It sounds complicated, but it works all right."

"Where is your switch?"

"That is the trick part of it. It is a remote control affair. The shutter opens and starts the machine taking pictures when the back door of the paying teller's cage is opened half an inch. There is also a hand switch in the line that can be opened so that you can open the door without setting off the camera, if you wish. When the hand switch is closed and the door opened, this is what happens. The shutter on the camera opens, the machine takes five thousand pictures during the next hundredth of a second, and then the shutter closes. Those five thousand exposures will take about five minutes to show at the usual rate of sixteen per second."

"You said that you had to get plenty of light. How are you managing that?"

"The camera is equipped with a special lens ground out of rock crystal. This lens lets in ultra-violet light which the ordinary lens shuts out, and X-ray film is especially sensitive to ultra-violet light. In order to be sure that we get enough illumination, I will set up these two ultra-violet floodlights to illumine the cage. The teller will have to wear glasses to protect his eyes and he'll get well sunburned, but something has to be sacrificed to science, as Dr. Bird is always telling me."

"It's too deep for me," said Carnes with a sigh. "Can I do anything to help? The doctor told me to stand by and do anything I could."

"I might be able to use you a little if you can use tools," said Casey with a grin. "You can start bolting together that light proof shield if you want to."

"Well, Carnes, did you have an instructive night?" asked Dr. Bird cheerfully as he entered the First National Bank at eight-thirty the next morning.

"I don't see that I did much good, Doctor. Casey would have had the machine ready on time anyway, and I'm no machinist."

"Well, frankly, Carnes, I didn't expect you to be of much help to him, but I did want you to see what Casey was doing, and a little of it was pretty heavy for him to handle alone. I suppose that everything is ready?"

"The motor reached full speed about fifteen minutes ago and Casey went out to get a cup of coffee. Would you mind telling me the object of the whole thing?"

"Not at all. I plan to make a permanent record of the work of the most ingenious bank robber in the world. I hope he keeps his word."

"What do you mean?"

"Three days ago when Sturtevant sweated a 'confession' out of poor Winston, the bank got a message that the robbery would be repeated this morning and dared them to prevent it. Rogers thought it was a hoax, but he telephoned me and I worked the Bureau men night and day to get my camera ready in time for him. I am afraid that I can't do much to prevent the robbery, but I may be able to take a picture of it and thus prevent other cases of a like nature."

"Was the warning written?"

"No. It was telephoned from a pay station in the loop district, and by the time it was traced and men got there, the telephoner was probably a mile away. He said that he would rob the same cage in the same manner as he did before."

"Aren't you taking any special precautions?"

"Oh, yes, the bank is putting on extra guards and making a lot of fuss of that sort, probably to the great amusement of the robber."

"Why not close the cage for the day?"

"Then he would rob a different one and we would have no way of photographing his actions. To be sure, we will put dummy money there, bundles with bills on the outside and paper on the inside, so if I don't get a picture of him, he won't get much. Every bill in the cage will be marked as well."

"Did he say at what time he would operate?"

"No, he didn't, so we'll have to stand by all day. Oh, hello, Casey, is everything all right?"

"As sweet as chocolate candy, Doctor. I have tested it out thoroughly, and unless we have to run it so long that the film wears out and breaks, we are sitting pretty. If we don't get the pictures you are looking for, I'm a dodo, and I haven't been called that yet."

"Good work, Casey. Keep the bearings oiled and pray that the film doesn't break."

The bank had been opened only ten minutes when the clangor of gongs announced a robbery. It was practically a duplicate of the first. The paying teller had turned from his window to take some bills from his rack and had found several dozens of bundles missing. As the gongs sounded, Dr. Bird and Casey leaped to the camera.

"She snapped, Doctor!" cried Casey as he threw two switches. "It'll take an hour to stop and half a day to develop the film, but I ought to be able to show you what we got by to-night."

"Good enough!" cried Dr. Bird. "Go ahead while I try to calm down the bank officials. Will you have everything ready by eight o'clock?"

"Easy, Doctor," replied Casey as he turned to the magnetic brake.

By eight o'clock quite a crowd had assembled in a private room at the Blackstone Hotel. Besides Dr. Bird and Carnes, Rogers and several other officials of the First National Bank were present, together with Detective-Captain Sturtevant and a group of the most prominent scientists and physicians gathered from the schools of the city.

"Gentlemen," said Dr. Bird when all had taken seats facing a miniature moving picture screen on one wall, "to-night I expect to show you some pictures which will, I am sure, astonish you. It marks the advent of a new departure in transcendental medicine. I will be glad to answer any questions you may wish to ask and to explain the pictures after they are shown, but before we start a discussion, I will ask that you examine what I have to show you. Lights out, please!"

He stepped to the rear of the room as the lights went out. As his eyes grew used to the dimness of the room he moved forward and took a vacant seat. His hand fumbled in his pocket for a second.

"Now!" he cried suddenly.

In the momentary silence which followed his cry, two dull metallic clicks could be heard, and a quick cry that was suddenly strangled as Dr. Bird clamped his hand over the mouth of the man who sat between him and Carnes.

"All right, Casey," called the doctor.

The whir of a projection machine could be heard and on the screen before them leaped a picture of the paying teller's cage of the First National Bank. Winston's successor was standing motionless at the wicket, his lips parted in a smile, but the attention of all was riveted on a figure who moved at the back of the cage. As the picture started, the figure was bent over an opened suitcase, stuffing into it bundles of bills. He straightened up and reached to the rack for more bills, and as he did so he faced the camera full for a moment. He picked up other bundles of bills, filled the suitcase, fastened it in a leisurely manner, opened the rear door of the cage and walked out.

"Again, please!" called Dr. Bird. "And stop when he faces us full."

The picture was repeated and stopped at the point indicated.

"Lights, please!" cried the doctor.

The lights flashed on and Dr. Bird rose to his feet, pulling up after him the wilted figure of a middle-aged man.

"Gentlemen," said the doctor in ringing tones, "allow me to present to you Professor James Kirkwood of the faculty of the Richton University, formerly known as James Collier of the Bureau of Standards, and robber of the First National Bank."

Detective-Captain Sturtevant jumped to his feet and cast a searching glance at the captive.

"He's the man all right," he cried. "Hang on to him until I get a wagon here!"

"Oh, shut up!" said Carnes. "He's under federal arrest just now, charged with the possession of narcotics. When we are through with him, you can have him if you want him."

"How did you get that picture, Doctor?" cried the cashier. "I watched that cage every minute during the morning and I'll swear that man never entered and stole that money as the picture shows, unless he managed to make himself invisible."

"You're closer to the truth than you suspect, Mr. Rogers," said Dr. Bird. "It is not quite a matter of invisibility, but something pretty close to it. It is a matter of catalysts."

"What kind of cats?" asked the cashier.

"Not cats, Mr. Rogers, catalysts. Catalysts is the name of a chemical reaction consisting essentially of a decomposition and a new combination effected by means of a catalyst which acts on the compound bodies in question, but which goes through the reaction itself unchanged. There are a great many of them which are used in the arts and in manufacturing, and while their action is not always clearly understood, the results are well known and can be banked on.

"One of the commonest instances of the use of a catalyst is the use of sponge platinum in the manufacture of sulphuric acid. I will not burden you with the details of the 'contact' process, as it is known, but the combination is effected by means of finely divided platinum which is neither changed, consumed or wasted during the process. While there are a number of other catalysts known, for instance iron in reactions in which metallic magnesium is concerned, the commonest are the metals of the platinum group.

"Less is known of the action of catalysts in the organic reactions, but it has been the subje of intensive study by Dr. Knolles of the Bureau of Standards for several years. His studie. of the effects of different colored lights, that is, rays of different wave-lengths, on the reactions which constitute growth in plants have had a great effect on hothouse forcing of plants and promise to revolutionize the truck gardening industry. He has speeded up the rate of growth to as high as ten times the normal rate in some cases.

"A few years ago, he and his assistant, James Collier, turned their attention toward discovering a catalyst which would do for the metabolic reactions in animal life what his light rays did for plants. What his method was, I will not disclose for obvious reasons, but suffice it to say that he met with great success. He took a puppy and by treating it with his catalytic drugs, made it grow to maturity, pass through its entire normal life span, and die of old age in six months."

"That is very interesting, Doctor, but I fail to see what bearing it has on the robbery."

"Mr. Rogers, how, on a dark day and in the absence of a timepiece, would you judge the passage of time?"

"Why, by my stomach, I guess."

"Exactly. By your metabolic rate. You eat a meal, it digests, you expend the energy which you have taken into your system, your stomach becomes empty and your system demands more energy. You are hungry and you judge that some five or six hours must have passed since you last ate. Do you follow?"

"Certainly."

"Let us suppose that by means of some tonic, some catalytic drug, your rate of metabolism and also your rate of expenditure of energy has been increased six fold. You would eat a meal and in one hour you would be hungry again. Having no timepiece, and assuming that you were in a light-proof room, you would judge that some five hours had passed, would you not?"

"I expect so."

"Very well. Now suppose that this accelerated rate of digestion and expenditure of energy continued. You would be sleepy in perhaps three hours, would sleep about an hour and a quarter, and would then wake, ready for your breakfast. In other words, you would have lived through a day in four hours."

"What advantage would there be in that?"

your standpoint. It would, however, increase the rate of reproduction of cattle might be a great boom to agriculture, but we will not discuss this phase now. it were possible to increase your rate of metabolism and expenditure of energy, in words, your rate of living, not six times, but thirty thousand times. In such a case you would live five minutes in one one-hundredth of a second."

"Naturally, and you would live a year in about seventeen and one-half minutes, and a normal lifespan of seventy years in about twenty hours. You would be as badly off as any common may-fly."

Agreed, but suppose that you could so regulate the dose of your catalyst that its effect would last for only one one-hundredth of a second. During that short period of time, you would be able to do the work that would ordinarily take you five minutes. In other words, you could enter a bank, pack a satchel with currency and walk out. You would be working in a leisurely manner, yet your actions would have been so quick that no human eye could have detected them. This is my theory of what actually took place. For verification, I will turn to Dr. Kirkwood, as he prefers to be known now."

"I don't know how you got that picture, but what you have said is about right," replied the prisoner.

"I got that picture by using a speed of thirty thousand times the normal sixteen exposures per second," replied Dr. Bird. "That figure I got from Dr. Knolles, the man who perfected the secret you stole when you left the Bureau three years ago. You secured only part of it and I suppose it took all your time since to perfect and complete it. You gave yourself away when you experimented on young Ladd. I was a track man myself in my college days and when I saw an account of his running, I smelt a rat, so I came back and watched him. As soon as I saw him crush and swallow a capsule just as the gun was fired, I was sure, and got hold of him. He was pretty stubborn, but he finally told me what name you were running under now, and the rest was easy. I would have got you in time anyway, but your bravado in telling us when you would next operate gave me the idea of letting you do it and photographing you at work. That is all I have to say. Captain Sturtevant, you can take your prisoner whenever you want him."

"I reckoned without you, Dr. Bird, but the end hasn't come yet. You may send me up for a few years, but you'll never find that money. I'm sure of that."

"Tut, tut, Professor," laughed Carnes. "Your safety deposit box in the Commercial National is already sealed until a court orders it opened. The bills you took this morning were all marked, so that is merely additional proof, if we needed it. You surely didn't think that such a transparent device as changing your name from 'James Collier' to 'John Collyer' and signing with your left hand instead of your right would fool the secret service, did you? Remember, your old Bureau records showed you to be ambidextrous."

"What about Winston's confession?" asked Rogers suddenly.

"Detective-Captain Sturtevant can explain that to a court when Mr. Winston brings suit against him for false arrest and brutal treatment," replied Carnes.

"A very interesting case, Carnes," remarked the doctor a few hours later. "It was an enjoyable interlude in the routine of most of the cases on which you consult me, but our play time is over. We'll have to get after that counterfeiting case to-morrow."

IN THE NEXT ISSUE

BRIGANDS OF THE MOON

Beginning an Amazing Four-part Interplanetary Novel
By RAY CUMMINGS

THE SOUL MASTER

A Thrilling Novelette of the Substitution of Personality
By WILL SMITH and R. J. ROBBINS

COLD LIGHT

An Extraordinary Scientific Mystery
By CAPT. S. P. MEEK

—AND MANY OTHER STORIES, OF COURSE